One Night with a Spy

Book Three in the Royal Four series

Celeste Bradley

St. Martin's Paperbacks

ONE NIGHT WITH A SPY

Copyright © 2006 by Celeste Bradley.

ISBN: 0-312-93966-3
EAN: 80312-93966-3

Printed in the United States of America

St. Martin's Paperbacks edition / April 2006

St. Martin's Paperbacks are published by St. Martin's Press, 175 Fifth Avenue, New York, NY 10010.

10 9 8 7 6 5 4 3 2 1

THE ROGUE

"Once you've read a Liar's Club book, you crave the next in the series. Bradley knows how to hook a reader with wit, sensuality (this one has one of the hottest hands-off love scenes in years!) and a strong plot along with the madness and mayhem of a Regency-set novel.   *—RT BOOKclub Magazine*

"Bradley continues her luscious Liar's Club series with another tale of danger and desire, and as always her clever prose is imbued with wicked wit."   *—Booklist*

"Celeste Bradley's The Liar's Club series scarcely needs an introduction, so popular it's become with readers since its inception . . . Altogether intriguing, exciting, and entertaining, this book is a sterling addition to the Liar's Club series."
       —Road to Romance

TO WED A SCANDALOUS SPY

"Warm, witty, and wonderfully sexy."
       —Teresa Medeiros, *New York Times* bestselling author

"Funny, adventurous, passionate, and especially poignant, this is a great beginning to a new series . . . Bradley mixes suspense and a sexy love story to perfection."
       —RT BOOKclub Magazine

"A wonderful start to a very looked-forward-to new series . . . once again showcases Celeste Bradley's talent of creating sensual and intriguing plots filled with memorable and endearing characters . . . A non-stop read."
       —Romance Reader at Heart

"Danger, deceit, and desire battle with witty banter and soaring passion for prominence in this highly engrossing tale . . . Bradley also provides surprises galore, both funny and suspenseful, and skillfully ties them all in neatly with the romance so as to make this story more than averagely memorable."
       —Road to Romance

MORE . . .

The Impostor

"Bradley carefully layers deception upon deception, keeping the intrigue level high and the tone bright . . . Readers will race through this delightful comedy of errors and eagerly anticipate the next installment."
                                                          —*Publishers Weekly*

"With delicious characters and a delectable plot, Bradley delivers another enticing read brimming with the mayhem and madness that come with falling in love when you least expect it. The devilishly funny double identities, witty dialogue and clever twists will captivate."
                                        —*RT BOOKclub Magazine* (Top Pick)

"Don't miss this second book of the Liar's Club series. With humor, passion and mystery, it's absolutely delightful in every way! I can't wait for the next one.
                                            —*Old Book Barn and Gazette*

The Pretender

"Totally entertaining."
                        New York Times bestselling author Julia Quinn

"An engaging, lusty tale, full of adventure and loaded with charm."
                —Gaelen Foley, *USA Today* bestselling author of *Lord of Ice*

"Bursting with adventure and sizzling, Bradley certainly knows how to combine engaging characters with excitement, sensuality, and a strong plot."
                                                      —*Booklist* (starred)

"Bursting with adventure and sizzling passion to satisfy the most daring reader."
                                              —*RT BOOKclub Magazine*

"A charming heroine and a dashing spy hero make *The Pretender* a riveting read . . . [E]ntertained me thoroughly from beginning to end."
                        —Sabrina Jeffries, *USA Today* bestselling author
                                                  of *After the Abduction*

St. Martin's Paperbacks Titles
by Celeste Bradley

Surrender to a Wicked Spy

To Wed a Scandalous Spy

The Rogue

The Charmer

The Spy

The Impostor

The Pretender

Every ruler needs a few men he can count on to tell him the truth—whether he wants to hear it or not.

Created in the time of the Normans, when King William the Conqueror found himself overrun with "advisors" more concerned with their own agendas than with the good of the whole, the Quatre Royale were selected from the King's own boyhood friends. Lords all, and bound by loyalty rather than selfish motives, these four men took on the names of ruthless predators while acting as the Quatre, keeping their lives and identities separate from their true roles . . .

. . . to act as the shield of deceit and the sword of truth in the name of the King.

Courageous as the Lion
Deadly as the Cobra
Vigilant as the Falcon
Clever as the Fox

The appointment is for life—the commitment absolute. Bonds of family, friends and even love become as insubstantial as a dream when each hand-selected apprentice takes the seat of the master. All else is merely pretense, kept for the sake of secrecy and anonymity. For it is true that the iron bars of duty cage the hearts and souls of . . .

. . . *THE ROYAL FOUR.*

This book is for my family members who were so devastated by Hurricane Katrina. You inspire me with your strength and resiliency. To Jack, Dave, Gretchen, Steve, Virginia, Claudia, Janine and all of your loved ones . . . thank you for making me feel at home again.

I would like to thank the Bad Pennies for their support, and I would like to extend special thanks to Darbi Gill, who listened to me talk about the story long past the point where I stopped making sense.

Prologue

The moon is full and swollen in the dark lapis sky. A bright path shines on the glassy lake, leading me in, calling me onward. I want to follow. I want to feel the lake on my bare skin.

A tingle on the back of my neck at the hint of sandalwood on the night breeze. No, there is no one there.

The water will be cold silver, slipping silky fingers into places it would never reach through a bathing costume. I reach to untie my wrapper—and his hands come about me from behind. "Let me." His voice is deep enough to make me quiver, but not a growl.

My breath catches in my throat. "I told you to never come here again."

"I cannot stay away."

I look down to where large, competent fingers slowly tug free the knot in the satin belt. He lets the ends fall and spreads his open hands over my belly. I close my eyes at the heat that sinks into my skin and let my head fall back against the firm shoulder there. He rises behind me like a fortress, a wall of strength and protection that will never fail me. He is wrong for me, but I cannot resist him.

He presses warm lips upon my temple and I turn into his arms, leaving my wrapper behind to slip to the grass. I am as naked as he. His arms come around me and for one, long perfect moment he holds me pressed close to his heat and strength. His embrace is a pledge, a vow, and I nod in understanding before I open my eyes.

I may look upon his form—I must look upon it, and caress and take pleasure in it. His great chest rises with each breath, which comes more quickly as I allow my fingers to explore the plates and cords of muscle that shape him. I slip my hands up to trace the thickened strength of his arms to his broad shoulders—those shoulders I do love to rely upon—and then back down. I especially love to trace the risen vein that throbs in each forearm, and to feel his blood jump at my touch.

Then I take his large, square hands in mine and press them to my breasts, giving him the weight of them in his palms. His organ rises between us, rigid and hungry, without shame. "Do you want me?" I know he does, but I need to hear him say it.

"I want you." His hands tighten on me, not cruelly but possessively. I close my eyes and let my head drop back.

"Tell me why."

"I want you because I was made to fit within you. I live to lose myself in your wetness and your heat. I love—"

No. Wait. She couldn't have him say that. Good heavens, love was the last thing she wanted on her plate! He was a plaything only. That thought sent a tiny shiver through her and put a naughty twist to her lips as she bent to scribble in her diary once more.

I stop him with trembling fingers over his lips. No. Not that. Even I dare not dream of that.

"*I need you.*"

That was better. Not as dangerous.

I flow against him, melting into his skin, wishing I might stay in the circle of his protective, urgent embrace forever.

He sweeps me into his arms, lifting me lightly from my feet. With me in his possession, he strides into the lake. The water is cool, not chill, on my heated skin and it slides over my nipples and between my bare thighs like a sweet invader, tightening my flesh and making me shiver. He spins me in the water, creating a wake of shimmering wavelets that continue onward to break up the flawless pale path to the moon. I won't be going there tonight. I will stay here, in my lover's arms.

He stops with the moon behind him, throwing him into silhouette, and only then do I look up to see his dampened hair curling about the shadows of his face. He kisses me and allows my body to slide down his until we are pressed breast to chest once more. My feet do not touch bottom, for I am weightless under the heat of his mouth.

I wrap my arms about his neck and my limbs about his waist. His erection presses demandingly to me and I ease myself down onto his thickness.

I close my eyes and press my face into his muscular neck. I don't want to see his features, for if he has a face he will also have a name—and I must never know it.

"Will you bathe, my lady?"

With a start Julia, Lady Barrowby, twenty-year-old wife of the elderly lord of the manor, looked up from her writing to where her maid, Pickles, stood tapping her toes impatiently.

Julia blinked as the fantasy faded into mundane reality. Right. It was only early evening, not midnight, and she was in her bedchamber as usual, not swimming naked in the lake. A twinge of guilt went through her. Her life in Derbyshire was wonderful, after all. Why did she feel the need to escape it into these diary entries? "So sorry, Pick. I'll put it away as soon as the ink dries."

"Always scribblin'. You'll lose your eyesight, my lady, see if you don't!"

"I know, Pick." Julia capped the ink bottle with a sigh. "Did his lordship mention that he might be joining me this evening?"

A glint of pity shone in Pickles's eyes. She turned briskly away to hide it. "Himself went straight to his room after dinner, as usual."

As usual. Julia lifted her chin. Aldus hadn't come to her in so long—and even when he had, he'd always been more embarrassed than amorous. She didn't care about the difference in their ages. She owed him so much. She would do anything for him . . . if ever he should ask.

"Humph. Good hot water gettin' cold, too." Pickles sniffed reproachfully, the moment of crusty pity past. "If you were still our little Jilly, I'd tan your bottom for wastin' my time this way."

"Yes, Pickles." Julia let a little Lady Barrowby creep into her voice. "You've made yourself perfectly clear."

Pickles subsided with a last irritated grunt and held out her hand for Julia's wrapper. Julia removed it and stepped into the now tepid water with another sigh. Pickles left the room, giving the door a decidedly miffed slam.

Julia closed her eyes. She'd pay for that one later—she likely wouldn't get a truly hot bath for a fortnight—but she couldn't allow Pickles to go too far. Aldus was adamant—simply because the woman had once been one of her mother's closest friends was no reason to allow her and the rest of the handpicked staff to badger the mistress of the grand house of Barrowby.

Looking back, she decided tonight's entry had been a particularly lovely fancy, full of beauty and titillation. The last line was a bit embarrassingly melodramatic—"if he has a face he will also have a name—and I must never know it"—but what did it matter? No one was ever going to read it but her.

She slid deeper in the bath and leaned her head against the back of the lavish copper tub, letting the fantasy take over her imagination once again.

The moon is full and swollen . . .

"My lady!" Pickles burst back into the room, graying hair astray and eyes wide. "My lady, it's his lordship—he's collapsed!"

1

Husbands came and husbands went, but dreadful hair lasted forever.

Julia, now the widowed Lady Barrowby, forced one last curling strand back into her severely restrained hairstyle and settled the black veil over it all. Her beloved Aldus had lingered for three long years in his efforts to stay with her after his initial collapse and although he'd been more mentor than husband, she had sworn to mourn him for one entire day before she took on the task he had set her.

Just as he'd wished, she had buried him today with no more fanfare than the baker of the nearby village of Middlebarrow might have received. Now, she must pull herself together and dry her tears, for the moment had come.

With a sigh, she saw that another pale wisp had come loose. Her hair refused to adapt to the role of highborn lady, a last holdout from the common Jilly Boots she'd once been.

She shoved the blasted thing into submission once again, using her customary excess of pins. At last, she

was ready to face down the three intimidating lords
who had gathered uninvited in her front parlor. She
pressed her fingertips to the locket about her neck for a
moment, then she turned and walked calmly from her
bedchamber.

All about Marcus there was chaos in the yard of the
coaching inn. The impromptu visit from the Prince Regent of England had sent the innkeeper into fits of
near-fainting and the people of this anonymous village
into goggle-eyed ineptitude. There was noise and madness everywhere as he tried to get his highness back on
the road, but deep inside him, there was a place of suspended silence.

Marcus Ramsay, Lord Dryden, was waiting.

Outwardly, he seemed well enough occupied by his
duties protecting the Prince Regent and securing his
prince's safe journey from Kirkall Hall in Scotland to
Brighton—George IV's preferred winter destination.
There was the prince's new mistress to consider, and
there were more servants and staff and Royal Minions
of the Midnight Kitchen Foray than any one man could
possibly need, and yet somehow Prince George still
overworked them all.

Marcus's duties to his demanding monarch aside,
there still remained a portion of Marcus's mind that sat
in that still, frozen moment of anticipation.

He'd been waiting all his life, it seemed. The second
son of a marquess, one boy child too many to hope for
more than Ravencliff, the minor estate left to him by
his mother's dowry, he'd spent his youth wondering
what the world would have left for him.

He'd spent his years in the army, hoping for the answers there, but mere combat didn't hold any thrill but the unpleasant one of danger itself. Marcus didn't want to be the man taking the hill, he wanted to be the man to choose the hill.

His vision seemed to extend beyond that of his general, as if he could see the field of battle from an eagle's view, as if he could outthink the enemy, and his own commanders. He'd waited for them to see what he saw, until he'd not been able to wait any longer. He'd been so frustrated by the useless waste of life perpetrated by shortsighted men—the men who chose the hills.

Finally, unable to bear one more day of slaughter for slaughter's sake, he'd salted his commander's meal with a powerful emetic and left the man puking out his ignorance and stubbornness in the company's latrine. Taking command through lies and persuasion, though he was a mere major, Marcus led his command through the gaping weakness in the side of the French army that somehow he'd been the only one to see.

They'd taken the hill without a single loss.

He'd been accused, tried, and acquitted—for no one could quite prove he'd done what he'd done, nor could they deny its effectiveness. He'd been ordered from the army with a black mark on his record and a furtive, fervent thank-you from his men.

The next day, he'd been tapped by the Royal Four. A blond giant of a man had appeared at his doorstep and offered him the chance of a lifetime.

Someday.

Someday he would take over as the Lion, someday he would assume a seat on the council of analysts and

spies who held the reins of England in their hands—
the Cobra, the Lion, the Fox, and the Falcon. Men whose
deathless loyalty to England superseded even their loyalty to their king.

Someday—provided his youthful and very lively
mentor died before him.

Nor did Marcus wish Dane Calwell dead. The man
was more brother than teacher, more friend than superior. But the Viscount Greenleigh had given Marcus the
taste of a future full of promise and power—not to glo-
rify himself, but to change the world.

To be a man who ruled kings—to be able to use the
vision he had, the mind he'd been given, the strength in
his spirit for something more meaningful than spending his inheritance and waiting for his brother to kill
himself with overindulgence? Now that was a future he
could scarcely wait for.

"Be patient," Dane had advised him, seemingly for
the hundredth time. "You're almost ready, but not quite.
You're too impulsive yet, too reckless. Yes, you saved the
lives of potentially hundreds of soldiers—but you did it
rashly, without thorough deliberation. You might have
killed more than you saved. Take this time to cultivate
some restraint—for you'll need more than you know."

Wait. Always wait.

Marcus had bitten his tongue, he'd beaten down his
ambitions, he'd settled into his role as protégé of the
Lion. Or so he'd thought.

Marcus closed his eyes against the chaos of the inn
yard. He should not allow himself to savor the excitement and satisfaction rising within him, yet he could
not contain it. The waiting was nearly done.

Even now, the Cobra, the Lion, and the Falcon journeyed to Barrowby, home of the Fox. All Marcus need do now was reach for a last bit of patience in a life filled with "wait." In a matter of days, he would have his dream—a seat in the ring of power. A seat on the Royal Four.

For the unthinkable had happened. The Fox had died without apprentice.

And the Royal Four were only Three.

In the most formal and luxurious parlor of Barrowby, consternation reigned.

For the first time in the history of that elite and powerful cabal that steered the course of England's past, present, and future, one of the Royal Four had neglected his most sacred duty.

The three lords, most concerned, accompanied by a very edgy Prime Minister, had set themselves the task of discovering which deserving gentleman had been selected by their venerable peer before his death. At that moment, this task seemed futile.

He had not trained a replacement.

More vital than an heir to a mere title, more important than even an heir to the Crown—for when had England ever had any shortage of those lying about?—the lacking heir to the seat of the Fox left the Four vulnerable to defeat from within.

Lady Barrowby was counting on just that.

Lady Barrowby, "Jilly" to her long-dead mother, "Julia" to her recently deceased husband, stood in the front hallway of Barrowby and listened without shame to the conversation being had in the first parlor.

It was her house, after all—at least until the distant heir to Barrowby could be found. And, although the four men in the parlor knew it not, their conversation concerned her greatly.

The crisp, slightly nasal voice of Lord Liverpool, the Prime Minister of England, was unmistakable. "I cannot believe Aldus could have been so careless! He had nearly forty years as the Fox to select a protégé— it is not possible. There must be someone—perhaps someone who tired of waiting and went about his business."

Not bloody likely, Julia thought.

A deep and powerful rumble disagreed with Lord Liverpool. That would be the blond giant, Lord Greenleigh, who held the seat of the Lion.

"I have never heard of someone choosing not to serve once selected—and don't give me Etheridge as an example. He still serves as spymaster."

"Barrowby cannot have believed he still had time," said a smoother voice thoughtfully. Julia guessed at Lord Reardon, the new Cobra. "He was over seventy years of age!"

The fourth man, Lord Wyndham, had not said much at all. Nor would he. Julia was well aware of the Falcon's cool, watchful nature. Aldus had prepared her well.

"You'd not have had a chance among the old roosters I served with," Aldus had told her, back when he'd been lucid nearly all of the time. "This new crop of fellows . . . perhaps they are of a more modern bent." Yet, he'd not truly believed it, she had known even then. Hoping was not the same as believing.

Julia believed. She had based the last five years of

her life on believing. Now the time had come to put that belief to the test.

She straightened, patted her hair once more just in case, then knocked briskly on the parlor door. With luck, the carved oak had left no discernible impression upon her cheek.

At the curt invitation—obviously Lord Liverpool had thought her to be a servant—she entered the parlor. The four men looked up in surprise and hastily stood.

"Lady Barrowby!" Lord Reardon bowed. He was easily recognizable from his appearances in Sir Thorogood's political cartoons. The other three bowed as well, although their expressions were less welcoming.

Julia decided at once that she approved of Reardon. She was not so sure about Greenleigh and Wyndham. Liverpool she knew too well to approve of. She curtsied. "My lords."

Liverpool stepped forward. Julia noticed that he did not come close to her. Perhaps he came close to no one—or perhaps he was unwilling to draw attention to the fact that she stood inches above him. Not vanity, she knew. Liverpool's motives were ever rooted in power.

How odd to see them all in person at last.

Liverpool cleared his throat. "Lady Barrowby, if you'll excuse my thoughtlessness in your time of grief—" He didn't sound any too penitent to Julia. "I wonder if you could tell us of any particular companion your husband might have had in his last years. A younger man, perhaps—a member of the aristocracy?"

Julia could answer that question with complete honesty. "No, my lord, I could not. Aldus has—*had* not seen anyone outside of our household in years."

Still, there was no point in keeping them in distress. *Breathe in, breathe out.* "Gentlemen, the fellow you seek does not exist. There is no younger man. There is only me."

She paused. Swallowed. Met their confused gazes with a serenity that did not truly exist.

"I am the Fox."

The uproar was immediate and unpleasant. Julia maintained her composure until the four men had sputtered and exclaimed and denied enough.

She cleared her throat. They fell more or less silent, although if Liverpool did not cease swearing beneath his breath, someone might think him better off in Bedlam.

"My lords, I am not requesting that you allow me to be the Fox. I am informing you that I *am* the Fox, and have been for the past three years. I know everything that my husband knew, and considerably more than any of you, excepting the Prime Minister, of course."

Liverpool sputtered. "Rampant falsehoods, all of it! I have been dealing with Barrowby for years! We came into the Four within a few years of each other. When I stepped down to become Prime Minister last year, it was after extensive correspondence with Aldus. I would have known had I not been dealing with him!"

She folded her arms. "You have been corresponding with me, Robert. I could prove it, but I do not think you would wish me to. I know more about you than merely the gossip one might read in the newssheets."

Liverpool went entirely still. "You tread dangerous ground, my girl."

She tilted her head. "I believe the correct address

would be 'my lady,' but I shall let that familiarity pass for such an intimate acquaintance."

Liverpool did not respond. It was obvious that he was thinking very hard, and even more obvious that one would not like to know what he was thinking. Not that she required a map. She knew these men, even the most recent member, Lord Reardon, better than their mothers could.

Julia turned to the other Three. "May I congratulate you on your recent marriage, Lord Greenleigh? I wish you and your intrepid lady the best."

Dane Calwell nodded graciously, but his eyes were narrowed. "You seem rather well informed, my lady, for being isolated at Barrowby for so long."

Julia nodded. "Indeed, I have found it necessary to set up my own network of informants. I could hardly take my case to the Liar's Club, could I?"

"So you admit to hiding the truth from us?" Liverpool was quick to sniff out discrepancies. Aldus had warned her of that.

Julia lifted her chin. "I imagined your response and acted accordingly. Aldus wished to remain the Fox until he could no longer function as thus. He entrusted me to decide for him when that time was." She was unable to hold back a sigh. "It came so much sooner than we'd feared."

There was not a flicker of sympathy in the granite expressions before her. Never mind. She would not fail Aldus. He had believed in her ability to hold the Fox's position, even to preparing her for this moment.

"They'll test your mettle," Aldus had told her. "You

won't know where it will come from or when, but you can count on being set with some sort of trial." He'd patted her hand. "No sense in worrying over it yet. Not a thing you can do but prove to the lot of them that you're made of good stern stuff."

So far, only her carpets were being tested by Liverpool's pacing.

"She is too young!" The Prime Minister was not going to give up easily.

Julia smiled gently at him. "There is a precedent. The eleventh Falcon assumed his seat at the age of nineteen in the reign of King Henry VI. I was all of twenty when I did so."

The Falcon nodded slightly. "That is so." His eyes gave away nothing.

Julia nodded respectfully in reply. "I realize that this is a shock to you all. You will require some time to adjust to the notion of a woman in the Royal Four." She curtsied and turned to leave the room. "Yet, pray do not forget this." She stopped and looked at them over her shoulder. "There is no one else."

She left, closing the door behind her. She made it around the corner of the hallway before the stiffening left her knees and they began to shake uncontrollably. She'd done it. She'd faced down the four most powerful men in the land—some might say the world. Nothing she had done so far as the Fox compared to this moment. She felt terrified and exhilarated and calm, all at the same moment.

She knew they would do their best to deny her. Liverpool was particularly dangerous, for he'd not taken kindly to her dig about the gossip. Then again, she doubted any of the others would stop at eliminating her if they truly believed her to be a danger. It was up to her to convince them that she knew what she was about. Being female had no influence on her mind or her loyalty.

"Oh, Aldus," she whispered, tipping her forehead against the cool wall. "You should have seen their expressions." A small, rusty breathless laugh broke through her reserve. "I wish I could see it again, myself."

Beppo rounded the corner, obviously looking for her. Julia straightened and nodded at the small wiry butler, her practiced composure instantly back in place. "Yes, Beppo?"

"Their lordships wish you to wait on them in the parlor, my lady. At your convenience, of course."

Beppo, who had come late in life to the serving of the "Quality," had added that last bit on himself, she was sure. "Their lordships" hadn't seemed too terribly concerned with her convenience. She lifted her chin and closed her eyes for a long moment.

Grace under fire.

She returned to the parlor to find the four men ranged like a firing squad, facing her. Fire, indeed. From the glare in Lord Liverpool's eyes, she rather thought brimstone might also be in her future.

"Gentlemen, have you come to the obvious conclusion?" Careful. She might have the upper hand, but they'd never work with her if she alienated them completely.

Lord Reardon bowed. "My lady, I fear the only conclusion we have come to is that we cannot currently come to a conclusion. We request a fortnight to deliberate upon it."

A thrill went through Julia. A tie vote, then? Who might be voting on her side—Reardon and Greenleigh? The two were reportedly very happily wed. They would likely have a higher opinion of a lady's abilities.

So . . . it was the Prime Minister, of course, and the sharply handsome Lord Wyndham.

She curtsied low in return. "Then I shall remain here at Barrowby to await your verdict, my lords."

If someone had been watching—and someone was— they would have seen four very thoughtful men leaving the grand house of Barrowby.

Now what in that house might have brought about such pensive brows?

The afternoon sun glanced off shining golden hair, drawing the watcher's attention to the woman standing at the top of the grand steps, watching her guests leave. His gaze passed over her, then was drawn sharply back.

No.

There was an unfamiliar sensation in the watcher's midsection. He spared a moment to analyze the feeling, only to determine that it was deep and bone-chilling shock.

He slipped silently through the trees, moving closer than was truly wise, but he must know . . .

She turned slightly, lifting her face to the day and letting her shoulders droop wearily for a moment. He could see her clearly now—the same eyes, the same chin, the same shimmering hair. It was impossible. How could this be?

More to the point, what had she to do with the men who were now riding away? After he'd followed them thus far the truth seemed no clearer. She was obviously the lady of the house and she wore black, so she must be in mourning. Had they been merely consoling the widow of a peer?

No, it could not be. It was merely a chance resemblance, some trick of the light, a similarity in bearing—

Then he saw the locket gleaming in the hollow of her throat. He knew that locket well, for he'd ordered the jeweler to make it just so, with the design of the golden serpent's coils cradling an emerald.

Ah, so it was true. When there was no other explanation for the impossible, one must accept it as possible.

His eyes narrowed as the woman turned to reenter the grand house.

Then one must consider how to turn it to one's advantage.

A new plan, a perfect new plan, blossomed in his mind. He would take her back with him—but he must take care that she went more or less willingly.

He could merely steal her away, but how to control her? He was a bit short of treasonous minions at the moment, nor did he have the gold to bribe the mercenary sorts.

On the other hand, she obviously possessed a plenty from her generous, elderly husband. He almost smiled, for he did appreciate such ruthless ambition. She could afford two passages on a fine, if highly illegal, ship.

If he could convince her to come away voluntarily, at least until he could imprison her aboard a ship and keep her drugged for the journey to Paris, then his long arduous penance might come to a close at last.

He could see the difficulties already. She would want to stay, for although he could promise much, who would leave such luxury unless they were forced to?

Then again, if the burden of playing lady of the manor became too much—

He would begin immediately, then, to make sure she would have no reason to stay.

Julia stayed where she was for a long moment as the four men on horseback rounded the turn in the long drive.

In moments, they were gone. She'd not been surprised when they'd refused the hospitality of Barrowby. They must have realized that every word they'd uttered would have been reported by her faithful staff.

Three large men, one slight. All handsome in different ways. All waxing territorial, their hackles raised. She'd not been around that much heady virility in a very long time. It would be enough to make a sillier woman giddy.

Luckily, she simply wasn't that sort.

2

Broad shoulders, blocking the firelight. The silhouette of cheekbone and jaw as he moves over me, his rhythm unrelenting, his power undeniable. I stroke my hands up his corded arms simply to feel the muscles moving beneath his damp, silken skin. I don't want to close my eyes, no matter how intense the pleasure. I wish I dared see his face, I want to see him watch me as I shatter. I want to be bared and naked in my lust. I want him to want me that way.

In the Chamber of the Four, a rather nondescript room among many in Westminster, Marcus Ramsay refused to allow his dismay to show before his mentor and the others—although he feared his hands were fisting at his sides. His confident hopes of advancing to his seat before he was white-haired began to slip away. "She actually believes she is the new Fox?"

Dane Calwell shrugged. "According to her, she has been making the decisions and suggestions in Barrowby's place for years."

Lord Liverpool snarled. "Bringing every action of

the Four into question for the duration of that time. Who knows what sort of fritterly female thinking she's injected into our—ah, *your* dealings?"

Marcus stared at the Prime Minister. "Pray, tell me you don't give a second's credence to such a claim? It's ridiculous. She must be lying. She found out about the Four somehow and is taking advantage of her husband's death!"

Reardon shook his head. "I know it seems unbelievable, but according to the staff, Barrowby has been entirely incapacitated for three years. The Barrowby physician concurred. The Fox has been without speech, without the ability to hold a quill, without even much recognition of his surroundings. Yet we believed the Fox was in fine form all that time."

Marcus scoffed. "She holds Barrowby now, which means she holds the lifelines of all those people in her hands. They will say what she commands them to say!"

Liverpool turned to the others. "Precisely what I have been saying!"

Dane nodded. "I suppose that is a possibility." Marcus couldn't believe the reluctance he saw in his mentor's expression.

"You cannot be seriously considering this creature's petition?"

Dane shrugged. "Were she a man, we would consider her to be more highly qualified than you."

Reardon nodded. "True enough. Three years' apprenticeship and three years' active duty. An excellent record for someone her age."

Marcus looked from one to the other. They were

barking mad, both of them. "Active duty? Ordering tea and toting her sick husband's chamber pot?"

"Precisely!" Liverpool nodded. "Somehow she wormed her way into Barrowby's trust, likely when he began to fall into senility. He told her too much. We ought to have been more suspicious of a young, beautiful woman who would wed a man his age!"

"We never sought much information on her. It did not occur to us that a mere girl could get the better of a wily old hunter like Barrowby." The Falcon, whom Marcus had trouble thinking of having an actual name, slid his gaze from man to man. "We need more information on the woman."

Marcus rather thought they needed to be sent to Bedlam, but he would support anything that prevented his position being usurped by an old man's arm ornament! "I'll do it."

Dane flicked his gaze sideways at Marcus. "And you'll be an objective observer? I think not."

Liverpool held up a hand. "Perhaps Dryden is a good choice. He is not objective. He is less likely to be swayed by her astonishing beauty than another man, for she threatens his advancement."

Lord Reardon grinned. " 'Astonishing beauty'? I didn't think you noticed that sort of thing, Robert."

Liverpool shot his own former protégé a dark glare. "I may be indifferent, but I am not blind. The influence of such a creature should not be underestimated."

Reardon reached into his pocket and tossed something small toward Marcus, who caught it neatly. He turned it in his hand. It was a miniature, painted carefully on a circle of ivory, framed in gilt.

Dane lifted a brow. "You robbed the widow, Nate?"

Reardon shrugged. "She won't miss it. There was quite a collection of them."

Marcus peered closely at the image in his hand. The lady there was fair, with eyes of gray and a sweet, vulnerable gaze. Her rounded face looked so young and her eyes so very hopeful . . .

Those eyes caused an unaccustomed ache somewhere within his chest. He closed his hand over the image quickly. "Pretty." He pocketed the piece. "I assure you all," he added dryly, "I am not about to be swayed by a pretty face—or even an 'astonishing' one."

Dane regarded him carefully. "And you'll return a true verdict, though it might mean you'll wait many years to take a seat in the Four?"

Marcus returned the gaze evenly. "If you don't trust me, then I shouldn't be here in the first place."

Dane watched him for a long moment more, then shrugged. "True. Very well, I am for it."

Reardon nodded. "It will be an interesting study, will it not? A woman in the Four. Our pool of potential members would widen instantly."

"God forbid," Liverpool said fervently. He nodded. "I am in agreement."

"You are all forgetting something," the Falcon said slowly. "If she is indeed well versed in the Four, she may very well know of Dryden already."

Dane narrowed his eyes thoughtfully. "Perhaps, although she did seem to think she was the only possible candidate. Of course, I have never used names in our correspondence."

"She has other means of gathering information, if

you recall." The Falcon tilted his head and regarded the ceiling. "Channels I would very much like to know more about." He dropped his chin to gaze at Marcus. "Go, but use an alias."

Marcus pinned on a jaunty smile and bowed briskly. "Marcus Blythe-Goodman, footloose and charming younger son, at your service, my lords."

Reardon grinned. "She'll think you a gold digger, man."

Marcus's grin soured. "It takes one to know one. And, once she labels me thus, she'll look no further."

The Falcon stood. "Excellent. We'll await your report in London in ten days' time."

Marcus bowed and turned to leave. He might be entrusted with all the Four's information and intelligence, yet when dismissed, he was most decidedly dismissed.

No matter. He would take a few days to ferret out Lady Barrowby's secrets—then he would be dismissed no more.

The knock on the door of her morning room surprised Julia. Nothing short of fire or famine would normally induce one of Barrowby's staff to disturb her when she was working.

Not that there was much to do at the moment. Barrowby was entailed to the next male heir and until one could be found through the patrilineal search that was even now being conducted by her—ah, Aldus's solicitor, there was little to do but count and store the harvest and see that the cottagers had sufficient wood and tight roofing for the coming winter.

The investments that Aldus had begun for her five

years ago were doing well enough, and although she would hate to leave the estate that had been her home, she would never want if she managed her concerns carefully.

Beppo entered, his mobile face a study in dismay.

Julia frowned. "What is it, Beppo?"

"My lady, you have callers."

She blinked. "Callers? Not the gentlemen who were here yesterday?"

"No, my lady. But they are gentlemen . . . most of them."

"Most? How many are there?"

Beppo hesitated and stared at the ceiling for a moment as if counting a great number from memory.

Indeed, as it turned out, there was a distinct possibility of famine.

The ravening hordes had arrived.

The inn at Middlebarrow was full to bursting. It had taken a considerable bribe to have Marcus's horse properly stabled. He elbowed his way to the barkeep of the public room through a sea of fellows.

"Ale," he called to the man who was filling tankards five at a time in his massive fist.

"Four pence," the man shouted back over the din.

Marcus blinked but dropped the coins on the bar without comment. It was a king's ransom as ale prices went, but the stuff must be excellent if the number of patrons was any indication. When his own tankard appeared before him, he drank deeply to erase the dirt of a hard day's ride.

Acrid. Weak. Bitter and raw. Marcus swallowed out

of fear of spitting on his neighbor and gasped. "This is horse piss!"

The man next to him glanced his way. "I've tasted horse piss and it's an improvement over this." He indicated the small circle of men about him, all nursing tankards of the heinous ale. "We've a bet down that we can find something that tastes worse. So far, no luck. Want to lay down a quid?"

Marcus wheezed and shoved his own tankard away. "I can't back a wager I don't believe in." He wiped his mouth. "So what is the attraction here if not the ale?" He grinned. "Does the innkeeper have a flock of pretty daughters?"

The other man shook his head. "No flock, just one. And not the innkeeper's daughter."

One of the other fellows nodded emphatically. "And she isn't pretty, either! She's the most beautiful woman in England!"

The first man snorted. "You'll have to forgive Eames, there," he said to Marcus. "He's a bit smitten."

Eames bridled. "And you aren't, Elliot?"

The man next to Marcus, Elliot, raised his tankard in salute. "I am indeed smitten, old man. I'm just too cynical to spout superlatives in public."

Oh, hell. This didn't look good. Marcus let his gaze travel about the room, taking in the occupants with a new eye. All young or youngish. All well dressed and groomed to a spit and polish—all watching each other with the wary acquiescence of predators sharing a watering hole. As far as Marcus knew, there was only one prize worthy of such a turnout in Middlebarrow.

"You're all here to court Lady Barrowby, aren't you?" Damn, and he'd thought it would be easy.

"What? Did you think it would be easy?"

Marcus shot his gaze to Elliot, whose lips twisted knowingly. "You thought you'd just trot down here and attach her affections with your good looks and your ebullient charm?" He gestured to the filled room. "As did we all." He tipped back his tankard and downed the dregs of his ale with a grimace. "Bog water, perhaps?" His brow creased thoughtfully. "Or castor oil?"

The other three men shook their heads. "No, we agreed that it has to be a naturally occurring phenomenon. No preparations from the apothecary!"

Elliot shrugged. "Castor oil occurs naturally, but I shan't press the issue." He turned back to Marcus and stuck out his hand. "Since we're here on a similar mission, I shall dispense with the niceties. I'm Elliot."

Mission? Marcus shook the offered hand warily. "I am Marcus Blythe-Goodman. Elliot . . . ?"

Elliot smirked again. "Simply 'Elliot.' It adds to my mystique. I need every advantage to stand out in this lot."

The other three offered their hands. Eames, Potter, and Stuckey . . .

"Are there any blue bloods in the game?"

Elliot narrowed his eyes. "Why, are you planning to claim some connections?"

Marcus regarded the other man just as narrowly. "Why, are you planning to refute them?"

Elliot watched him for a long moment, then shrugged easily. "Sabotage is not my style. I'm more the sort to dazzle her with my charm until she's blinded to yours."

Marcus fought the urge to laugh. A true younger son desperate for some advantage in the world would take this game very seriously. In fact, if he had any hope of getting close to Lady Barrowby, he ought to start taking it more seriously himself. He looked about the room. "There must be some way to cut the herd."

The other four men riveted him with their gazes. "We're listening," Elliot said. "I've tried everything, even telling tales of the man-eating Beast of Barrowby."

Marcus folded his arms. "Rumor is effective. Shall we spread the word that the heir to Barrowby has been found? That will send home the ones looking for more than a widow's portion."

Elliot smiled slowly. "I'm in."

Eames bridled. "Lie? Never! I am a gentleman."

Marcus widened his eyes innocently. "It isn't a lie. I heard it myself, just before I left London. He's on a ship from the West Indies even as we speak." To be truthful, there was a possibility that Barrowby's lost heir lived in Johannesburg—then again, there was a possibility that he did not.

Either way, it was not Marcus's problem.

So it was in unspoken and temporary truce that they all moved into the crowd, spreading the word.

In the elegant halls of Barrowby, Julia heard voices coming from her parlor and pressed herself against the wall at the top of the stairs, keeping out of sight of the entrance hall below. They were back.

She pressed a hand to her forehead. Perhaps if there weren't so damned many of them. Or perhaps if they weren't so attentive.

She'd tried speaking very little, then not speaking at all. She'd instructed her cook, Meg, to lessen the supply and quality of the refreshments, and the same of Furman, the innkeeper in the village. Now there was no food and no fire and still they came!

She'd tried pleading ill once, only to be deluged with notes and gifts wishing her well, all of which then had to be politely answered, which only encouraged the lot of them. She daren't try it again.

She'd always understood the mourning process of the upper classes to be rather isolating, but since each and every one of the gentlemen insisted they were merely here to "console" her, she could not in politeness turn them away.

She was desperate, even contemplating a sudden, vigorous attack of the pox and sneezing on them all.

"Never lie," Aldus had instructed her. "Not if you can possibly help it. It is too difficult to keep track of the ripples in the water. It is better to tell part of the truth and behave as if you've told it all."

She sighed. So many rules to remember and follow. Over the years most of them had become second nature . . . but now she was faced with something she'd never experienced.

Male attention was not something she'd had aplenty in her life. She'd been a gawky girl and an unprepossessing bride. True, she'd improved somewhat in the following years, but by then she'd been lady of the manor. Hands off.

She was still lady of the manor, and more importantly, she was the Fox, wily manipulator of countries and kings. So what was so difficult about a roomful of adoring fellows unsubtly seeking her favor?

The difficulty was that she missed Aldus. She missed his conversation when he was well and his need for her when he wasn't. For the first time in ten years, she felt alone.

Igby, one of her footmen, passed her in the hallway and gave her pert smile and an encouraging wink. Julia mustered up a smile and nod in return. She wasn't alone. Barrowby was her family, all the staff and cottagers who had become so dear to her.

She sighed and pushed herself away from the wall. There was no help for it. She must face the mob.

She entered the parlor with her head high and the merest of polite smiles on her face. Surprisingly, there was no mob in sight, only a bare dozen fellows— the most persistent of the former crowd and one other.

The tall stranger stood back from her faithful coterie as they moved forward as one to greet her. He remained clearly visible to her, as if the others instinctively left him a path to her side.

A small tremor went through her, surprising her into examining him more closely. He was beautiful. With his sculpted cheekbones he might have been almost too pretty, but for the bump on his nose that gave one the impression that there was a brawler beneath the polished exterior. That impression was substantiated by a small scar that cut through one eyebrow.

His green gaze caught her short, causing her to pause in her unenthusiastic greetings. His eyes were a riveting emerald that seemed to turn darker when his gaze rested on hers. When they briefly turned away, she was able to take notice of his broad shoulders and generally superior manly physique.

A ringing like that of the village fire bell sounded within her. *Danger.*

She was attracted to him, whoever he was. How alarming—and absolutely perilous. Then Elliot, who held the distinction of being the only one to ever make her laugh, stepped between, cutting the stranger from her sight.

Who was he? He was different, she could tell instantly. There was something about the way he stood there, unwilling to compete with men who were clearly his inferiors, completely confident that *she* would go to *him.*

That unconscious bit of arrogance broke her trance. She increased the brightness of the smile she bestowed on dear Elliot. "How glad I am that you could visit again today," she said clearly, not looking at the newcomer by force of will.

She was desperate to find out who he was and somewhat less desperate but still interested to find out what had happened to the rest of the mob. Had Furman gone so far as to actually poison the ale this time?

"I'm afraid the faint of heart have returned to their usual hunting grounds," Elliot whispered into her ear as he took her hand to lead her to "her" chair—well, she couldn't very well allow them to fight out who sat with her on the sofa!—and he winked at her with his face turned away from the others. "Now all I must do is kill off the others and you'll be mine, all mine!"

The corners of Julia's mouth twitched. Elliot spotted her response, although she covered it with an imperious nod. His eyes lit triumphantly.

She ought not to encourage him, but at least his company was not as tiresome as that of the more earnest Mr. Eames. "Can you make it look like an accident?" she replied, her voice no more than a breath.

He squeezed her hand briefly. "A veritable act of God."

"Here now," huffed Mr. Eames from behind Elliot. "Her ladyship is in no humor for your senseless jests, Elliot!"

"Perhaps her ladyship is in no humor to be told what sort of humor she's in."

The stranger's voice was deep and powerful, reminding Julia of the rumbling growl of a predator.

Mr. Eames huffed once more, which seemed to be his primary form of communication. Julia noticed Elliot eyeing the new gentleman with watchful amusement. The fellow gazed calmly back at him, clearly waiting for Elliot, or someone, to remember their manners and present him to her.

Elliot dragged the moment out a bit more, clearly amused. Then he shrugged and turned back to Julia with a smile. "That looming brute over there is Marcus Blythe-Goodman. He rides a fine horse and tends not to talk overmuch about himself. A highly suspicious character. I suggest you bar him from your house immediately."

"But then I should have to bar you all, for I know nothing more about you than I do about him." She stood and held out her hand. "Mr. Blythe-Goodman."

"If that's even his name," Mr. Eames muttered.

Mr. Blythe-Goodman approached her and bent over her hand. Blimey, he was tall.

Julia immediately heard Aldus in her mind. "Don't say 'blimey,' Julia. Say 'goodness!' or 'heavens!'."

The reminder of Aldus pierced her sharply. She must have paled, for Mr. Eames cried out. "Lady Barrowby, are you ill?"

Bloody hell. Not more notes! She shook her head quickly. "No, do not concern yourself! I am quite well! It is only that I—" There was no reason to hide it. "I was only thinking of his lordship."

All the gentlemen murmured sympathetic things, but Julia caught a flash of something else in Mr. Blythe-Goodman's expression. It was gone before she could define it, but it made her uncomfortable.

Marcus gazed at the woman coolly, then released her hand and stepped back.

He'd been warned. He ought to have known that if Lord Liverpool waxed eloquent about a woman's beauty—eloquent for Liverpool—that she would be truly extraordinary.

Extraordinary didn't even begin to cover it.

Exquisite. Perfect. Dazzling. All applied, yet none portrayed the additional attributes that kept this motley crowd of men coming back for the crumbs of her attention.

Voluptuous. Graceful—in a coiled-spring sort of way, like a feline at rest. *Jaw-dropping.*

Arousing.

Oh, yes. That word said it all quite well. Before them all stood the single most arousing woman Marcus had ever had the painful pleasure of being gobsmacked by the sight of.

The miniature in his pocket must be years old, the image of a mere girl. Before him now was a creature who was entirely a woman.

She was demurely clad in deepest mourning and, until now, Marcus had never seen a woman who wasn't washed to a sickly pallor by that particular dull black. On Lady Barrowby, the drab color only made her golden hair shine more brightly and her fine, alabaster skin gleam like moonlight.

She'd worked the moment nicely as well, with the touching declaration of mourning and the tears that had misted her eyes just enough to make them shine. She was very lovely, the picture of bereaved grace and elegance.

That didn't mean she wasn't lying.

"Tell me, Mr. Blythe-Goodman, what brings you to our far corner of Derbyshire? Are you here on business?"

Marcus leaned back casually on the sofa. "I'm interested in a position that has recently become available."

Well, that was refreshing. Most gentlemen abhorred the very idea of actual work, although most of them surely would end up taking some sort of employment if they couldn't marry well.

Then it struck her that he was making reference to taking Aldus's place as her husband. His arrogance irritated her anew. She lifted a brow. "I'm sure there are others in pursuit of such a choice position. I do hope you are not out of your league."

For some reason this made him flush darkly, the most honest reaction she'd seen yet. Could she have been mistaken? If he was actually in pursuit of employment, her comment was unforgivable. Julia looked away. She'd not meant to injure him.

She wished he would smile again. One of his front teeth was slightly imperfect. She liked that chipped tooth. It said, "I am a man, not merely a pretty plaything."

Not that she would be playing—nothing of the sort!

Oh, dear. The timing of Mr. Blythe-Goodman's arrival into her life was dreadful. There was so much at stake right now. She could not afford such an exceptional distraction!

If only he had come . . . well . . . *never.*

3

His riveted gaze reminds me of a hunting beast with the prey in sight. Oh, let me be your quarry . . .

Marcus was having a bit of difficulty concentrating on what Lady Barrowby was saying to her paramours.

Above her modest neckline he could see the bounty of her breasts still swelling, as if the bodice were a bit too tight. In addition, the waist was cinched more than the current classically draped fashion dictated, so that the curve of her rounded hips was revealed to a group of men who hadn't seen a woman's waist since boyhood.

Although Marcus's own mother had worn such a fashion, it suddenly seemed a deliberate tease aimed at his entire generation. A woman's true shape, revealed!

Perhaps the style will catch on, he found himself fervently wishing.

"God, I hope so," whispered the man standing next to him.

Marcus clenched his jaw tight. Had he actually spoken aloud without thinking?

She would not surprise another such response from him. He forced himself to look at her with detachment. Was it her large, heavily lashed blue eyes that drew the other men, or the perfection of her even features? Her cheekbones were high enough to be coolly Slavic, but her eyes had a sleepy downward slant that made one think of damp, rumpled bedsheets that smelled of sex.

That is, if one were susceptible to that sort of thing.

Then again, it might be those full, pink lips that she moved with the slightest extra emphasis when she spoke, as if she savored the feeling of the words— which was a ridiculous notion, indeed. Her speech was merely a bit slower than Marcus was accustomed to, having recently spent weeks in the company of those sprightly chatterboxes, the Ladies Greenleigh and Reardon.

Ladies, indeed, through and through, unlike the seductively catlike Lady Barrowby, who looked as though she could bed an entire battalion of soldiers and then walk away from their spent bodies looking cool as buttermilk.

To his astonishment, Marcus was angry. He could feel his fists balling at his sides and cold fury eating at his gut. He'd meant to come to Barrowby and charm its lady, gain her confidence, endear himself with flattery and blandishments, much the way Elliot had.

He couldn't do it. There was far too much at stake for him to achieve that kind of distance. For years he had waited and worked for his chance, sacrificing more than he even wanted to think about—and this mendacious beauty was trying to steal it away. What had she to offer the Four but trickery and a superior bosom?

Worse imaginings surfaced. The Falcon, Cobra, and Lion had already seen her, spoken to her, heard her plea for the Fox's position. They were virile sorts all— and if she affected *him* thus, what might she have gained from men without his own rivalry-induced resistance?

For a single breathless moment, his future stretched before him as the protégé of the Lion. Servitude without power, obligation without advantage, forever and once again second best.

He shook himself slightly. There lay dangerous ground, for the Four were not supposed to look to their own advantage. That was one of the reasons why they were chosen from the highest born, from the ruling class—for there was less likelihood to need social advancement or monetary compensation. It was much more difficult to bribe someone who already had everything.

And he'd known when he'd taken the Lion's offer that he was pledging service to a young, healthy man who might well outlive him.

His gaze fixed on the source of his fury where she sat allowing Elliot to tease a smile from her "I devour men for breakfast" lips.

Instantly her face was transformed by a gamine's grin, changing her from unattainable, if exquisite, statuary to a warm accessible female.

Every man in the room held his breath. Marcus felt his own chest grow tight and forced himself to exhale.

Old Barrowby might have fallen for her wiles, more the fool he, but Marcus was on to her game. She would find that her claws had no purchase on his flesh.

Her soft laugh crossed the room to crawl beneath the skin on the back of his neck. His mind might be resolute against her but his body wasn't listening very well. He could feel the glow of her beauty on his flesh like the heat of the hearth fire behind him. Appallingly, he felt his groin swell.

He stepped away from the mantel—too bloody warm over there anyway—and strode to look out the window onto the chill, gray day. Rather, he aimed his vision in that direction, but he found his gaze caught by the golden reflection of her sitting in the lamplight. The wavering glass did not reproduce her exactly, thank God, allowing Marcus's body to submit to his will once more.

He toyed idly with a decorative box that rested on a side table, distracting himself with the intricate inlay until his heart slowed and his cravat did not feel quite so tight.

At last he felt able to turn back to the party in the room, only to find her gaze fixed on him.

"Is it too warm in here for you, Mr. Blythe-Goodman?"

Marcus met her curious gaze with measured calm at last. "Fret not, my lady. I find the atmosphere most congenial."

"The atmosphere is, but you are not." Elliot was also gazing at him curiously. "Have you spoken more than ten words since entering this house?"

Marcus shot Elliot a glance. "I just did."

Lady Barrowby smiled at that. Marcus felt a momentary flash of ridiculous pride that he had brought it into being once more. He strangled that emotion and buried it deep.

"Mr. Blythe-Goodman, I must correct you," she said with a subtly teasing tone. "That was precisely ten words, not 'more than ten.'"

The measured melody of her voice threatened to inspire a permanent craving for it within Marcus. He could well see why she had such a following of devoted suitors. She was an actress of the highest caliber, to know precisely what would most appeal to a particular man. She was truly waxing professional over Elliot now.

Marcus burned to know why.

You mean, why is she paying attention to Elliot and not you?

Very well, if Elliot had already claimed the role of fawning, inoffensive charmer, then Marcus would take on the part of rousing, haughty challenger.

He bowed. "Very well. I accede to your superior tallying ability, my lady." His words replied appropriately enough to her gentle ridicule, but his tone said he doubted she could count above ten without the removal of her shoes.

Clearly taken aback, Elliot seemed without words for once.

Lady Barrowby's blue eyes flashed icy warning and Marcus was rewarded by her full and complete attention, just as he'd wanted—er, required—for his mission, of course.

"As long as you realize your inferiority, Mr. Blythe-Goodman, then we shall have no disagreement."

He met her gaze with arrogant assurance. "Did I not already denounce my own error? Or should I call for a recount, simply to be sure?"

"Are you sure you can survive the strain?" she said tartly. "I fear the effects of such heavy labor on your alleged mind."

Marcus could feel the eyes of the other men upon them, watching them volley words, but her ladyship's attention seemed entirely focused on him. Excellent. "My mind is quite present, my lady, I assure you."

"Oh, really?" A fine brow arched high. "I see no evidence of such. What have you to prove this?"

"My mind is telling me that you are of four-and-twenty years, your accent comes from the south of England, and your butler's is from the Sicilian Alps."

Her eyes narrowed. "I am but three-and-twenty, thank you." Then she shrugged and let a rueful smile cross her expression. "Until two weeks from tomorrow."

Amid a burst of birthday congratulations—good God, could those fellows be any more obsequious?—Marcus found himself once more at the point of her ladyship's surprisingly focused attention.

"All of that could have been gathered from common talk in the village," she retorted. "Does a propensity for gossip now equal intelligence? If so, I must promote my lady's maid to replace the Dean of Oxford."

The crowd murmured their appreciation for her jab. Both Marcus and Lady Barrowby ignored them. "There are other things my mind tells me," he replied. "However, I do not discuss a lady's personal business before other gentlemen."

"Meaning you discuss it before other ladies? Or perhaps you mean before men who are *not* gentlemen." Her tone was that of a teacher to a slow student.

Marcus felt his face darken and tamped down on his

temper. He would not allow her to control this dis-
course, no matter how ridiculous the turn of it.

"I mean that if I were to discuss the fact that you are
wearing another woman's mourning dress, then I would
not be behaving like a gentleman."

She started slightly at his revelation, then raised her
chin. "Mine are still being made," she said calmly.
"This gown belonged to Lord Barrowby's first wife."

Elliot and the others turned back to Marcus with
looks of "dare you to make something of that?" in their
eyes, but he saw a new respect rising in Lady Barrowby's gaze. If nothing else, she knew the value of
good observation.

Respect was not enough. He needed to get closer, to
find out more, to discover her weaknesses and gain
proof of her manipulations.

So he smiled at her just the way he'd wanted to
when he'd made her laugh.

Oh, my. Julia blinked. If Mr. Blythe-Goodman was
a fine-looking fellow when he was sulking, then he was
a veritable god when smiling. She touched one hand to
the back of her neck.

If she'd ever thought him dark and remote, she'd
been wrong. His green eyes had sparked when she'd
teased him and the intensity of his regard had made the
other men disappear, even her friend Mr. Elliot.

He was less distant than he was . . . caged? Yes, that
was it. He reminded her of a wild creature long
caged—one with eroding patience, waiting for its opportunity to escape. Not tame, never docile, merely
endlessly, ruthlessly patient . . .

What a fancy. Mr. Blythe-Goodman was nothing

more than another handsome young gentleman without means of his own, looking for a rich wife to see him clear of his debts.

From his attitude so far, he didn't even like her!

Abruptly, she tired of the verbal sparring and glanced at the ormolu clock on the mantel. Heavens, was it so late?

She stood. The gentlemen leaped to their feet as well.

"I fear I must now return to attending my duties," she said politely. "It was lovely of you all to call."

Eames and Stuckey backed out at once. Elliot lingered a moment, sending her a considering glance. "I am glad you were able to spare so much time for us today," he said, but his tone and expression implied that he was not entirely happy about it.

Julia had never spent more than a quarter of an hour in their company before. She was appalled to realize that she had been conversing with Mr. Blythe-Goodman almost exclusively for much longer than that. Elliot was clearly sorry he'd brought his friend along and Julia wasn't much happier about it.

Her life had no room for diversion.

The journey down the hedge-lined road back to the inn promised to be a quiet one for Marcus, at least until Elliot opened his mouth.

"What possessed you to be so rude to her ladyship?"

Elliot was furious with him, Marcus could tell. Perhaps it was the way Elliot kept shooting deadly glares at him as they kept apace on their ride back to the village. Or perhaps it was the enraged silence that had lasted so blissfully until this moment.

Marcus remained bland. "Was I? So sorry."

"It isn't I you should be apologizing to, you lout! What a thing to say, about her wearing another woman's gown! How could you be so sure of such a thing, anyway?"

"Tight bodice, twenty years out of fashion, an inch of unmatched fabric added to the hem," Marcus replied easily.

"The hem? The *hem*? What sort of man are you? With such a creature before your gaze, you were looking at her *hem*?"

Marcus sighed. He ought to allow Elliot to doubt his masculinity. There was value in being underestimated but it rankled to leave it.

"*I* noticed the entire set of attributes, Elliot, which is how I remarked the bodice was too tight." He couldn't resist another dig. "She ought to have added another inch to that hem, for I saw a pair of very pretty ankles as well."

"Humph." Elliot subsided, although Marcus noted that the fellow looked a bit envious that he'd missed her ladyship's ankles.

"Well, be careful," Elliot continued. "Several of the others are quite upset with your behavior. I've no doubt you'll hear more about it back at the inn."

"Oh, dread. The inn." Marcus pulled his mount to a halt. "I don't think I can bear another drop of that pig pizzle."

"Pig pizzle, eh?" Elliot looked thoughtful. "No, I believe Stuckey already disproved that submission."

Marcus made a face. "Then I'll take his word for it." He rolled his head on his neck for a moment. Lady

Barrowby brought out a new tension in him—surely
due to the gravity of his mission. The very future of the
Four rested on his shoulders, after all.

He raised his gaze to see Elliot sitting easily in his
elegant but worn saddle, on his elegant but elderly
horse, the very picture of a dandy on his last stretched
bit of credit.

"You ought to move on, you know," Marcus said
abruptly. "She isn't going to wed anyone so soon after
her husband's death. There must be dozens of other
ladies who would welcome your suit."

Elliot smiled slightly. "Rich ones? Young, lovely rich
ones who like me above all the others?" His eyes narrowed slightly. "Or used to." He tilted his head. "How
did you do that? How did you know she'd respond to
your insult as a challenge and not simply take offense?"

Because she is so much more than you think she is.

The thought came from nowhere—and a ridiculous
notion it was. She was tricky and cunning, but Marcus
could not believe that she was anything more than that.
He refused to consider that she might be any sort of
real competition for the seat of the Fox.

"I didn't," Marcus said finally. "I simply tired of you
lot buzzing about her like flies on taffy. It's sickening.
Have a little dignity, man."

He reined his horse around and took the lesser-
traveled fork. He glanced back to see Elliot stand in his
stirrups.

"Don't have any dignity!" Elliot called out. "Never
did, never will!" He sent Marcus a jaunty wave.

Marcus rode hard for about two miles before his
tension began to ease at last, soothed by the cadence of

hoofbeats. What he needed was a slant, a secret doorway to Lady Barrowby's confidence.

What he needed was information not available by common gossip.

When the road began to curve back in the direction of Barrowby Hall, Marcus took it.

Elliot watched Blythe-Goodman ride away with narrowed eyes. He claimed to be just another down-on-his-luck second son, but Elliot wasn't so sure. There had to be a dozen ladies of good fortune simply panting to be courted by a great, square-jawed lout like that.

And that horse—that was a very fine horse. Of course, Elliot had met a few gentlemen who put good horseflesh over good tailoring, though rarely.

Yet it was something both more and less than the exterior that didn't seem quite right.

The fact of the matter was, as odd as it sounded even in Elliot's own mind, the bloke walked like a lord.

Elliot rode back to the inn lost in thought. Lady Barrowby seemed rather impressed as well. Elliot had meant to outshine the other suitors and so far had done so with ease. Yet the minute old Blythe-Goodman had begun to speak, Elliot and the rest of the worshipful multitude had faded into nonexistence.

Her ladyship had actually glowed, animated by the spirit of battle. Damn, he ought to have thought of that tactic himself. After all, this was his chosen profession. Yet nothing seemed to be going to plan.

He'd come here hoping to do what all the others did, to get close to the Widow Barrowby. Now that he'd come to know her a bit, he'd stopped seeing her as a means to an end and begun seeing her as a woman, a lovely and amusing person in her own right.

He hated it when that happened. Now he'd be forced to think about how his actions influenced her, and her feelings, and all that rot. He let out a long sigh. Was there no end to the obstacles in his way?

4

"All my days are consumed by thoughts of my nights . . ."

Evening came more quickly with the passing days. The sky darkened and the fires were lighted for warmth instead of show. Barrowby was empty of callers, but for once that isolation did not soothe. Peace and quiet did not always bring peace of mind.

Julia became aware of the trail of petals she'd left zigzagging down the fine carpet of the gallery behind her as she'd restlessly picked at the posy Elliot had given her.

Dismayed, she gazed down at the stripped bunch of twigs she now held in her hands. Oh, dear. And he'd probably spent his last shilling on it, too.

It was all Mr. Blythe-Goodman's fault!

She thrust the wreckage of the posy into her pocket and absently continued her pacing. "Another woman's dress." What a terrible thing to say! Of course, it was true, but that wasn't the point. The present Lady Barrowby had nothing but colorful clothing to wear, for it had pleased Aldus's fading vision to see her brightly clad. She hadn't had even a yard of gray silk to her name when Aldus had died.

Which was silly as Aldus had been dying for some time. She ought to have been thoroughly prepared. Yet she'd not been able to bring herself to order mourning clothes—as if it would hurry his end somehow.

She tipped her head back and closed her eyes. "Oh, Aldus, how do I make them go away?"

More importantly, how did she make Mr. Blythe-Goodman go away?

Choose one.

She stopped, her breath caught. Choose one? Could it be that simple?

But it was. All she need do was indicate her preference and the others would go away, taking their noise and their appetites and their brooding, disturbing presences with them.

Yet that would be cruel, wouldn't it? To raise a fellow's hope in such a way? There were words for women like that. She'd certainly never applied them to herself before and she found it distasteful now.

That thought led her down a different path. What if it were not false hope? What if she did marry again?

For the first time, it occurred to her that her current popularity might not be temporary. If Barrowby's heir wasn't found, then custom demanded that she live out her days on the estate and its rents, until the Crown seized it upon her death.

She pressed one hand to her throat. A lifetime of being pursued by money-hungry men? She nearly staggered at the sheer exhausting possibility. Heaven forbid!

So marriage might be in her best interest. After all, members of the Four were encouraged to have unremarkable lives, and what could be more unremarkable than a widow who remarried to a respectable man?

Part of her cried out against it, for she still thought of herself as Aldus's faithful wife, but the logic was inescapable. Once her mourning period was ended, the barrage of suitors would only increase a hundredfold.

Or worse. She knew from her own position as the Fox that Napoleon was on the run and the end of the war was imminent, which meant that England was about to be deluged with restless young men fresh from the war looking to marry

Good God, what a horrifying thought. She shut her eyes against the vision of wall-to-wall redcoats, voracious, competitive, elbow-jostling ex-soldiers, all earnestly vying for her attention and her wealth.

It made one long for a nap, that's what it did.

What she ought to do was arrange an informal agreement now for a quick wedding in two years' time—take on a consort, so to speak. A clear message to other suitors that the position had been filled.

The thought of the peace and quiet that would ensue took the idea from outrageous to charming in an instant.

Choose one.

But which one?

Eames was a good man, and more inclined to verbosity than passion—would she never be allowed to have passion? No, unworthy thought. Passion was too complicating—but he was also inclined to be officious and Julia had never been inclined to mindless obedience.

Stuckey was rather nice, and he'd be easy to please . . . but he wasn't altogether bright and might make stupid children—

Children! A bolt of joy went through her.

But no . . . she might be forced to put her duties before motherhood, which was fair for no one.

Her elation fell flat. Ah, well. She'd never really thought children would be part of her future, not after Aldus had stopped making even the monthly obligatory trip to her bed.

Nonetheless, she had no desire to endure stupid conversation across the dinner table for the rest of her life, so Mr. Stuckey was out.

What about Mr. Blythe-Goodman?

Damn, she ought to have known he would come up.

For a moment, she allowed herself to imagine having lifelong access to that admirable form—those shoulders!—that restless energy, that quick wit . . .

Her breath quickened, until she caught herself short.

No. Too good-looking, too intense, too distracting from her duty. She needed someone interesting, but not absorbing. Someone easily managed. Someone as unconcerned for life's heavier subjects as she was herself concerned by them.

She needed someone like Elliot.

She turned the thought around in her mind, doing as Aldus had taught her, examining it from all angles.

Amiable. Light-minded but not stupid. Amusing. Unlikely to pry into anything he found tedious, such as the running of Barrowby, or the origins of its staff, or the mysterious work that occupied his wealthy and very generous wife.

She narrowed her eyes, thinking on Elliot. Good-looking enough to be pleasing. Though not as tall or as broad as Mr. Blythe-Goodman, Elliot had a lean, poetic appeal. His fair hair was most attractive and his blue eyes—or were they gray?—shone with sarcastic wit. She would not mind sharing a bed with such a man—

Not that her libido was a factor in any of this. Those days of wasteful fantasy were long over and had been ever since Aldus's collapse. She had duties to attend to.

Of course, Lord Greenleigh had a pretty new wife, as did Lord Reardon. If they could please themselves with an attractive spouse, then could she not as well?

Another point in Elliot's favor was that she would never be tempted to bear children with him. She knew his kind—"the flash sort," as Pickles would say. Good fathers that sort did not make.

Yes, she finally decided. It was a good idea.

She turned and swiftly strode from the gallery, kicking her skirts high with her hurry and sending the pitiful torn petals astir with the breeze of her passing.

Just as Aldus had always said, she took her time to come to a decision, but once made it was as good as done.

From the point slightly uphill from the manor house itself, Marcus could see all activity in the stable and kitchen yards. The Barrowby servants were an odd bunch, that was sure.

When one of the young footmen cartwheeled easily from atop the round cistern cover to land neatly on his feet on the cobbles, Marcus chalked it up to too much youthful energy.

When another footman, identical to the first one, did the same to land upon the shoulders of the other as securely as if he were standing on the ground, Marcus began to wonder.

When the third footman—they must be brothers, Marcus could not tell them apart—took a running leap to bound off the cistern and form the top of a human tower, Marcus was forced to restrain his applause. If milady wasn't careful, she'd lose the three of them to a traveling fair!

The small, swarthy butler hustled from the house and admonished the three for their play with much Gallic waving of hands. Chastened, the boys bowed their heads. The butler, Beppo, stood giving them what for, the picture of exasperation with his hands pointing and gesturing.

Beppo obviously ran a tight ship, proven by the gleaming condition of Barrowby itself. Marcus watched, amused, as Beppo delivered three identical ear boxings. Those three wouldn't shirk their duties for—

Abruptly, the portly Beppo further illustrated the point he'd been making by taking a running jump at the cistern himself.

The butler, livery tails flying, performed an inspiring double flip in the air, then landed with a flourish, arms high. It was as if a penguin had suddenly learned to fly.

Marcus blinked, his jaw dropping. What the hell was going on?

The sound of pounding hooves brought Marcus's attention back to the front of the house. He moved along the hillside several yards until the front drive came into view.

When Marcus saw Elliot arrive at the steps of Barrowby at a pace punishing for such a mount, his first thought was that there was some emergency. He had the impulse to run up the steps himself to rescue the fair maiden, until he cynically recalled that there were no maidens here.

He saw candlelight brighten the window of the front parlor and then double as a housemaid scurried about to prepare the room. She even pulled the draperies closed tightly against the night, covering the window completely from view.

Marcus smiled. "Why, thank you. I don't mind if I do," he murmured.

Wasn't it convenient that he'd unlatched that very window when he'd stood there earlier pondering the gray afternoon?

Now, with it properly concealed, he could wedge it open a crack and listen quite easily from outside. He quickly descended from the hillside—keeping within the cover of the ancient tree trunks—and made his way from the shadow of the trees across the dark lawn to the planting bed beneath the front parlor window. A push of a finger was all it took to open the window enough to hear the conversation within.

Two voices, one deep with a lazy cadence that was unmistakably Elliot, one light with that succulent pronunciation that sent unwanted tingling up Marcus's spine.

Elliot certainly seemed surprised about something. "Me, my lady? But I thought Blythe-Goodman—"

Lady Barrowby cut off Elliot's astonished voice. "I hardly know the man," she said briskly. "Now, I know you have a realistic grasp of the situation."

Damn, he'd missed something important.

"Of course." Elliot's surprise was no longer apparent. He did seem the sort to bounce back quickly. "I can provide you with a valuable service. You will provide me with compensation."

Marcus blinked. Service? Compensation? Elliot had no skills to offer that he could think of, other than his charm.

Lady Barrowby laughed softly. Marcus's nape hairs rose in reaction.

"No, Mr. Elliot, you do not understand," she said. "I do not wish a merely temporary solution to my problem. I would like to make it permanent."

There was a moment of silence. Marcus burned to know what was to be permanent. *Bloody hell, answer her, Elliot!*

"I know you are not interested in false protestations of love, my lady," Elliot said slowly, "but at this moment I do believe you are my favorite woman in the world."

Marcus heard that soft laugh again, like cream on his tongue.

"Mr. Elliot, if you agree to this, I had better remain your favorite woman in the world, till death do part us."

"That will not be a hardship . . . Julia."

No. Marcus couldn't believe it.

Till death do part us?

Julia?

She was going to wed that useless, pretty boy? That mooching, shallow, debt-ridden tea leaf—

All right, perhaps "tea leaf" was going a bit far, but for pity's sake, Elliot was a blot on England's masculine population! He was a lazy, overdressed, undermotivated, frivolous gnat! Julia was far too intelligent and lovely to waste herself on such a person of little consequence—

Julia?

Marcus realized he was standing ankle deep in the soft soil of Barrowby's flower bed, cursing soundlessly under his breath, absolutely enraged at the idea of his target wedding another man—er, *a* man.

If he was worried about anyone's welfare, it ought to be Elliot's. After all, Elliot had no previous—dead!—spouses under his belt.

Then again, if he was going to worry about anything, he ought to be worried about how he was going to accomplish his mission and save the Royal Four from contamination now that Lady Barrowby had neatly foiled his plan to ingratiate himself.

There were no more voices coming from the parlor. In his moment of fury, Lady Barrowby and Elliot must have made their good-byes.

Damn.

Without a second to spare, Marcus threw himself to the ground behind the naked thorny trunks of the rose-bushes, just as the front door opened to emit Elliot. Marcus watched from his concealment as Elliot coolly strode down the stately entrance stairs of Barrowby to wait for his horse in the drive.

As soon as the door behind him closed and cut off the golden triangle of light, Elliot threw back his head, threw out his arms, and hoarsely whispered, "Thank you!" to the heavens.

Then he performed a brief, elated jig on the gravel drive.

He's a poor winner, Marcus thought sourly.

And you're a poor loser.

Which was absurd, for he'd lost nothing. This was a minor setback, that was all. Lady Barrowby could wed a thousand dandies and it wouldn't stop Marcus from accomplishing his mission.

He wasn't jealous. He was . . . merely disappointed. For the sake of his mission, of course.

Ridiculous, that's what it was. Simply ridiculous.

Elliot?

Elliot rode his weary mount slowly back to Middlebarrow, basking in the moment.

He'd won. Over all the others who'd fought for Julia's attention, *he* was the one she'd chosen. Bloody hell, she'd not only promised her hand, she'd proposed the union to *him*!

He'd thought for sure the battle was lost when Blythe-Goodman had come along. Suddenly thoughtful, Elliot realized that, in some indefinable way, he *had* lost when Marcus had come. Yet here he was, engaged to Lady Barrowby, scarcely a week after he'd arrived.

She didn't love him, thank heaven. God, what a burden that would have been. Ah, well. No worry on that score now. Whatever her motive for choosing him—and however suspiciously tied to her obvious attraction to Marcus—Elliot was comforted by the lack of real feeling between them.

That would save a great deal of trouble when he was forced to betray her.

Elliot urged his exhausted horse to a slightly faster

dragging walk. He couldn't wait to see Blythe-
Goodman's face when he told the great, handsome lout
that he'd lost the lady!

It was after midnight when Marcus returned to Barrowby. He'd made an appearance in the taproom to
allay any suspicions, although the numbers of Lady
Barrowby's faithful were lessening by the moment. Elliot obviously had a knack for spreading the persuasive
rumor.

He'd played the morose, disappointed suitor rather
well, if he did say so himself. All he needed to remember was how much his alias would have suffered from
such misfortune—and top that off with the image of
Elliot undressing Julia on their wedding night—and
he'd had no trouble brooding aplenty over his foul ale.

After sufficient misery, he'd made noises about getting to bed and left the inn by way of the window in his
room. He'd left his horse behind as well, preferring to
stay off the road and in the shadows while on such an
errand.

He'd realized while watching Elliot work the taproom that he was going to have to be a bit more direct
in his approach. He needed information on milady and
he needed it now.

Unfortunately, the house was as tight as a miser's
fist. There wasn't a single reachable window unlatched,
not even the one he'd unlocked himself earlier that afternoon. The doors of course were tightly locked, as
was the coal chute and the kitchen ash pit.

There was also far too much light. It was as if every

sconce in every hallway still held a candle—lavish
spending for simple convenience, or was it? This had
been the house of the Fox, by all accounts one of the
wiliest members of the Four in all its history. Such a
man would never allow a simple thief to breach his
walls.

*Yet you think he would allow himself to be swayed
by a lovely face?*

Marcus brushed away that niggling doubt. Any
man—no matter how intelligent—could fall victim to
his baser urges. The two aspects had nothing to do with
each other.

He shoved thoughts of the seductive Lady Barrowby
to the back of his mind and regarded the house intently.
He might be able to scale the wall by clinging to the
seams between the stones with his hands and feet. He
might be able to steal secretly into the house tomorrow
and wait for nightfall. He might—

He might grow old and die before he ever got into
the house undetected. He pulled his handkerchief from
his pocket, wrapped it twice about his knuckles, and
punched out the nearest pane of glass.

"Done." It was crude but effective. He only hoped
the Three never learned of it.

He let himself in. The window led to a chill room
containing a spinet and a few settees for the listeners. It
was lovely and tasteful in a manner more befitting the
last century than the current one. It looked as if it
hadn't been used in years. Marcus grunted softly to
himself. "She doesn't really seem to be the spinet sort,
does she?"

He listened carefully at the door before entering the

hallway. He began to move silently down the hall, pinching out the candles with his fingertips without pausing as he passed them by. He left only a few burning in case he needed to run for it.

Where to start? Obviously the lady's bedchamber would hold the most secrets—some ladies more so than others—but since the lady in question was undoubtedly sleeping in that room—

I wonder what she wears to bed? Would her hair be loose or braided? Did she bathe in rosewater before bed—

Marcus stopped still long enough to banish such unruly thinking, then continued on his way. He would begin with the obvious, in the spirit of elimination—the study.

It was a spacious and manly room, all gleaming wood panels and velvet drapery. The enormous mahogany desk caused Marcus a pang of acquisitive lust, for it was a lord's delight of elegance and function. It was also entirely empty, containing not even a stump of pencil.

There was nothing in the safe box but a note. "Amateur."

He found a promising hollow portion of the desk. He worked free the secret drawer. Another note. "Oh, go home. You lack imagination."

He had to laugh. Someone had a wicked sense of humor. Surely it could not be the ice carving, Lady Barrowby?

He realized that the study was too obvious, and that she rarely seemed to frequent it anyway. Where did she spend most of her time?

He worked his way back down the hall, taking each

room into closer consideration. He knew it the moment he found it. There was a pleasing little withdrawing room off the music room with a view of the garden and a writing desk, a comfortable chair and hassock, topped by an embroidery basket.

There was nothing in the desk but estate records, kept in a precise hand that surpassed his own. Lady Barrowby seemed to keep every detail herself, with no steward in her employ. She was doing a bang-up job of it, too, except that she kept far too many servants even for this vast a house.

The embroidery basket drew his eye once more.

He couldn't explain why its presence struck him as so odd, except that, once again, Lady Barrowby didn't seem the "embroidery sort."

The basket certainly had an air of neglect about it, although the desk saw hard use. He bent to brush dust from the handle of the basket. Curious, for he simply couldn't picture the vital, energetic Julia settling down to a long evening of stitching, he lifted the lid to see what he assumed were the usual accoutrements of such a pastime. Colored floss, needles, tiny golden scissors . . . and in the bottom of the case, a false bottom.

Most people would not have seen it as such, but it was obvious to him. The outer dimensions of the basket extended a good half-inch farther than the inner dimensions. He fiddled with the bottom of the basket for a long moment—he was beginning to feel a bit silly about it in fact—when he flipped up the bottom to reveal a shallow compartment that contained simply a key.

Not a door key, not a safe-box key—it lacked the sturdy importance. It was a pretty key, the shank ending in a carving and a tiny jeweled eye. The key to some sort of luxury item . . . a box? Perhaps the sort that ladies used to keep dried bouquets and the left-behind handkerchiefs of solicitous gentlemen?

Like the one he'd seen in the . . . where? Music room? First parlor? Surely not. Not left so negligently in plain sight, day after day, where any stranger could spot it?

Unless . . . unless she was counting on just that sort of reaction. God, her thinking was twisted.

He returned to the parlor where he'd borne that excruciating jousting session with her other suitors. There it was, on the side table with a pair of dainty spectacles carelessly laid on the top. He slipped the key into the lock and turned. With a click, the lid lifted slightly, released.

Inside the box, things were much as he'd expected. There was a dried bouquet, a shell from the sea, a curling, faded ribbon . . . and another key.

This one had the heft and authority the other key had lacked. It was definitely the key to a room. Nor was it the plain, unadorned key of a larder or a silver case. This ornately carved key was meant to be seen by more than mere servants.

He could discount the master's bedchamber and— much to the regret of his inner voice—the mistress's bedchamber, for he was in the presence of a mind that would never be so obvious . . . so what did that leave him?

Barrowby was huge, but it was also full of staff and was beautifully maintained—better than Ravencliff, in fact. What room in this house would see no traffic of guests or servants?

He looked down at the key in his hand and smiled slightly. Only a woman . . .

The journey up the stairs took too long, but he dared not allow a single squeak in such an overpopulated house. Two painstakingly silent floors later, he quickly searched the halls until he found what he was looking for.

The nursery was every bit as neglected as the rest of the house was looked after. Dust coated the empty shelves that would have held toys and the sheet-covered cribs were positively saddening.

Then again, children had obviously never been Lady Barrowby's goal.

There was a small dusty trunk standing in one corner of the room. Careful to disturb the accumulated dust as little as possible, Marcus crossed the room to kneel by it. The keyhole was tiny. Marcus tried the same key he'd used to open the ornate box in the parlor and was rewarded by a click.

Inside there were several leather-bound books with plain covers, the sort used for diaries or sketching. At last, her records. Marcus adjusted his candle for maximum lighting and opened one at random. The looping script was easy to read.

"—*his thickness drove into me with increasing fury as his hard hands lifted me above him again and again*—"

Marcus nearly dropped the book in his surprise. "What the *hell*?"

The records were a diary—but what a diary! Page after page was filled with raw, sexual description and erotic darkness. Marcus read faster and faster, his own breath coming quick at the erotic daring on the pages.

He forgot to look for code, he forgot to scan for secrets, he only wanted to live each fevered page of her
exploits and then the next, and the next. By the time he
neared the end of the final volume, he was dripping in
perspiration and his cock was as hard as iron.

It was going to take an hour of cold cloths on the
back of his neck and a hundred press-ups before he
was sure he would not have to take himself in hand to
relieve the pressure!

Absorbed, he lost all awareness of the passage of
time. A sound came from outside the house. Dear God,
it was nearly dawn! Marcus put aside the last, unfin-
ished volume and concluded that the only thing revealed by the diaries was that Lady Barrowby was no
lady, no matter how highborn she was.

She was unchaste and unfaithful. He was repelled.

*Oh, really? Repelled? Is that what you were thinking
when your trousers nearly lost their buttons?*

That wasn't the point. The point was that he had
gained nothing useful in his night raid of Barrowby. He
could try again, but he'd been most thorough.

He was going to have to start all over again.

In the meantime, the morning brightened. It was
past time to leave.

5

The garden is warm and the sunlight glows through the petals and leaves of the roses. The sweet, delicious scent turns my senses to fire, making my skin tingle for my lover's touch. He walks beside me and I can tell that the perfume is affecting him as well, for his steps have slowed and his fingertips linger on the blooms as we pass. "They feel like you," he tells me huskily. "Like the inside of you."

I turn and walk slowly backward before him. I dressed to tantalize him and his gaze falls victim to my décolletage. "Are you sure of that?" His eyes meet mine. "I mean to say, don't you think you might need more experience to make such a comparison?"

He laughs, a low, heated sound that matches the passion rising in his eyes. With one hand, he pulls the petals from a few blown roses, then tosses them to fall about my hair and shoulders like ruby-red snow. "Perhaps you are right. It would not do to compare them without further investigation—"

He grabs my hand and we run for the ruined Roman temple at the back of the garden. He pulls me through

*one of the arched windows, lifting me easily. Then I see
that he has covered the floor of the tiny temple with
rose petals of all colors. He lays me down upon them.
"My goddess," he whispers. "My Artemis, my golden
huntress."*

*"My Adonis," I reply with a smile. "Now, enough
with the pet names. You have important research to
conduct."*

*He laughs and throws petals in my face. "Then shut
up and let a man work."*

I close my eyes and let him do just that . . .

Julia opened her eyes to the dimness of early morning
in her bedchamber, then sighed in frustration. She
could not seem to break the habit of predawn rising.

There wasn't a sound from the house and only the
palest of morning light crept past the draperies. She
could sleep for hours yet, if her habits allowed it.

Once these had been the hours she'd spent at Aldus's
side, reading the reports aloud to him and discussing
her opinions on every one. After he'd first collapsed,
that had been his best time of day, before the confusion
and mind-wandering would steal his attention.

He'd been unable to speak, but she'd seen the understanding in his eyes, and he'd been able to signal her
with small hand motions . . . at least for a time.

By the end, he'd been slipping away from her for so
long that she knew he no longer heard her, but still she
had sat there every morning, setting her own mind in
order and feeling as though somewhere, somehow, he
was listening.

She drew a deep breath, feeling the void in her heart.

There was no one to speak to now and for the first time she realized the true lot of the Fox. No one else could share the burden and the knowledge that a member of the Royal Four held close. No trusted servant, no companion, no family member could ever know.

No wonder each member kept an apprentice! Otherwise one would go mad from the isolation of it!

Julia felt twitchy with restlessness. For some reason, her thoughts kept returning to those diaries she'd kept years ago. Honestly, she'd thought she'd banished that portion of herself quite thoroughly!

It was all Mr. Blythe-Goodman's fault. He made a woman think of hard hands and urgent heat. And those eyes, darkening like night in the forest when he looked at her . . . perilous night in a dangerous forest.

Aldus had touched her as if she were about to break from his handling. How could she have told him that she wanted more, that she longed to *feel* a man's hands on her?

She was not like the fragile ivory carvings from China that Aldus had compared her to. Pain was simply something she'd lived with all her life, from hard work if nothing else.

This world, the luxurious realm of Lady Barrowby, was only part of the mask she'd donned upon her marriage.

She'd spent her childhood in the rough-and-tumble world of the traveling fair folk. They were a loud, boisterous lot, prone to fits of arrogance and temper and just as prone to acts of astounding generosity and good humor.

Her life had been colorful and mostly unkempt,

except for when her more subdued mother had managed to pin her down long enough for a bath and combing.

Now she was a lady, just as her mother had dreamed for her. Those dusty wild days were nothing but fading memory. Only Julia's resilient nature remained the same.

So there was nothing Aldus could have done to cause her more than the most momentary discomfort, yet he had insisted on treating her as if his intrusion were more than mortal woman should be forced to bear.

The gentlemen who called on her now were much the same, treating her as if she might blow away if they spoke too forcefully, as if she might collapse beneath the pressure of their slightest touch.

Gentlemen were bloomin' annoying that way.

Of course, Elliot might be open to a bit of rousing bed play. Unfortunately, Julia wasn't so sure any longer that she would enjoy being with Elliot. His reaction when she'd outlined her proposal had been rather luke-warm. He'd begun to seem a bit . . . depleted, somehow. As if he were half a man—

As if he were half the man that Marcus Blythe-Goodman is.

She slapped away that annoying thought the way she would a gnat. Marcus was a boor and a lout and a great deal too distracting—

Marcus, eh?

Damn, she was doing it again.

And who said the man was even pursuing her? He had called on her, just like all the others, yet he'd scarcely spoken until she had addressed him first, never joined in with the social chatter, done nothing but watch her with those eyes . . .

She shivered. Sometimes she had felt as though he hated her, then she would catch a glimpse of heat shimmering like the green light in a jungle—

Ridiculous. The man was simply not to be borne. She had much more important things to think about.

Before Aldus's death, she had been running her own investigation into the man the Liar's Club called the Chimera. The Liars were very good, but she had sources in a world that they could not touch.

No one could penetrate the tight, nomadic society of the fair folk unless one was one of them.

There was no way to infiltrate, investigate, or otherwise gain access to the traveling fair folk. Not the finest of the Liars could pass in that world . . . but she could.

From the center of her web at Barrowby, the strands of her intelligence-gathering spread out over England and all of Europe—for what did festival players care for wars and borders? Her information came fast and fresh, spread like lightning through the ranks of the showmen, the accuracy preserved in the long-standing oral tradition of the "Say."

As there was nothing to do now but wait for the final decision of the Three, she might as well take up the threads of her latest investigation once again.

The Chimera had last been seen on Cheltenham lands in Durham County and she knew the Liars and the Three considered the man to have drowned beneath the wheel of a crumbling mill.

Julia was not so sure.

The Chimera had slipped through their defenses again and again. He'd assumed the guise of a young bag

man of the streets and insinuated himself into the household of the previous spymaster, Sir Simon Raines. He'd
then been passed from household to household among
the more highborn Liars as a valet until Rose Tremayne,
the first lady Liar—and Julia had been very interested
in the career of the young housemaid Rose Lacey from
the beginning—had become suspicious of him.

Trust a woman to see through the man's disguise.

In addition, it had been the Falcon's operative, his
cousin Lady Jane Pennington, who had been the one to
realize that the uneducated young valet, Denny, was in
fact the French spymaster, the Chimera. The fellow
was a brilliant master of disguise and seemed to have
an eerie ability to sense and recruit England's dissatis-
fied and aimless for Napoleon's cause.

Yet such a man had died beneath a mill wheel? Julia
didn't think so.

The body had never floated to the surface—
something the Lion had explained away by the fact that
the bottom was riddled with years of accumulated
grasping sunken branches.

The Liars were making inquiries, she knew, but the
fact remained that the Liars were still undermanned
from the Chimera's attacks and only the first class of
new trainees had graduated from the Liar's Academy.
With man—and woman!—power so short, Julia somehow doubted that the Liars were expending their ener-
gies searching for a dead man.

Enter the traveling players.

In every corner of England and Europe, a "Say" was
being spread about an evil man who could change his
face and manner at will, a man of small stature, who

might even now be ill from a near-drowning. The showmen loved such a tale and even the tiniest child would soon be on the lookout for such a man as they played the last of the harvest fairs of the year.

There was nothing to do now but wait to hear from them as well as from the Royal Three.

She slipped from her bed and pulled her wrapper about her. Pickles was used to her doing for herself in the mornings and doubtless assumed that Julia would be having a bit of a lie-in now that there was no need to rise early.

The heavy draperies still covered the window, keeping out the light and the chill. Julia tugged one aside to peek out at the day.

It was gray and misty outside, which was no surprise. The hills were nearly revealed now that the trees stood naked in their carpet of fallen leaves. There was little doubt the winter would be—

Something moved between the stables and the house. Not a deer, not a servant about his business. The motion had been furtive and quick. Someone did not want to be seen.

Julia blew out an irritated breath. Her suitors were truly pressing her patience! She tugged the belt of her wrapper loose and moved quickly to her wardrobe. Someone evidently hadn't taken Elliot's claims seriously!

It was a good thing that Sebastian was safely in bed.

Marcus made his way back down the wall of the house without incident, until he was only ten feet from the ground.

Then a great bestial roar shattered the dawn's stillness.

Marcus would never admit it later, not even to himself, but he flinched. Very well, it was more than a flinch. He went rigid with shock, lost his grip altogether, scrabbled uselessly at the wall for a split second, and then fell to the ground like a rock.

Thud.

He landed flat on his back, no wind left in his lungs. His teeth snapped hard on his tongue and his brain rattled in his skull.

First thought—*Ow.*

Second thought—*What in the hell was that?*

The Beast of Barrowby? Surely not. Yet, whatever it was, it was undoubtedly large and predatory and Marcus had no intention of being prey. He dragged air back into his lungs and scrambled to his feet with his back pressed to the wall of the house.

How could anyone have slept through that horrible noise? Unless they were used to it—or, more likely, knew the source and discounted it? Which meant that everyone in this house knew something he didn't.

Marcus just hated that.

The roar did not repeat. He almost wished it would. Fleeing—er, making a strategic retreat—from a beast would be easier if one knew where said beast was located.

Searching through the shadowy grounds of a strange estate for some mighty beast—as rabidly as his curiosity twitched within him—proved too stupid a concept for even his rash nature.

No, better to leave while he still had the chance. He

carefully, silently left the way he'd come, a mere shadow among shadows. The secret of the beast could wait.

A stick cracked behind him.

Julia was still fuming over the invasion of her valued privacy. It seemed some of her erstwhile suitors would take more convincing than others.

Now fully dressed, she pulled one slipper over her stocking foot and reached for the other. If it was that overeager bore Eames, she was going to stuff his pompous—

Suddenly a great roar shattered the morning quiet— a roar that most definitely wasn't coming from the specially heated stable addition she'd had built as far from the horses as possible.

Nor was that the "I'm bored and need entertainment" roar, or the "someone forgot to feed me" roar.

That was the hunting roar.

She jumped to her feet and ran from her bedchamber, hopping on one foot to pull on her other slipper as she went. She was joined in the hallway by Beppo and Pickles, moving at a run. There was no need to exchange words—the entire staff knew what to do.

Sebastian was loose—and there was a stranger on the grounds.

The beast stood on Marcus's chest, its great weight pressing the life from his lungs, its hot, stinking breath bringing up primordial instincts of fear, its mighty jaws opening wide to—

There wasn't a single bloody tooth in its mouth. Not even one lone, ivory survivor.

Oh, this was just perfect. "Bloody hell," Marcus wheezed. "You're someone's blasted *pet,* aren't you?"

The lion leaned down and snuffled his face, drooling enthusiastically on his cheek. Marcus gasped for air as the great weight shifted to press more heavily on his chest.

"Ge-orff!" He shoved at the broad muzzle with both hands. Stars were beginning to spin before his vision but he noticed the lion's miffed expression as its friendly overtures were refused. Maybe if he kept offending it, it would go away.

"You're molting"—gasp—"and you drool"—gasp—"and you really ought to chew mint leaves for that breath—"

The sound of lightly running steps came closer. "Oh!" A feminine noise of disapproval followed. "Shame on you, Mr. Blythe-Goodman! What a terrible thing to say to a poor, defenseless animal!"

Marcus rolled his eyes upward to see an upside-down Lady Barrowby glaring at him with her fists on her hips.

"It isn't"—gasp—"listening anyway. Get the bloody thing"—gasp—"*off!*"

Her expression told him quite plainly that she considered him to be the greatest pansy ever to walk the earth, but she knelt to the grass and held out her arms.

"Sebastian," she cooed to the colossal, malodorous creature. "Come to Mummy, my darling!"

The beast finally climbed off Marcus. Unfortunately, it traveled in the direction of its mistress, which meant that the enormous hind feet also left permanent impressions on Marcus's rib cage and he saw more of the undercarriage of the great cat than he truly cared to. It was enough to make a man bloody insecure.

"Unhh." He rolled to one side and spared a moment to drag sweet, lovely, untainted-by-beast-breath air into his tortured lungs. At least now he knew the secret of the Beast of Barrowby. Alas, the answer only raised more questions.

His breathing returned to normal and his rib cage apparently still operational, Marcus looked up at the Beauty of Barrowby where she sat with her Beast. His mouth went dry, for she wore a morning gown of some filmy pale blue fabric that draped closely to her curves as she lounged half over the golden beast to scratch the thing on its opposite ear. Her bodice barely won the day against the bounty of her creamy bosom and her golden hair hung loose on her shoulders. Marcus's wayward mind flashed on some of the more erotic passages he'd read in her diary, pelting him with thoughts of bare, wet breasts and round, eager thighs that wrapped hungrily about his waist—

Yet imagination could not compare with the real woman before him. She was a bountiful pagan goddess of fire and ice—one that made a man consider abandoning his religion to worship at her feet.

That or ravaging her unto mutual madness, preferably on a lion-skin rug.

Both were dangerous thoughts for a man on a mission.

She took her attention off soothing the hurt feelings of the lion long enough to shoot him an assessing glance. "What brings you to Barrowby so *early* today, Mr. Blythe-Goodman?" She laid her head on the beast's broad skull and gazed at Marcus coolly.

"My deepest apologies, my lady." Marcus made to stand, but one look at the great cat's eerie, alert, golden gaze cautioned him to stay where he was.

He arranged himself on the ground with somewhat more dignity, leaning on one hand with his other elbow supported by a raised knee. A casual, picnicking sort of pose, not at all as if he feared another round with the Breath of Death. "I was taking my morning constitutional and I fear I strayed too close to Barrowby in my enjoyment of the day."

The excuse was weak as hell, a fact that could not have escaped her, considering that Barrowby extended for miles in every direction, but she only nodded slowly. "It is lovely in the morning, isn't it?" She smiled down at the lion in her embrace. "Sebastian couldn't bear to stay in his stable on such a warm day."

"It was a most memorable walk." He gave her his best careless grin. It wasn't as good as Elliot's but it had worked more than once.

To his surprise, she looked away, small spots of color rising in each cheek. It was the sort of response one might expect from a schoolgirl, not a wicked widow. It caused an answering, protective response in himself. *Defend the maiden.* He examined that response with detachment, decided it was only to be expected from a gentleman of his caliber, and dismissed it.

Nonetheless, he went on his guard. The chivalrous man within didn't seem to have many defenses against her gamesmanship. That man saw a sweet, untarnished beauty who needed protection and devotion.

Stupid fellow. Marcus knew better.

But damn, she was good.

She'd had a lover, perhaps many. She'd likely drawn in man after man with that dewy, "protect me now" façade . . .

"Oftimes the best way to play a target is to use their own game."

Wise words from the Prime Minister—and quite probably the answer to Marcus's dilemma. He had the advantage. He knew her deepest weakness, her lustful nature . . . he also knew she found him attractive despite her caution.

There might be a reasonable explanation for the exotic pet. There might be a rational purpose behind the strange household staff. There might even be some sort of understandable reason for the wicked diaries—although he doubted it.

Yet he would never know unless he became closer to her—much, much closer.

As usual, he acted instantly.

He stood smoothly, one eye on the lion, who did not object this time. Marcus bowed deeply, smiled, and held out his hand. "My lady, would you care to walk with me through the garden?"

Julia blinked at the inviting light in his green eyes. *The garden?* There was little to see there but mulch and brown vines . . . yet her hand rose to nestle into his anyway.

"Yes," she heard herself say. "That would be lovely."

6

The scent of the rose petals beneath seep into my bare skin until I feel steeped in perfume and passion and him.

Well, damn. Marcus looked about him in alarm. The garden was a mess, all brown and dry. The rose garden he'd pictured from her diary entry was nothing but rows of skeletal sticks, truncated a foot from the ground. There was nothing but stripped vines covering the grim stone walls and nothing but yellowed grass and gravel on the ground. In the pearly morning light it looked more like a graveyard than a garden.

How was a bloke supposed to stage a seduction in such surroundings?

Lady Barrowby walked slightly ahead of him down the gravel path, her hands clasped behind her back. He noticed that her fingers were twisting together. Another display of girlish nerves from the Beauty of Barrowby?

That was reassuring, but also a reminder of their other companion, the great Beast who padded along at the lady's side, his tail twitching ominously.

Why was he having so much trouble with this

mission? He knew what he needed to do and he knew how to make her respond to him. He was a charming fellow usually, prone to making ladies smile and flip their fans his way. What was it about Lady Barrowby that left him tongue-tied with mingled lust and fury?

Lust he'd felt before, so it must be the fury. He'd charmed the knickers off a few widows in his time, but he'd never faced one who held the power to destroy his dreams.

He was going to have to put his mission from his mind, that was all. He was going to have to pretend that she was just another pretty widow, albeit one with a penchant for lions and making love out of doors.

He bottled his fury, stoppered it and put it away for the day he would need it—the day he destroyed her. Finally, with a mind cleansed of anger, he stepped smartly up to her side and smiled down upon her with easy sincerity. "Lovely day, is it not?"

She blinked in surprise. Surely he'd not been all that much of a bear?

"Well," she said slowly. "It is chill and damp, I don't have a wrap, and I think I smell something dead over in the alliums."

"No," he said firmly. "It is a lovely day." He shrugged free of his coat and slipped it over her shoulders. "You do have a wrap." He steered her away from the alleged deceased down a pretty path lined by small trees whose arching branches in the summer must have met over-head in a charming shade. "And I don't smell anything but roses."

Thankfully, the Beast preferred to investigate the

smellier portion of the garden and left them to their own devices.

She snorted. "Nicely done. The roses, however, exist only in your imagination, I fear."

He leaned close and inhaled deeply. Her eyes grew wide at his forward behavior.

"No," he said, his voice a caress. "I most definitely smell roses."

He saw her swallow hard and hot triumph flared within him. He fought it down. He was Marcus Blythe-Goodman now and Blythe-Goodman actually *liked* Lady Barrowby.

He straightened and grinned down at her. "Your name is not Julia," he declared, apropos of nothing.

She went very still. "W-what did you say?"

Interesting reaction, but to be stored away for later review. Now, he lightly touched a gloved finger to the tip of her nose. "I dub thee Helen, or perhaps Persephone."

Her breath gusted in a small, relieved laugh. "Oh, you are stuffed like a sausage full of blarney, Mr. Blythe-Goodman. And here I thought you a more discerning sort." She turned away, shaking her head.

He caught her hand and pulled her back to him. "Why?" He moved closer. "Because I compared you to legendary beauties?" He kept his voice low and intimate. "Or because I think you are a woman to tempt the gods?"

Her eyes locked on his. He felt her fingers tremble in his and felt his own body answer her shiver. Her lips parted and her warm breath feathered against his mouth.

"And are you tempted?" she whispered.

Hot need ignited in him and this time he let it flare.

There was no chill now. Instead, there was heat, between them and around them, until Marcus feared they would set the desiccated garden aflame.

There was a ruin ahead, a garden affectation that had been fashionable a generation ago. Marcus took her hand tightly in his and dragged her several feet down the path until he came to the raised dais of the Roman-style temple.

Then he turned and wrapped his hands about her waist and lifted her to stand on the dais. She gasped, breathless from their run. Her cheeks were pink and her blue eyes alarmed. He liked her that way. "Mr. Bl—"

He couldn't wait another moment. He kissed her hard, with his hands in her hair and his body pressed to hers.

The hell of it was, she kissed him back.

She was going to hell, there was no doubt about it. Here she was, a widow of only a week, kissing another man.

And oh, sweet heaven, what a kiss!

His mouth was hot and needful and his hands were pulling her hair too hard and she felt his erection pressing into her belly through the layers of her gown—

She became aware that her own hands were fisted white-knuckled in the front of his weskit and she was making sure that her lower body didn't miss a bit of his.

And she'd never, ever heard that pleading hungry sound come from her own throat before.

No. I am not that woman.

She pushed him away, shoving hard against his shoulders until he staggered back. He stood there, his gaze blank with lust for a long moment.

"Sir, I fear you've gained the wrong impression of me."

He shook his head sharply and passed a hand over his face. "I am most assuredly impressed, my lady, but I think I am in the wrong." He laughed regretfully. "Have no fear, Lady Barrowby, I think I am definitely going to pay for overstepping so severely." He bowed. "My deepest apologies and my most heartfelt thanks. Good day."

With that confusing remark, he turned briskly on his heel and strode away, leaving his coat about her shoulders and a small helpless smile on her face.

Impressed, was he? And here that had been her very first kiss.

Marcus strode from the sleeping garden with his head down, fighting his own compulsion to return to the heat and pent-up passion that was Julia.

She'd kissed him as if she'd been waiting all her life for his lips on hers. God, she was a seductive creature. He reminded himself of all the men who had come before him. She had filled volumes with her exploits, for pity's sake!

The hell of it was, he ought to go back for the sake of his mission. He ought to press her, to work his advantage, to seduce the seducer—

"You bloody piker." There was no mistaking Elliot's supercilious drawl. Marcus lifted his head to see Elliot standing in the drive with the reins of two horses in his hands. A groom came forward to take them from him, but Elliot shook his head sharply. "No, Mr. Blythe-Goodman was just leaving."

Marcus narrowed his eyes, for it certainly seemed that he was about to embark on a journey. There stood his stallion alongside Elliot's nag, fresh and shiny from his pampering in the Middlebarrow stable, fully saddled and packed with what looked to be everything Marcus had brought with him on this mission.

"You really orta let me take them 'orses, sir."

Elliot ignored the groom, who shrugged helplessly and turned back to the stables.

"You cleaned out my room at the inn." He turned his gaze back to Elliot. "How thoughtful of you."

"Yes. I stopped by there late last night to tell you 'no hard feelings' and what did I behold? You weren't in bed as you'd claimed. I waited, thinking you'd decided to visit the privy after all the ale you drank, when it occurred to me that you spent the evening nursing a single flagon. And if you weren't drowning your sorrows, you had a reason to make me think you were."

"You came up with all that on your own?"

Elliot did not ease his glare. "I'm smarter than I look."

Marcus folded his arms. "One would hope."

"So I searched your room."

Marcus blinked. "You're bloody cool about it."

Elliot nodded slowly. "Do you know what I learned about you last night?"

Not a bloody thing. He'd made sure there was no evidence of his real identity in his belongings.

"Not a bloody thing," Elliot said. "No letters, no medals from the war, no miniatures of your mother. Tell me, what sort of fellow carries nothing personal with him?"

An idiot, apparently. Damn, he ought to have fabricated Blythe-Goodman more carefully. And he sure as hell ought to have investigated Elliot No-surname immediately!

"So I decided to give you a hand with your packing. No real point in you staying on, after all." Elliot held out the reins. "Mount up. Your visit to Middlebarrow is over."

"Leaving so soon, Mr. Blythe-Goodman?"

Marcus turned to see Lady Barrowby exit the garden. He was about to answer her when Sebastian followed her through the open gate.

The two horses went instantly mad with fear. Elliot was pulled from his feet as both his nag and Marcus's stallion reared and spun about to race away down the drive. The groom came running back at the equine screams, but he was too late to do anything but help Elliot from the gravel as they all watched the shiny haunches of the horses disappear down the long drive. All except Elliot, of course, who gaped at Sebastian, blinking forcefully as if he were trying to convince himself that he wasn't really mad.

"Told you I orta had took them 'orses," the groom muttered.

"Thank you, Quentin," Lady Barrowby said with warning in her voice. "Do put Sebastian to his breakfast, if you will."

Quentin sighed heavily. "Yes, milady. Come on, 'Bastian. Let's get you a leg o' mutton from Cook."

The groom strolled off, hands in pockets, followed by the lion with long, eager strides that boded certain ill for some mutton's leg.

Elliot remembered to inhale at last. "My lady, I must inform you that your pet cat is not what you think he is."

Julia smiled. "Do tell, Mr. Elliot."

Elliot blinked, then glared at Marcus anew. "You weren't surprised at all!"

Marcus sent a nonchalant glance after Quentin and Sebastian. "Oh, about the lion? Heavens, no. Sebastian and I are old friends."

Lady Barrowby's lips quirked. "Absolutely ancient. In fact, Mr. Blythe-Goodman was just about to help me bathe him. It seems Sebastian found something deceased to roll in."

Marcus blinked. "Er, yes . . . well . . . I would, you see—can't think of anything I'd like to do more, but now I must chase down my horse. Elliot would be more than happy to assist you, I'm sure."

Elliot blinked. "Er . . . ah . . . I fear my horse has run off as well. I hate to leave you in the lurch, my lady, but—"

"Shall I call Quentin back to aid you?" She turned to call after the groom.

"No!"

She turned to look at Marcus, surprised by the force of his refusal. The thought of Quentin strolling back with lion in tow was more than he was truly able to cope with at the moment.

Elliot was violently shaking his head as well. "Thank you but no, my lady. I'm sure Quentin has more important matters to attend to."

Lady Barrowby shook her head. "Oh, go on. Run off like a pair of spooked horses. You may return for luncheon later, if you like."

Elliot bobbed a quick bow. "I shall return, my lady, but I'm sure Blythe-Goodman wishes to get an early start—"

"I'll be but moments, my lady," Marcus said briskly. He slid a glance at Elliot. "My mount won't run far. He is well trained, unlike some."

Lady Barrowby put up a hand. "Do stop growling at each other and go fetch your horses."

They quieted, but not before Elliot got the last word in. "My horse won't run as far as yours because he can't."

"Now that I believe," Marcus shot back, as they watched Lady Barrowby stroll away.

When Julia had settled Sebastian back into his quarters—he stank after rolling in the dead thing, so she rubbed him down with dried mint leaves, leaving him smelling like something that had died from eating too much mint—she made her way slowly back to the main house.

She'd kissed Mr. Blythe-Goodman. Really, truly kissed him—open lips, battling tongues, urgent hands and all. That was a terrible thing to have done, especially since only last night she had promised herself to Mr. Elliot.

Mr. Blythe-Goodman brought out the worst in her. Every person had some devil inside them, be it drink or rich foods or the compulsion to collect great numbers of small yapping dogs. Her devil was apparently Marcus Blythe-Goodman.

The only cure for such an affliction was complete abstinence. She was going to have to avoid him most diligently in the future.

Except for luncheon, of course. But after that, she would be on a strict diet of Elliot and Elliot alone.

Blast it.

"I don't know why you had to show up." Elliot had a marvelous grasp of the acid glare.

"Now you see, that is the wrong take on matters," Marcus said conversationally as they rode back to Barrowby together on their exhausted but now-calm mounts. He was still in a very good mood after the pleasure—er, triumph—of this morning's kiss. "A man should keep his competition in plain view."

Elliot smirked. "You don't believe that her ladyship and I have come to an agreement."

"Oh, I believe you. I'm simply not sure that she does." He gave his horse a kick, pulling ahead.

"Now what is that supposed to m— Oy, hold up there, Blythe-Goodman!"

It wasn't sporting to outrun Elliot's nag. It was only that Marcus felt the pull to see her—to complete his mission.

Oh, bloody hell. He wanted to see her and he shouldn't hide it, not if he wanted to win her confidence. He should allow Marcus Blythe-Goodman to have his infatuation, for it would only make his efforts more persuasive. Look at what the fellow had accomplished with a simple stroll in the garden!

Talking about your alias as if he were real? Not sane, old man.

Nor did he care. She was less than a mile away and he wanted to see her.

Now.

When informed that her guests had arrived, Julia felt her heart leap for a single perfect moment. Then she remembered that she didn't want to see Mr. Blythe-Goodman ever again.

Yet there he was, emerald eyes gleaming above his white, intimate smile, looking very nearly as glad to see her as she was to see him.

She became aware that she hadn't breathed in several moments. She put a hand to her cheek to find that her own face held a welcoming smile as well. Immediately, she turned it on Mr. Elliot.

"Have you given your horses to Quentin? He will check them for injuries while we luncheon." She turned and gestured for the gentlemen to come along, all the while with the smile in place. She must not let him know it was just for him.

Still, Julia walked ahead of Mr. Blythe-Goodman and Mr. Elliot as she led them down the hall. She didn't mean to be rude, but one never knew . . .

Sure enough, from the open library door she heard a suspicious "Hut, hut, hut!" She increased her pace slightly so that she came level with that door before the gentlemen did. With a quick sidestep, she shut the door on the human tower, three footmen high, that was tossing books from hand to hand, passing them to be put away on the top shelf—twenty feet from the floor!

"There was an unpleasant draft," she called over her shoulder to her guests as she moved quickly on. She wanted to get to the dining room first, for Beppo had an uncanny habit of—

"Beppo!" Her hiss was nearly silent, but the butler,

who was hanging from the chandelier by his knees—in order to dust it thoroughly, he maintained, but Julia knew he simply loved to swing ten feet above the floor—had time to flip over twice and land on the center of the table with a flourish before the gentlemen entered five strides behind her.

Julia nearly panicked, but when she turned, Beppo was standing sedately at her side, every bit the dignified servant.

He bowed deeply to them all. "Shall I bring wine as well, milady?"

Julia smiled with relief. "Yes, Beppo, that would be lovely. I'm sure the gentlemen wish some refreshment after their difficulty this morning."

Mr. Blythe-Goodman was watching her. His green eyes—how could anyone's eyes be that perfectly green?—missed nothing, she could tell. She smiled to cover her moment of alarm. "And how have you found our little village, sirs?" She waved them to their chairs and seated herself with Mr. Elliot's help. "Is the innkeeper taking good care of you?"

"Exemplary." The big man folded his length into the dainty dining chair like a fellow who intended to stay. Julia tore her gaze away from the muscles rippling in his thighs, encased as they were in snug breeches.

Mr. Elliot was more effusive. "I believe Furman's ale improves by the day," he said.

Julia shot a glance at Mr. Elliot, who was gazing at her with his tongue thrust firmly into his cheek. She'd been found out, it seemed. Ah, well. No bit of maneuvering lasted forever, no matter how ingenious.

Besides, the local fellows had begun to complain that their own beer was being tainted by proximity to the "piss" ale.

She smiled back at Elliot. "I'm pleased to hear it." He would get no more satisfaction than that from her. She had no regrets about trying to get rid of the throng of gold diggers.

Of course, Elliot was just as bad, but at least he was an amusing gold digger. Mr. Blythe-Goodman, however . . .

He was dressed simply enough, and the cheap fabrics and inexpensive buttons lent him an air of financial instability, but the way he wore them—as if he were dressed by the Prince Regent's own tailor.

He said all the right things, and he said them well, but there was something in his eyes . . . Julia felt challenged, stimulated, frustrated, and gratified, all at once.

Which was ridiculous. What did she care for his good opinion? He was looking for a wealthy wife so that he might live out his days without a moment of honest work!

Which is nothing at all like you, correct?

Julia's indignation lost all inflation at that thought. Who was she to point shame at someone who was trying to improve their situation through marriage?

Not that anyone knew that but her vast and loyal family here at Barrowby.

No, Mr. Blythe-Goodman had no reason to gaze at her so critically, as if his judgment might actually sting her somehow! She raised her chin and matched his gaze, judgment for judgment. "What is it that you see, sir? Am I turning blue, perchance?"

Elliot sputtered protest, and Julia could tell that her friend was truly worried that she'd been offended, but she never took her gaze from Mr. Blythe-Goodman's. He watched her for a long moment, then finally let his eyes drop.

Julia might have taken a bit more comfort in her victory if she wasn't very nearly sure—no, she was quite sure!—that his gaze was now pausing at her bosom. Insulting and impertinent!

And you weren't watching the way his long strides flexed the muscles in his thighs? Or were you too busy looking a bit higher?

This time it was her gaze that slid away.

If only it weren't for that blasted kiss. She'd been doing so well, cementing her plans with Elliot and having confronted the Royal Three—which she'd done nicely indeed—and settling Barrowby after the loss of its lord.

How could all that stability have been so befuddled and confused by the mere touch of a man's lips on hers?

Warm hungry lips that had swept over hers and possessed them—hot invading tongue that had battled hers, hard hands on her flesh, strong arms about her back—

She swallowed forcefully and glanced up at the suddenly silent room. Mr. Blythe-Goodman was gazing at her with naked hunger in his eyes. Mr. Elliot was regarding them both with half-lidded eyes.

Beppo arrived with the wine. Mr. Elliot leaned into

the path of Julia's absentminded gaze. "My lady, are you unwell?"

Outside the house, something exploded. *Boom. Boom, boom.*

7

To be sheltered and protected, not from life or danger or travail, but from the way such can wound the solitary heart—is that more than I have the right to ask?

The glass in the windows shivered and the crystals tinkled in the chandelier above their heads. Mr. Elliot and Mr. Blythe-Goodman froze in the act of lifting their glasses.

Beppo's gaze shot to hers. *Privies,* he mouthed.

She nodded quickly. *Go.*

He was right, she knew. If there was one thing travelers knew, it was the sound of fireworks in the privy. It was a common revenge upon the landowner who did not allow his lands to be crossed by the fair folk, who considered their right to passage granted from time immemorial.

"Stay here!"

At Mr. Blythe-Goodman's terse order, Julia turned back to him in surprise, but he was already following Beppo, Mr. Elliot close on his heels. Left behind, Julia was safe to roll her eyes in exasperation. All that manly heroism, wasted. When a privy blew—oh, heavens, the perpetrator had blown up all three!—there was nothing to be done but the cleaning up.

She followed more slowly. She wasn't truly interested in slipping in the inevitable muck that would coat simply everything, but she was highly interested to know who would do such a thing.

There wasn't a showman or Gypsy in Europe who didn't know that Barrowby was a good host to the travelers. It was only good estate management, after all, to provide good meat and plentiful firewood to prevent the folk from poaching—er, procuring it themselves.

None of them would do this to her, of that she was certain.

An angry suitor, resentful of her choosing Mr. Elliot?

She sighed. It was possible. Those boys were desperate enough to attempt some sort of sabotage—

Sabotage.

As she stood in the gravel drive, her skirts inches away from the limit of the foul stuff sprayed from the main house privy, she gazed sourly at the mess surrounding her. Now, who might try to discomfit her in the midst of her mourning? Someone with a knowledge of sabotage techniques? Someone who knew she was vying to be confirmed in her position as the Fox?

No. That was a ridiculous notion. This was not the work of the Three. It was only the childish vengeance of a disappointed swain, she was sure of it.

Mr. Elliot was mincing through the muck to where Mr. Blythe-Goodman was examining the remains of the privy shed where it had landed on its side several feet from its previous resting place.

From the look of the splintered mess, they'd be needing new sheds as well. Julia sighed and signaled to Igby, one of her juggling footmen. He came, holding his filthy hands wide so as not to mar his livery. The showmen took their roles as household staff very seriously and cared for their "costumes" well.

"Clean up and go to the village to fetch a carpenter or two and a wagonload of sawn lumber," she told him. "I want new sheds up by tomorrow eve."

Igby nodded gratefully. "Yes, my lady. Right away, my lady."

Julia turned back to watch Mr. Blythe-Goodman kneel carelessly in the filth to get a closer look at the scorched interior wall of the privy shed. Her curiosity twitched, both at the cause of the blasts and the fact that this alleged dandy was entirely absorbed in the mystery himself, much to the detriment of his wardrobe.

"For pity's sake, Marcus, don't touch it!" Elliot, who persisted in lingering over Marcus's shoulder, had gone green with nausea at the smell.

Marcus ignored him. Curiously, the interior surface of the privy shed was clean, burned to the grain by the fireball that had tossed it aside.

"That was no mere firecracker in the privy," said a soft melodic voice behind him.

Marcus controlled the tremor that went up his spine at that delicious intonation and shot Lady Barrowby a considering glance. She'd hiked her skirts and waded through the slime to his side and bent over the shed.

"What do you mean, no mere firecracker?" It had been his own conclusion, as well, but she was not behaving in any way as he'd expected a lady to behave in this situation.

Then again, Elliot was being lady enough for both of them.

She was gazing at the blackened wood. "We dig new privies on a regular schedule. There was no gas buildup to cause such a flame. Someone used—" She leaned closer to the wreckage and inhaled deeply. Elliot went into silent paroxysms of revulsion behind her.

"Someone used gunpowder," she stated with certainty. "And lots of it." She straightened, her expression grim. "If we were like most and let the privies overfill, this could have been much more serious. Stupid boy!" She glared at him as if it were his fault. "One of my people could have been gravely injured!"

Marcus stood and looked about them. "Are you sure one of them wasn't?"

She shook her head, not bothering to glance about. "I would know if they had been."

Marcus gazed at her for a long moment. She paid no attention to him as she stood gazing at the splintered wood with narrowed eyes. She chewed her lower lip when she was thinking hard, he noticed. When she released it, it was plump and pink and wet—

He forced his gaze down to his own muck-covered boots. *Mind on the job, you idiot.*

She was the target of his investigation. Targets did not have lips, plump or otherwise. Targets were objects, not people. She was an unknown species that required analysis, not a woman.

She was a target whose property had been vandalized. She might be unqualified and unsuited for the Fox's seat, but she was still a lady and he was still a gentleman. Someone had pulled a nasty prank that could have had deadly results. If, somehow in some future he didn't want to contemplate, she was confirmed as the Fox, he would not be found lacking in his duty to protect her.

For a moment he wondered if she had done it to herself for some nefarious reason, but he discounted the thought immediately. She was far too angry about the danger to her people. She did seem to care about her dependents, he had to give her that.

His mother had often told him that you could tell much about a person by how they spoke to the lowest maid in their household. Was this caring attitude some sort of pleasing façade Lady Barrowby wore or did she take her responsibilities seriously?

"You and Mr. Elliot must return to the village," she told him abruptly. "Please tell the innkeeper to charge your cleaning to me." She turned and began to stride off—to the center of the mess, he noticed, not away from it.

"I believe I shall remain a while longer," he said easily. "You need all the hands you can get at the moment, I should think."

She halted and turned to him in surprise. She would have denied his assessment, he could tell, but there was no denying the sheer magnitude of the damage.

She nodded sharply. "If that is your wish, then I would appreciate the assistance."

She glanced at Elliot, who sighed deeply. "I shall remain as well."

Her lips twitched and she glanced back to Marcus—as if to share a private joke? He gazed at her impassively

instead of answering her amused glance, for he still
fought the wave of lust heating his belly. Her expression fell slightly, then she turned away and busily
marched to where the servants were hauling buckets of
water to wash down the nearest buildings.

Elliot came abreast of Marcus and watched her walk
away. "She rolled her eyes at you," he said smugly.

Marcus shot him a dark glance. "She did not."

Elliot chuckled. "Yes, she did, as she turned away.
She thinks you're an idiot." He turned to grin at Marcus. "I do like that about her."

"Well, she thinks you're a useless dandy."

Elliot nodded amiably. "Oh, yes. That's what she
likes about me."

Elliot ambled away, rather off course if he truly intended to help. Marcus gazed after Lady Barrowby,
eyes narrowed. She'd chosen Elliot of her own free
will. Could it be that she *wanted* a feckless, light-
minded husband?

The respect for her that had been reluctantly growing
took a bit of a slide down the muck-covered hillside.

There was nothing here!

While the household ran about trying to clean up the
filth he'd showered them with—most deservedly,
indeed—he'd ransacked the study and the library.

To hell with precision and secrecy—he wanted her
to know she'd been searched, after all—he tossed
books from the shelves and took a knife to the uphol-
stery, a fast and dirty search for something, anything
that would tell him what she was about.

He found nothing. In the morning room off the

music room he found her desk and all the accounts for
the estate—everything that one would expect from an
intelligent lady who knew how to run her household,
but nothing at all to indicate why those particular lords
had visited her, nor any proof that she was who she
could not be, but most obviously was . . .

Then again, he'd seen the locket for himself. It was
the only proof he needed.

And the lack of information relating to those
visitors—well, that was all to the good. If she was
merely the widow of a peer, then it could be expected
that lot might pay their respects. They'd not stayed
overlong, after all, and had immediately made their
way on to London.

He had his doubts, but as far as he could tell by what
he'd not found, she was nothing more than what she
appeared—the lovely, capable widow of the late Lord
Barrowby.

She'd done quite well for herself, he had to admit,
though it chafed him. Then again, all the more reason
to think she could be made to see the advantages of his
plans for her.

He shattered a vase against the wall in an uncharac-
teristic burst of temper. He closed his eyes and took a
breath. She was a tool, nothing more. He would use her
and discard her afterward.

Of course, there was no law against enjoying the destruction he would cause in the course of it.

By evening, the mess was somewhat under control.
One of the tumbling footmen was sluicing buckets of
lake water over the cobbles, while another one swept

the grime away from the house. The yard reeked, and likely would until the next good rain, but the Barrowby staff had the worst of the filth scraped away.

One thing still bothered Marcus. "How well do you really know Elliot?"

Lady Barrowby started as Marcus came up behind her. She raised a brow at his impertinence, then turned away. "Better than I know you." She lifted a hand to direct several of her people to work on the next area of grime.

"But what do you know of his background? Of his history? He could be a—" *French spy.* Then again, he wouldn't want her to wonder what he knew about French spies. "A criminal!"

She made a derisive sound. "Elliot isn't a criminal. He may be lazy and a tad spineless and more than a little vain, but he's a good man, deep down."

"How can you know that about him?"

"How can I know that about anyone? How can I know that about you?" She shrugged delicately. "I may not know Elliot, but I know his sort, and his sort is usually most trustworthy."

Marcus opened his mouth, but she held up a hand. Damn, she did have a commanding air about her sometimes.

"I can absolutely trust that Elliot will forever and always see to his own interests. Knowing that, I will be sure to never put more pressure on his fragile ethics than they can bear. Furthermore, I trust my instincts and my instincts tell me that there is more to Elliot than meets the eye."

Marcus snorted. "Of that I'm sure."

"Oh, stop. He is harmless. All a fellow like Elliot wants from life is comfort and amusement. Although it is a terrible waste for someone so intelligent . . ."

Hearing her praise Elliot made Marcus uncomfortable. Oh, very well, it made him want to smear Elliot's face in the muck after a prolonged and satisfying brawl, but that was simply the strain of lust—er, *waiting* building up inside him.

Furthermore, he found her reasoning faulty in the extreme. He would be sure to include her response in his report to the Three. Instincts were all well and fine, but to depend solely upon such?

Beside him, Lady Barrowby sighed. "I suppose that is all we can do today. With any luck, we'll have some rain soon. At least the cistern was covered when the sh—when the dirt rained down."

Marcus glanced over to where the large stone well pierced the yard like a squat fortress itself, well away from the privies. "You haven't modernized the manor?"

She nodded. "We've pipes to the kitchens, of course. Aldus didn't hold with piping the bathwater in. He thought it was too extravagant." She smiled at Marcus. "Men."

While Marcus himself had nothing against regular bathing, he felt compelled to defend his sex. "Well, I could see where it might become wasteful."

"More wasteful than paying three footmen to carry water buckets to the second story?" She looked down at herself in dismay. Her gown was ruined to the knees and there were streaks of unspeakables in her hair. "Which I shall have to make them do tonight—and they are so weary."

"Well, that is what you pay them f—"

She grabbed his arm and towed him away from the others. "I require something from you, Mr. Blythe-Goodman. I don't want my staff to know, for they'd insist on carrying bathwater for me, and you're the only other person I—"

Marcus tilted his head at her pause. "The only other person you what?"

She huffed an impatient breath. "Suffice it to say that I know you had no hand in—" She spread her hands. "Well, this. Yet someone did, and they might still be about."

"What about Elliot? You just said you trusted him."

She laughed. "Elliot disappeared hours ago. Hadn't you noticed?"

He hadn't. He laughed. "That's Elliot for you."

She nodded. "Precisely my earlier point. Your discretion about . . . this morning . . . leads me to trust you. Will you be my bodyguard while I bathe in the lake?"

The moon is full and swollen in the dark lapis sky. A bright path shines on the glassy lake—

The memory of what followed those lines struck him like a fist in his gut and his mouth went very dry. He nodded jerkily and swallowed. "It would be my pleasure, my lady."

"It will be a service, Mr. Blythe-Goodman, but it will not be a pleasure. Are we quite clear on that point?" She crossed her arms, raising her bosom and causing rather more devastation to his equilibrium.

Good God, man, she's covered in privy muck!

He thought about that for a split second. Did he care?

Most decidedly not. Which meant trouble he wasn't prepared to think about right now.

She led him around the house, grabbing up a pile of old, worn clothing the servants had brought out to use as rags when the old rags had been turned to rubbish. "A shirt and breeches for you, and here's a maid's dress for me." She held them at arm's length, for the rags were still cleaner than both of them, and led him down a well-kept path.

There was no full and swollen moon, thank God. Only a faint glow on the water from the many lanterns that had been hung around the area of destruction.

"If you will wait for me here, I shall step around this bank and bathe quickly. Then I shall stand watch over you."

Again Marcus found his mouth very dry. He managed some sort of assenting grunt, which satisfied her. She left him standing there, very glad of the darkness that hid the tent in his trousers and doubly glad he'd not finished reading the account of her lover by the lake.

The water was very cold but Julia could hardly feel the chill for the fire beneath her skin. Simply knowing that he was nearby watching—for he was watching, she could feel it—and knowing that he felt it too . . .

Felt what? They were both filthy and exhausted, and they'd hardly exchanged a dozen words all afternoon. She ducked her head to rinse her hair and to wash away such woolly thinking. She was a new widow, he was a gold digger. The only things he was thinking about were the size of her accounts. The only thing she ought to be thinking about was returning Barrowby to order.

A splash nearby brought her attention back with a start. She whirled in the dark water, spreading her hands out. There was nothing to see.

"Mr. Blythe-Goodman? Are you there?" There was only silence from the bank.

Alarmed, she began to work her way back to the water's edge, keeping low. "Mr. Bl—"

He erupted from the lake no more than an arm's length away, his bare wet chest gleaming in the scarce light.

8

His form is like a god's, rippling with strength beneath my touch. Cool skin, hot hands, the rush and flow of the water between us . . .

"Eek!" Julia abruptly sank into the water up to her chin.

He jerked at the sound of her voice and nearly fell back into the water. *"Bloody—"*

He was obviously as surprised as she was. Julia fought the urge to giggle as he scrambled for footing on the gooey bottom. Instead, she put on a scowl.

"Sir, I beg you, explain yourself! This is most improper!"

He whipped the hair back from his face. "I'm improper? What of you, my lady? What sort of woman sneaks up on a man when he's bathing!"

"I didn't!"

"You did."

"You were supposed to wait for me to finish!"

"Well, I couldn't bear myself one moment longer! I'm not accustomed to being covered in sh—muck, you know."

Abruptly, she smiled at him. "Since it is my muck, and you've been such a help to me today, then I must forgive you." She moved to pass around him. "If you'll turn your back, I shall get out and leave you to your swim."

"There's no need for that." His voice was low, rumbling up her spine and causing the hairs to rise on the back of her neck. "The lake has water enough for us both."

She stopped and gazed at him uncertainly. His eyes were in shadow, his jaw tensed. The intensity of his gaze could be felt like fire on her skin. Time stretched as she lost herself in the darkness of his spell.

He swam about her slowly, his circling path growing smaller every course. She kept him before her, turning in the water, matching his speed. She could not tear her gaze from his. "I—I suppose I . . ."

"You are a most unusual lady."

She didn't want to be—or at least, she knew she shouldn't be. For a swift, endless moment, she wished she were precisely what he thought her—simply the widow of a wealthy man, a lady by birth and raising, free to make choices with her heart and not cold logic.

He was closer now, so close she could read the want in his eyes. He truly wanted her. Not only her position and wealth, although that might be as well. But this heat—she did not think this was simply yearning for an easy life. His desire flared between them, igniting her own.

It crawled over her skin like flame, only stimulated further by the cold water. She was naked and alone with this man, and yet he stayed his distance—nearly. Clear in his gaze was a question, one that she was answering by her own lack of protest.

And yet he did not complete the last spiral to press that smoldering heat to her chilled naked body. He stayed, waiting, floating inches away, forcing her to act instead of simply allow.

There was no sound but the wavelet lapping at the shore and her own heartbeat thudding in her ears. Even the sounds of the cleaning of Barrowby had died down as the darkness grew.

They were alone, entirely private.

Secret.

And no one ever need know.

Her heart thudded and she could hardly breathe for the ache in her lower belly. She need move only inches, need drift a mere moment closer—

It would be wonderful. Heaven on earth. Everything she'd never had and always dreamed of. She didn't know how she knew that about him, but she would have serenely wagered Barrowby itself on this man's knowledge of a woman's pleasure.

He would melt her in his hands. He would drive every fantasy from her mind with his hard, hungry reality. He would make her his forever . . .

But she was not hers to give. She belonged to the Royal Four and would for the rest of her life. A man such as he would never be satisfied with the half of herself she could afford to bestow. A man such as he would own her attention, would captivate her heart, mind, body, and soul.

And she would give them over to him, willingly, gladly, joyously—

If she were simply the woman he thought her.

She pulled away slowly, letting the cooler water

rush between them. "I must be getting back," she said, her voice strange and husky to her own ears.

"Must you?" A breath of a whisper, but it pulled at her like a chain around her chest. She blinked and swallowed and stepped farther away.

"I must."

He let her go. For a moment, she'd wondered if she'd misjudged him, if he would fall upon her and make her stay.

Then it would not be your decision. Then you would be free to be his—taken, not given. Blameless.

But then he would not be the man she thought him, and it was that man, the one who stayed where he was, alone in the water, respecting her decision—it was that man she wanted now more than ever.

Marcus watched her go. Perhaps he ought to have pressed his advantage and forced her to submit to the hunger he'd read in her eyes. Perhaps he ought to have urged her harder, persuaded her more passionately—

Perhaps you should have conked her on the head and dragged her off by the hair! That would have accomplished precisely nothing.

The goal was not to merely get into her knickers. He needed to gain her confidence, to cajole her into betraying herself by telling him how she truly became the Fox's apprentice.

Maybe she went swimming naked in the lake with him. It certainly worked with you.

If his rigid, throbbing erection was any clue, then yes. Yet, he was seducing the seducer. He was bound to get scorched by a bit of heat along the way. He could bear it. After all, it wasn't as though there were any real attachment.

He waited for the cold water of the lake to ease his tension. A splash behind him caused him to turn automatically, defensive instincts always to the fore.

She was half out of the water, bent forward wringing out her hair. Diamonds of water dripped from her nipples, making his blood leave his brain with such force it dizzied him. His cock swelled, harder than ever. He sank lower, keeping only half his face above water, watching her. Damn. This lake wasn't nearly cold enough to make a dent in his iron hardness.

She swung her hair back over her shoulders, arching back to shake it out, jutting her breasts high. She was so lovely, so luxuriously rounded, so athletically lithe. She turned away, walking from the water, lifting her knees high as she waded. His heart beat faster. Her bottom swayed, luring him, baiting him . . .

She bent to retrieve her dress from the bank—

Marcus convulsed as his ejaculation erupted. He gasped harshly, clenching his eyes shut to stop it, but it was too late. She'd brought him there without so much as the touch of his own hand, just by looking at her.

"Are you unwell, sir?" she called from the bank.

"Um-hmm." He hadn't done that. It wasn't possible. Never in his life—

Well, there was that pretty housemaid he'd been obsessed with when he was twelve, but not since his boyhood!

"Do you need assistance?"

God, even her voice from the distance of the bank made him ache, though by all rights he deserved a grace period of at least an hour after a release as powerful as that!

"I'm fine, my lady," he gasped. "I merely . . . stepped on a sharp rock." He opened one eye carefully, but she was fully dressed now, the overlarge maid's dress hiding her luminous, exquisite flesh.

Yes, well, get out of the water, you lout. Are you waiting for another orgasm?

She turned her back as he approached. "I must have dropped the other piece of toweling," she said apologetically. "You may use mine."

Rub woman-scented toweling all over his naked, wet, aching flesh? Was she trying to kill him?

He threw the worn shirt and breeches on his wet body and grabbed his boots. "I should return to the inn." He started up the path. Perhaps if he didn't look directly at her, he could erase one of the most unbearably embarrassing, delicious episodes of his male existence.

"Don't be silly." She caught up to him easily. "It is far too late. You'll stay at Barrowby tonight."

Oh, she most definitely had Marcus-murder on her evil female mind. He opened his mouth to decline her invitation on the grounds that it might incinerate him.

You're on a mission. You should accept and stay the night.

She tossed him an amused glance. "You can sleep with the Igbys."

"Thank you, my lady," he heard himself say, before he'd come to any real decision. "I appreciate your hospitality."

She grinned up at him. "It is the least I can do." That

saucy tip to her lips startled him once again. What secrets lay beneath that elegant exterior?

Lush, curving, delectable—

Damn. He was going to die from permanent lack of blood flowing to his brain.

Something ahead caught her attention. "Igby? Igby, what is wrong?" She picked up her skirts to run forward, leaving him behind to contemplate his certain demise by perpetual arousal.

Ah, but what a way to go.

Then the alarm in her voice penetrated the fog of his lust. Marcus broke into a run.

Julia stood speaking to an Igby at the door of the kitchens. "Are you sure there's no one in the house now?"

Marcus halted. "Someone was in the house?"

Igby nodded, his freckled face pale. "The 'ole place is done up, sir!"

"Are you sure there's no one still in the house?"

Julia shot him a sour glance. Marcus realized he'd just repeated her own question. Right. This was Barrowby, not Ravencliff. He was only a guest. A friend—ah, no. An *observer.*

He stood back, willing himself to release his desire to take control of the situation. Then again, Lady Barrowby seemed more than up to the job herself.

She immediately sent teams of staff through the house armed with knives and sharp tools. Marcus had to admire her restraint, for he himself would have been at the head of the first team, despite the danger.

Still, she twitched irritably at his side as she waited.

"Blast it," she muttered. "If someone hurts one of my people—"

Finally, Beppo gave them a wave from an upper-story window and they entered.

Julia stepped through the kitchens, gazing about her. Meg should be there chopping up something tasty for dinner. Instead, there were pots congealing on the stove and no meal in sight.

She made for the front hall, hoping to find that it was all some Igby-type exaggeration.

The wreckage extended all the way down the hall, from the stairs to the front door. Every room in the main area of the house had been quite thoroughly and professionally—and vindictively—tossed. It took one to know one, after all.

The servants were milling about, hands filled with debris, their expression aghast. Beppo saw her first. He held up the pieces of Aldus's favorite rare porcelain vase.

"My lady, what could this mean?"

Julia knew precisely what it meant. Someone—and who else could it be but the Royal Three?—someone wanted her to know she was being investigated. Aldus had warned her that they would not roll over easily and it seemed he'd been quite correct.

She folded her arms defiantly. If the Cobra, Lion, and Falcon thought she was the sort to quail at a rain of shite on her property and a bit of broken pottery, they obviously had no idea who they were dealing with.

She smiled through her fury to reassure the staff. "This means nothing. There was nothing of value in these rooms." Thank heaven Aldus had taught her how to keep all the affairs of the Four in her head and not on paper. "It is a mess and an annoyance and that is all. Igby, Igby, and Igby, bring some canvas sacks to gather the rubbish into. Pickles, you and I will see what can be repaired. Meg, do see to your pots, dear. I think our supper is burning . . ."

The staff rushed to work, thankful for direction and her calm assurance. Julia smiled and shrugged off the import of it all, while inside she was fuming.

Damn the Three. Of course, she probably would have approved such action herself had the positions been reversed, but once she was confirmed in her seat, she certainly hoped they didn't plan to ask her for any favors for the first year or so. Or twenty.

Mr. Blythe-Goodman stood at her side, like a wall she could lean upon. It was very good of him not to spring into manly officiousness. The last thing she needed right now was an interfering man.

Something else occurred to her that lightened her mood considerably. If nothing else, she knew that Mr. Blythe-Goodman was innocent of this invasion.

She just wished she could be so sure of her fiancé.

9

Our mounts thunder side by side, my white mare, his dark stallion galloping as one horse. The freedom and wildness of the gallop infects me, heating my blood, sensitizing the place between my thighs. I ride astride with my legs wrapped about my mare's bare back, as does my lover on his mount. I lean down and urge more speed from her, laughing over my shoulder as she and I leave our lovers in our wind.

I believe I have won, until a black nose enters my side vision. I cry out for more speed but it is too late now. A long arm reaches about my waist and pulls me from her back, letting her free of my weight. She wins the race without me, for I am wrapped in my lover's arms, lying across his lap, his stallion slowing to a swinging walk.

"You lose," my lover whispers into my hair with a laugh.

I twine my arms about his neck. "I win." I kiss him hard and wet and openmouthed, our tongues battling for yet more supremacy. I am strong, he is stronger. I am intelligent, he is also. He is my equal in all things and every battle ends in victory and delight for us both. My true match in all things . . .

The kiss heats us both after the stimulating race and our bodies deny the confines of our clothing. My hat is lost, the jacket of my habit disappears, his cravat flutters away on the breeze as the stallion carries us on . . . Soon my lover's chest is bare beneath my hands and my gown is rucked up to my hips as he lifts me to sit backward, astride his lap. I can feel his erection pressing hard to my damp center, only the wool of his trousers between us. The rocking motion of the stallion's walk brings me to orgasm as I ride both the man and the stallion, my breasts bared to the open air as I cry out in my release.

"Can you feel how much I want you?" His voice is husky with need. I have been selfish, taking my pleasure first. He prefers it that way. Now I reach between us as he holds me securely and guides the stallion. I free my lover's thickened rod and wrap my hands about him, letting the rocking rhythm set the pace for my pleasurable torture.

He moans and drops his head to my shoulder. I move my fingers and he shudders tightly, unable to stop me. "Shall you be my stallion to ride, then?" I release him and wrap my hands over his bare shoulders, using him to steady myself as I mount his cock and impale myself with its hard length. He gives a harsh shout of ecstasy as I take him deep into my tight, wet heat. I use the strength in my thighs to raise and lower myself in counterpoint to the horse's walk, clutching my own stallion's bare shoulders as I ride him until we both burst into flames.

Julia woke and stretched luxuriously for a moment before opening her eyes. She felt the efforts of the day before in the ache in her shoulders, but nothing could quench the joyous mood she felt bubbling up from within.

Of course, the evening before had been a disaster. The damage to the house was going to take days to repair and she wasn't any too sure they would ever get the smell out of the yard . . . but she felt truly marvelous nonetheless.

He'd held her hand last evening when he'd said good night. He'd taken her fingers in his hand and wrapped his big warm ones around them and just held gently, letting her hand rest in his for a long moment.

It was better than a kiss. Oh, very well, not better, especially not better than that hungry embrace in the garden—but it was something else altogether. It was caring and reassuring and it made her feel as though she could depend upon him to understand absolutely everything . . .

Which was girlish silliness and impossible to boot. She was going to have to make him leave as soon as possible, for she could not afford any more moments of temptation like the lake . . . or the garden . . . or that long silent moment of communion outside her bedchamber door late after the servants had rightfully gone to their rest . . .

She smiled and extended her toes into the cooler portion of the covers. Her room was so warm—

Her room was never warm when she rose. She never slept past five on the clock, and it took an hour for the fire to truly banish the chill.

She opened her eyes to see daylight pouring into the room through the opened draperies, a fire popping merrily in the hearth, and a real breakfast awaiting her on the side table, steaming gently from beneath the polished silver covers.

"It's about time you had a proper lady's rising," Pickles said as she exited Julia's dressing room with a gown over her arm. "Although it's still only nine."

"Nine?" Julia sat up. "I slept until nine?" She started to push back the covers. "Oh, dear. There's so much to be done!"

"And them that's paid to is doin' it. You let that silly ropewalker earn his butler's name for once. Him and Mr. Blythe-Goodman's got the lads buildin' privy sheds that'll outlast us all."

"Truly?" Julia settled back uneasily against the pillows as Pickles laid the tray across her lap. A leisurely breakfast? She wasn't accustomed to such an existence . . . but the food smelled lovely and the fire crackled so brightly and the steaming tea—

Julia drew back sharply. "Pickles, the tea smells like privy water."

The maid blinked. "What a thing to say! I brewed it myself, from the kitchen spout—" She leaned forward and sniffed. Then she paled. "Oh, my lady—"

"The well."

For the second morning in a row, Julia ran from her room half-dressed. She met Beppo coming up the stairs, wringing his hands worriedly.

"I don't know how it happened, my lady. We kept all the waste well away from the cistern—"

"I think I know how." She ought to have foreseen it. An iron lock on the cistern cover would have saved so much effort, but then they simply would have come at her from another direction. Julia pressed her fingertips to her eyes. "How bad is it?"

Beppo shrugged helplessly. "The well must be bailed and let fill fresh, at least twice. Even then, we'll be straining every cupful for a month at least—"

Julia's knees went weak. She sat down on the stair abruptly. Barrowby was huge, with an excess of staff to support because she couldn't bear to turn her friends away. How were all those people to do without water for so long?

Her hair fell forward as she dropped her head to her knees. Absently, she realized it still carried the fresh green scent of the lake.

Her head shot up. "Could we strain lake water now, while we cleanse the well?"

Pickles sniffed. "Best boil it, too, to kill the taste."

Beppo shook his head slowly. "It will take too many wagons and barrels to bring enough to last us all."

Julia shook her head. "No, we can send some of our people to stay in the village. Furman has shed the last of those young men, hasn't he? He can put them up at the inn, four to a room if we must. It isn't far to come if we need them. Cover and shut up every room that isn't in use, and let the gardeners go home early for the season. Only the main house staff will stay. Will that do?"

Beppo's brow wrinkled. "If we put the horses to the

north pasture with the dairy cows where they can drink from the lake as well . . ."

Julia smiled with relief. "Excellent. I'm sure they'll enjoy the rest after hauling water all day."

"Why are we hauling water?"

The deep voice behind Julia sent a jolt of deep pleasure through her. Before she thought, she'd turned and beamed a wide, welcoming smile up the stairs at Mr. Blythe-Goodman, the man she'd sworn to stay away from.

Marcus. After all, she had kissed him and bathed naked with him. It wasn't such a presumption—and she liked his name. It was strong and noble, like him.

Then she remembered that she could not afford such a challenge to her balance. He seemed harmless, standing there with a small intimate smile of greeting on his lips just for her, but she could not underestimate the danger he presented.

The danger of falling in love.

And, dear God, she could fall forever into those deep forest eyes—

"My lady." He interrupted her absorption with the way his green eyes caught the morning light. "The water?"

"Hmm?" She saw Marcus's lips twitch. He was laughing at her! Julia snapped her attention back to the problem at hand. "The well has been fouled." She stood, shaking out her skirts, thankfully in control of her wandering thoughts once again.

Marcus sobered at once. "Was it due to last night's damage?"

She shook her head. "Meg checked the water before bed. Someone did it after we retired for the night."

Bloody hell. Destroying an estate's source of clean water was a grievous offense, far beyond the inconvenience of a privy bomb. It was frankly an act of war.

Yet, as he watched Lady Barrowby—surely he could think of her as Julia? It would save so much time— organize her people, he saw that she was more than up to the challenge. If this was some sort of test by Lord Liverpool, it seemed the Fox's protégée would pass yet again.

So she had brains aplenty. That didn't mean she wasn't also cunning and ambitious.

Qualities that sound a bit familiar, don't you think?

Intelligence was not the only requirement for the Four. Any accomplished criminal had the essential mental capacity. Their primary enemy, the French spymaster known as the Chimera, was alleged to be entirely brilliant. What was needed—what absolutely radiated from the three men now in office—was a deathless loyalty to their country that outshone every other thought and commitment.

Something Julia had yet to prove to him she had.

Someone rapped on the front door of Barrowby. Quick as a flash, Beppo was down the stairs. Julia and Marcus followed more leisurely.

Elliot stood in the hall, tugging his gloves from his fingers. "Here I am, my lady!" He smiled brightly, only to let the smile slip when he spotted Marcus. "Blythe-Goodman, what the he—heavens are you doing here so early?"

Marcus grinned easily. "Her ladyship was kind enough to offer the hospitality of Barrowby when things ran late last evening."

Elliot grimaced. Marcus could almost read his mind. Advantages of cutting out of the wretched labor versus advantages of staying overnight in her ladyship's house . . . The resulting conclusion was evident in Elliot's sour expression. As Julia greeted him calmly and sailed on past, Marcus clapped the other fellow on the shoulder.

"Don't take it so hard, old man. We can't all be heroes."

"You're treading on my territory, Blythe-Goodman," Elliot said with surprising ferocity. Then again, even a dandy had his own sort of hill to defend. Her ladyship's income was quite a prize.

Marcus spread his hands. "I didn't impose. I was plainly invited."

Elliot narrowed his eyes. "She's pledged to me."

Marcus couldn't help it. He pursed his lips. "Is she reconsidering that decision after yesterday, do you think?"

Elliot looked a bit worried. "Well, I am here now."

Marcus nodded. "Yes, just in time to haul many, many heavy awkward barrels of water from the lake."

Elliot paled. "Haul?"

"Come on, man." Marcus gave him a sympathetic clout on the arm. "A bit of hard work never killed anyone."

He turned to follow Julia, but not before he heard Elliot grumble, "Ballocks. Hard work kills people every day."

Julia couldn't help but return to her earlier sunny mood once the work had begun. The autumn day was fair and her two swains were supplying an excess of high entertainment in their efforts to impress her. Men and their muscles—how adorably obnoxious.

Surprisingly, Mr. Elliot was holding his own. Who would have thought there was actual strength beneath that vibrant waistcoat? She paused in her bucket-toting to watch Elliot and Marcus combine their brawn to load a full cask onto the wagon. The great cart had to stand high enough on the drier bank so that its wheels would not sink into the earth. They never ceased their arguing, even as they worked effortlessly together to bring home more water to Barrowby than she'd dared to hope for.

It had been Elliot who had argued that they ought to dip from the far side of the lake so as to avoid any contamination from the privy mess. It had been Marcus who had initiated the idea of using Barrowby's copper bathing tubs to hold some of the water so that the barrels could return to the lake for another filling. Julia didn't know what she would have done without the two of them.

Not to mention the fuel for fantasy as the day wore on and Marcus removed his jacket and weskit to work in his shirtsleeves. Of course, it was inevitable that some barrels would slosh over on that shirt, wetting it to his rippling chest again and again. Julia nearly chewed her lip right from her mouth as she watched him, hair damp, nearly bare-chested, as he flexed his impressive strength on her behalf.

His gaze caught hers numerous times—hers guilty, his knowing—speaking volumes across the silence that never seemed truly quiet between them.

Really, it was a lovely day . . .

At last, the final barrel was filled and rolled away, leaving the exhausted Elliot, Marcus, and Julia behind. It wasn't until the wagon was well out of sight that Julia clapped a wet hand to her cheek.

"Oh! We ought to have ridden on the barrels! Now we'll have to walk miles back to the house." How could she not think of that? Then again, with Marcus rippling and flexing before her, who could have been thinking?

The look on Elliot's face was priceless, truly, but Julia was too upset to laugh. "How thoughtless of me, and after you have helped me so today!"

Marcus only grinned and put two fingers to his lips to emit a piercing whistle. A quarter of a mile across the pasture, his stallion, a fine creature the color of Julia's evening cup of chocolate, raised his head but didn't move a step to leave the other horses.

Marcus frowned. "I fear he's grown fond of that pretty mare." He whistled again. The stallion snorted and then began to reluctantly trot in their direction. Marcus smiled, then bowed to Julia. "May I offer you transportation, my lady?"

She raised a brow. "It doesn't seem that you shall have to, sir." She gestured to where her milk-white mare, Miel, had begun to follow his stallion like a schoolgirl with a crush.

She and Marcus laughed to see the two horses in the depths of infatuation. Elliot gave a whistle of his own. His aged mount continued to graze with great absorption. Elliot put his hands on his hips. "Filthy nag."

Marcus laughed. "You may double with me."

Elliot folded his arms. "Thank you, no. I'll walk. My magnificence has taken enough of a beating today.

The last thing I want is for her ladyship to see me thumping along on your stallion's arse." He stomped off in the direction of the herd.

Julia turned. "Mr. Elliot, you may ride with me," she called after him. He sent her a careless wave and continued on his way. She turned back to see that Marcus had darkened at her offer. So he did not wish her to ride with her arms about Elliot's waist? How gratifying.

Stop that. Remember, Marcus is not what you want.

Except that wasn't true, was it? He was precisely what she wanted.

Moreover, she needed him at the moment. His help had been invaluable, and Aldus had taught her to prize such an asset. She would send him on his way once this crisis was over with.

Cold and cruel.

Yes, most definitely. But then, she was not just the benevolent lady of the manor. She was the Fox. And he was useful.

And you don't want him to leave.

Lady Barrowby on horseback was truly a sight to behold. She and her mare moved as one, despite the lack of saddle and her position astride—or perhaps because of it. With the skirts of her practical dark gown covering little below her knees, she rode unashamedly, laughing as she and her mare left him and his mount behind.

He let her ride on for a moment as a thought wandered across his mind. This was so very like one of the entries in her diary that he had to wonder if she had planned it thus.

Yet, how could she know that her well would be

fouled and that the horses would be in the pasture with them?

So, was it merely a happy accident? Marcus bent low and encouraged his stallion to more speed. If so, then he meant to take advantage of it.

He easily came abreast of her. She cast him an exhilarated smile. The path entered the wood and he edged his mount closer to hers.

Abruptly, he leaned in and swept her from her horse with one arm. She squeaked in alarm, but nimbly twisted as he sat her across his lap. He slowed the stallion, letting her mare run ahead.

She brushed her fallen hair back from her face. She was plainly furious. "Why ever would you do such a thing? You could have harmed Miel!"

Marcus blinked. Well, hell. *Women!* He thought fast. "Branch," he said, cocking his head back the way they'd come. "A very low branch."

Her eyes narrowed and she leaned to peer behind them. "I saw no branch. And I ride this way often."

He nodded emphatically. "A branch. Very large. It had to be done."

She wriggled a bit in his lap and his eyes nearly crossed.

"Well, we must catch Miel."

"Will she not merely return to the stable looking for her oats?" Marcus tugged very carefully on the reins. The stallion's walk slowed to an amble. "I hate to press my mount when he must carry two."

As he'd suspected, her concern for his horse overrode her uneasiness. "Oh, of course you shouldn't."

Marcus said nothing more, only letting his easy,

respectful hold and the rhythm of his horse's walk soothe her fears. Of course, in his mind he'd already thrown her to the leaves and divested her of her gown, but that was a harmless diversion. His intent was not to ravish, but to ensnare.

" 'Tis a lovely evening," he observed mildly. Damn, she smelled remarkable. For the rest of his life, he was going to become aroused by the clean scent of lake water.

Julia felt what was happening near her hip, but Marcus was behaving so admirably she forgave him for what he certainly could not help. Besides, it was lovely riding along in his arms, the gentle rocking of his horse allowing her to relax against his broad, hard chest.

"You were wonderful today," she told him. "I cannot thank you enough."

He smiled down at her. "It was nothing. I enjoy a bit of toil now and again." He chuckled. "I think even Elliot enjoyed himself, although he made sure we wouldn't think so."

Julia laughed. "Elliot fears if we catch him enjoying it, he'll be made to do it more often."

His laughter rumbled up through her and she felt a tiny quiver run over her skin. His clean manly scent was all over her and his heat burned off the chill of her dampened gown.

"Are you cold, my lady?" His arm tightened slightly about her. She allowed it, for she longed for nothing more than to drop her head on his shoulders and close her eyes to the world.

Dangerous.

It was odd how that reproving voice grew fainter and

fainter by the hour. Now it was hardly more than an
echo in her mind.

Absently, she noticed that the stallion was scarcely
moving now. Marcus's heart was beating faster, she
could feel it. The heat and tension between them rose
in the silence and cocooned them from the real world.

She drew back to gaze up into his eyes. He was looking down at her, his hunger apparent and ferocious.
She waited breathlessly for his control to break, for she
longed for him to remove her from doubt and logic, but
again, he did nothing but watch her.

She licked her lips. His gaze shot to her mouth. She
felt him swell against her—heavens, who would have
thought it could become yet *larger*?—but he did not so
much as twitch in her direction.

He could be hers. All she need do would be to reach
out her hand . . .

She was promised—to the Four and to Elliot, although for the life of her she could not remember why
she thought she could bear to wed Elliot. However, she
was not the sort to break a promise.

She swallowed. "Marcus, you are a fine man and
I . . . admire you a great deal. But Mr. Elliot and I have
an understanding—"

"I know. He told me."

She nodded regretfully. "It would be for the best then
if you and I did not . . ." She drew a breath. "If we did
not share this . . ."

"This what?"

God, he was without mercy! "This attraction. Yes,
that is the word. Attraction." She straightened away
from him. "I will not break my word to Mr. Elliot."

The stallion stopped. Marcus dropped the reins and took her by the waist. She gasped and pressed her hands to his chest, gazing up at him in alarm.

He smiled slightly. "My lady, I am not going to assault you. We are but half a mile from the house. I am going to dismount to walk the remainder and I don't want you to fall."

"Oh." She blinked. "I do not fall off horses," she added, by way of awkward explanation.

His green eyes were so close. "You will if you do not release me," he said, a teasing tone creeping into his voice.

She looked down to see that her hands were fisted tightly in his shirt. She released her grip with a small embarrassed sound. "My apologies—"

He slid easily from the stallion, leaving her feeling cold and alone and very, very disappointed.

He took up the reins and stood at the stallion's shoulder, looking up at her. "I admire you as well. You are intelligent, capable, and stunningly beautiful. I desire you, my lady, and I will not deny it. I think you're a fool to wed a fop like Elliot simply because you believe you can control him. A woman who keeps a lion for a pet need not be afraid of a man like me. I would lend you my strength and I would contest you when required. You would not find me convenient, for I will not be dismissed. I would never be your lapdog, but I would be much, much more." He moved closer. "I would be your lover and your mate. I would inflame your nights and own your dreams. I would tire you to exhaustion and never, ever get enough of your luscious, naked, lovely flesh or the look that you have in your beautiful storm-sky eyes right now. You would never find me easy, Julia, but you would find me passionate, voracious, and entirely mad for you."

She stared down at him, her eyes wide and her mouth dry. He pressed the reins into her stunned hands and bowed. "Good evening, my lady." He turned and strode away, leaving her on his horse in the middle of the path.

"Wait!" It was only a choked gasp, but he turned.

"Wait for what, Julia? You said it yourself. You belong to Elliot now."

She didn't remember making a move, but the stallion stepped forward, bringing her to him like an offering. The horse stopped when she was directly before Marcus once more.

"I—" She couldn't breathe. Oh, God, he was so hazardous for her, but she could not let him walk away. She tried to draw breath into her lungs but the need inside her was like an iron band about her ribs. "I don't want Elliot," she managed. "I want y—"

Her next word was drowned out by the harsh clanging of the alarm bell at Barrowby. She jerked her head up to see a black cloud rising over the treetops just ahead.

"Fire!"

10

He is the flame inside me, that cannot be doused, that will not be stifled. When he is within me, I burn to joyful ashes in his arms.

The stables were afire. The stored hay was dry from the previous autumn and burned like paper in the high loft above the stalls. Smoke poured from the square hay door above, and the top of the large double stable doors below.

There were no horses within, Marcus was happy to remember, for the bucket brigade from the lake was nearly useless. There weren't enough hands and the water was too far.

Marcus turned away in an agony of frustration and spotted the cistern cover awry. "The well!"

Beppo shook his head miserably. "No, sir! We spent half the day pumping it dry!"

Julia turned to them, her expression rigid. "Beppo, bring out the casks."

"But my lady!"

"Now! Hurry!"

Beppo bobbed a bow and ran away to gather the bucket line back into the yard. They began to roll out the carefully collected water casks in a mad scramble that cost many a barrel on the cobbles.

"There will be no water tomorrow," Marcus said.

"Then we will fill them again," she said harshly. "I will not capitulate."

"What?"

But she was looking about suddenly. "Quentin! Quentin, where is Sebastian?"

Quentin's head jerked up, horror in his eyes. "Oh—oh, my lady!"

Marcus heard her draw a sharp breath. It was the sound of a hurt child. Then she lifted her skirts and pelted toward the stable. *"Sebastian!"*

Marcus caught her a few steps from flinging herself into the smoke-filled building. "Julia! You cannot save him now!"

She fought him, fists and nails, but he would not release her. She grabbed at his shirtfront.

"Marcus, he might still be alive! His pen is at the far end from the flames!"

Marcus eyed the burning building. "But you cannot reach it without burning to death."

Unless . . .

Elliot appeared riding his ancient mount, his eyes wide at the inferno before them. "Good God! I cannot leave you lot for a moment!"

Marcus forced Julia's tearstained gaze from the fire to his face. "Stay. Right. Here. I have an idea."

He grabbed up some of the rope that had earlier

bound the casks to the wagons and whistled for his stallion. The horse came, wild-eyed and reluctant, but he came. "Elliot! With me!"

He pulled himself up in a running leap and tore around the other side of the stables, to the newer addition. Elliot followed at a stumbling gallop. "Who are we rescuing?"

They were out of the smoke now and could hear the panicked roars. Marcus cocked his head. "Him."

"Oh, joy." Yet Elliot didn't retreat.

Marcus used his mount's height to tie the ends of two ropes securely about the eave supports. He dismounted to fashion the other end into a sort of harness to utilize the most powerful portion of his stallion's chest. Elliot watched for a moment, then did the same with the other rope.

"I hope you know what you're doing," Elliot said warily. "I don't fancy being cat food."

"He'll be too worried about the fire." At least, Marcus hoped so. He didn't cherish hopes of being a lion's dinner either.

They led their mounts to the ends of their tethers. "Now!" Marcus cried, and pulled the reins.

The two horses strained obediently, but the stable was too sturdily built. "Again!"

This time they could hear the lumber groan over the lion's roars, but the wall stood firm.

Julia came around the side of the stable on her mare. She knew instantly the plan wasn't working, Marcus could see it on her face.

She rode closer. "Sebastian!" Her voice rose commandingly above the din. "Sebastian, come!"

The lion's noise ceased for a moment. Julia rode closer.

"Julia, not too near!"

But she wasn't listening. She raised both hands to cup her mouth. "Sebastian, *come*!"

A mighty impact shook the wall before them, then another. The beast was trying to get to his mistress. Marcus noted the rhythm of the thudding blows. "Now!" he cried.

The horses heaved at the same moment the lion threw himself against the wall. With a groan, the nails gave and a corner of the planking pulled free. Immediately, a giant golden paw was thrust into the gap.

"Pull!"

The horses' hooves slid, cutting deep grooves in the grass. Marcus took hold of his rope to add his strength. The gap widened and a great golden head pressed outward, twisting into the narrow space.

Elliot's horse slipped to one knee. The gap in the wall narrowed, trapping the lion's head.

"No!" Julia rode forward, forcing Miel into Elliot's rope. The tension allowed the lion to pull his head back inside just before the wall fatally compressed his throat.

Elliot's horse was done, however. The gelding's head hung low and his ribs bellowed.

The smoke was worsening on this side, which meant the fire was moving fast through the straw and wood of the stable. Julia slid from her horse and began to tug at the knots securing Elliot's mount. "Quickly! We can use Miel—"

Marcus covered her hands with his own. "Julia, there's no time!"

She was crying now, tears running unnoticed down her face. "No! We can—we can—" She halted, unable to muster any more ideas. Her face crumpled and she staggered to lean against the mare's white side. She threw back her head. *"Sebastian, come!"*

The lion gave a cry that nearly matched hers and the wall shook as never before. Marcus saw the gap miraculously widen once more.

He handed his reins to Elliot. "Pull on three!" Then he ran to the wall and pulled himself up by the eave supports.

"Marcus, no!" Julia's voice followed him. "Sebastian is panicked! He won't know what he's doing!"

Marcus locked one leg over the gable and braced the other foot against the still-sturdy portion of the wall. Wedging his fingers into the gap, he made ready to pull. "One! Two!"

"Marcus, no!" There was real fear in Julia's voice. "Leave him!"

A giant paw forced itself through the gap, inches from his face. "By God, you better not eat me, you stupid overly endowed floor rug!" He took a breath. *"Three!"*

For a long moment, nothing happened. Then, somewhere in the wall, a single crucial nail lost its hold and Marcus felt everything give way at once. He kicked off hard, hoping to get free of both the falling wall and the escaping beast, but to no avail.

Julia's voice rose in a wail. "Marcus!"

The wall fell, pinning him by one leg. The shock of the fall knocked the breath from his lungs, and then the pain in his leg did it again. He lay on his back for an eternal instant, unable to inhale.

Above him, nearly on top of him, the lion planted himself on the fallen wall and roared loud enough to flatten Westminster Palace.

Just then, in that perfect moment of quiet when the lion's roar had frightened even the insects into muteness, Marcus's breath came back in a strident wheeze.

The already distressed beast started madly, then whipped his great head around to glare at Marcus with panic-maddened eyes.

Nice kitty. It would have been a lovely insouciant remark, fit to show the world his unconcern, but Marcus was scared spitless and could only muster a stutter. "N-nn—"

Sebastian sniffed deeply of him, then snorted a great gust of revolting predator breath and mucus spray. Marcus didn't dare so much as wipe at his lips.

"Sebastian." Julia's soothing voice came from far too near. "Sebastian, come away, pet."

Marcus jerked his head back to look at her. *"Get. Back."*

The lion growled at Marcus's hissed command. Then something caved in the stable fire and a scorching, spark-laden wind exploded from the gap in the wall. The lion leaped from the fallen wall and bounded into the darkening twilight as if he had the hounds of hell behind him.

Elliot and Julia rushed forward. "Marcus!" She knelt at his side. "How badly are you hurt?"

"Wipe my face! Wipe my face!"

She did so with her sleeve pulled over her hand, laughing damply. "Don't be such an infant, Marcus. It's only a bit of lion slime."

Elliot managed to shift the wood and Julia helped Marcus scramble backward from beneath it. As he limped away, supported by the two of them, Marcus could feel the heat on his back as the fire roared into the space recently occupied by His Heinous.

"That creature owes me greatly," he informed Julia.

She smiled at him gratefully, making him feel like a giant. "We both do."

"I like fur rugs," he said. "Big, hairy, yellow ones."

She laughed and thumped him in the ribs. "Be nice. It isn't his fault. He was so very frightened." She sighed and looked over her shoulder at the darkness.

"He'll come back," Marcus said.

She turned back to gaze up at him, worry in her eyes. "Will he?"

Marcus smiled down at this mad, odd, astounding, splendid woman. "How could he stay away?"

There hadn't been enough hands to stop the flames, only contain them. The stables were naught but blackened wreckage, wisps of smoke still drifting up from the piled char.

Julia stood in the yard, gazing at the debris. Her face was as pale as the ash in her hair.

"Who is doing this?" Her choked whisper carried back to Marcus as he came up behind her. "Who would hate me so?"

"You are only asking that now?"

She turned to blink at him dully. "I thought I knew who—or at least why. There are some people who do not wish me to succeed at something I am attempting . . ."

She believed the Three would do this to her? Well,

yes, they might do such a thing if the situation warranted it, for mercy was not truly their business, but there was no reason for the malicious turn of the things that had happened at Barrowby.

She went on. "Yet I do not believe they would do this . . . at least not in response to anything I have done."

Her thoughts matched his own, yet Marcus wondered. Lord Liverpool had been so very adamant . . . and the Prime Minister was not known for his mercy, either. Of course, he was back in London now, but everything was for hire, if the price was high enough.

Even murder.

Alarm shot through him. "If this thing you are attempting is so dangerous, perhaps you ought to consider ceasing."

She shook her head. "That is not a possibility. This is not the sort of commitment I could shed on a whim."

"A whim? You're under attack, Julia!"

"No. No, it could not be because of that. The people I spoke of . . . no, this is not them. I *know* them. This is not the tack they would take. More likely they would send someone to worm their way into my confidence—"

Oh, hell. He must distract her from that thought at once. "Julia, listen to me!" He turned her to face him, both hands on her shoulders. "You are in danger." He realized the urgency he heard in his own voice was not feigned.

Liverpool was not to be trifled with. The man still had much of the influence and power he'd garnered in his years of serving in the Four.

God, if anything happened to her—

Icy dread struck deep within him. "Julia, you must

leave Barrowby! Go somewhere safe, somewhere isolated, where no one can find you. Can you think of such a place?"

Her gaze focused on him. "I can, but I won't. I cannot leave my people here to face this alone."

"I will stay." It was a rash promise, but he realized that he would keep it if it meant she would flee to safety. "I will stay here and run Barrowby for you."

She blinked, her brow creasing. "Marcus, I know you mean well, but you have no idea of the requirements—"

"I have a dim grasp of the concept," he assured her. "And I am very experienced in the art of defense."

She raised one hand to his cheek. "My soldier." Then she seemed to realize the intimacy of the gesture and dropped her hand to turn away. "My thanks for the generous offer, Marcus, but you simply don't understand. I *cannot* leave. I was ordered to remain here to await a decision."

Marcus felt his fists clench at his sides. How convenient. Liverpool had commanded her to sit here like a lone pheasant in the park, awaiting the hunter.

Like him.

He ran a frustrated hand through his hair. He could not seem to keep his role in mind here. Was he investigating her or protecting her?

Protect her. Forever.

Unmask her. Win.

It did not matter. Either way, he would guard her from further interference. This was not Lord Liverpool's decision to make—something that doubtless rankled the Prime Minister ever more—and Marcus would not allow anyone to meddle with matters of the Four.

◆ ◆ ◆

The watcher in the trees was well satisfied with his work. While it had not gone precisely as planned, in the end, he'd accomplished his objective. Her husband was dead, her pet was gone, her house was nearly empty of dependents, and there was a rumor in the village that she would soon lose the house itself when the heir came to claim the estate.

Matters were nicely in hand. She had nothing left to keep her here, as far as he could see. And should some other attachment become apparent, he would take care of that as well.

He took a deep satisfying breath. He'd almost forgotten how enjoyable it was to make a woman like her suffer.

11

Marcus clenched his jaw so hard he thought his teeth might crack under the pressure. She was going to drive him mad. "I will not leave you here unprotected."

Where she sat elegantly in the room where he'd first seen her, poised like a queen upon a throne in her chair, Julia gazed calmly back at him. "I do not wish to be unprotected. I have my people."

"Servants and grooms and . . . I'm not entirely sure what some of them are, but they are obviously not bodyguards."

She raised a brow. "If I were to hire bodyguards, how could I be sure of their loyalty? How could I be sure they were not part of what has been happening?" She looked thoughtful. "I could send for more of the fair folk, I suppose. Harvest is over, for the most part. Work is slight during the cold months."

"Not more charity—you need protection!"

"Do not underestimate the travelers. It is a rough life and they are a hardy breed."

"Do you mean Gypsies?"

She shook her head quickly. "No, the Rom are

nothing like the fair folk. Except for the traveling, of course. And the wagons. And sometimes sharing camp-sites—" She shrugged, frustrated. "The Rom are a peo-ple, like the Chinese. The fair folk are Englishmen, or Italians like Beppo, or another nationality. The thing that keeps them together is the fair. Traveling showmen move from fair to fair in the spring, summer, and au-tumn. Jugglers, sights—"

At his puzzled expression she explained. "The giant man or the tiny woman. They aren't performers so much as attractions themselves."

He blinked. "I saw a lady with a beard when I was a lad."

She rolled her eyes. "You saw a man in a dress, more like. True bearded ladies are very rare."

He snorted. "Well, you needn't punch a hole in my tender childhood memories."

She grimaced. "Sorry. But true sights pride them-selves on their authentic uniqueness. Have you seen my cook?"

He shook his head. "Can't say that I have."

"Meg has more tattoos than anyone in Britain," she said proudly. "If the staff were to go on the road to-morrow, they'd get top billing, for Meg also swallows swords."

"So everyone at Barrowby is one of these 'fair folk'?" That made them sound like Irish fairies. He stifled a superstitious shudder. He wasn't so sure he wanted to fall asleep in this house again. He might not awaken for a hundred years!

She nodded. "Even Pickles, my maid. She was the

wife of Hiram Pickles, the show's owner. And she used to dance, in her day."

Marcus covered his eyes. "Stop." It was too late. The indelible image of the withered Pickles kicking up her petticoats was imprinted on his mind's eye. He made an impatient noise. "Then hire them, but get them here quickly."

She chewed her lip. Marcus wasn't supposed to be so fascinated by that action, he knew, but he found himself riveted as always.

"It will take a few days to spread the word. Which suits me fine. It will take that long to have the well usable again."

"Well, it doesn't suit me!" God, she was the most stubborn female! "I will stay until they come."

"Why are you staying and not I?" Elliot was leaning on the doorjamb, openly eavesdropping. "I'm the one with the 'understanding,' after all."

Marcus barely glanced at him. "Because I'm the one who can protect her."

Elliot darkened. "You are not the only one about who can shoot a pistol."

Marcus folded his arms and glared at Elliot. "I am a soldier. You are a coatrack."

Elliot narrowed his eyes. "Just because a fellow has a bit of style—"

"Oh, stop it!" Julia let her head fall forward in exaggerated weariness. "You may both stay. You may draw a chalk line down the center of the house and divide it between you, if you must, but for pity's sake, stop arguing about it!"

"We cannot *both* stay," Elliot muttered. "What would people say?"

Julia sighed. "If you insist on propriety—and I cannot imagine being less interested in that at the moment—then we could formally announce our engagement, if you like. You can tell people Marcus is your cousin."

Marcus made a protesting noise. She glanced his way, but he subsided and looked away. Surprisingly, even Elliot shook his head.

"People will be very shocked if you become engaged so soon."

Julia threw up her hands. "People will think the worst of me no matter what I do! I'm the young widow of a wealthy old man—I'm an endlessly potential scandal as it is! Still, I am a rich widow, not a sheltered maiden, and money has the most interesting way of making scandal disappear."

She planted her fists on her hips and glared at both of them. "Which do you think is a worse bit of gossip—that I became engaged again too soon, or that I'm enjoying my own little *ménage-à-trois*?"

Elliot could not argue that, although Marcus looked as though he wanted to. Part of her wished he would. The female who could not resist his male wished that he would demand that she break her promise to Elliot and claim her as his own.

Which was the worst possible thing that could happen, of course. Which was why she was glad he did no such thing.

Very glad. Definitely.

Elliot reluctantly went back to supervising the

preparations for the second water excursion but Marcus lingered for a moment after he'd gone.

"Ménage-à-trois?"

She fought back a smile. "Don't worry. I won't tell anyone I said that."

He shook his head. "Most ladies have never even heard of such a thing."

Julia slid her gaze up to meet his. "I have recently retired from the 'most ladies' club, or hadn't you noticed?"

He laughed. "Yes, I had. I think it was the lion that convinced me . . . or perhaps the juggling footmen."

She blinked. "You saw that?"

He winked at her. "Don't worry. I won't tell anyone I saw that." Then he tilted his head and regarded her curiously. "Your French is exquisite, you know."

"Thank you." She looked down at her desk. "I learned from a Frenchwoman . . . when I was quite young."

"Hmm." He continued to gaze at her. "Is there nothing you cannot do?"

"Sing," she replied instantly with a tiny smile. "Not a single note. Squawking parrots flee my voice."

She kept smiling as she heard his laughter follow him down the hall.

Elliot kept a close eye on Marcus as the two of them directed the final effort to clean the well. He'd not foreseen Marcus's doggedness in pursuing Julia. Elliot grimaced. It was alarming how she seemed to be veering away from him by the moment.

Igby, Igby, and Igby—Julia had assured him that it was not necessary to attempt to differentiate them. "I'm not sure even they remember which is which"—had spent themselves at the two-man pump, trading off seamlessly with one always at rest.

The bald, tattooed cook, Meg, had created a straining box filled with clean sand so that every pail of water could be quickly purified before ever leaving the well area.

"That's a fine job," Elliot told the man, giving a clout to one bare, hairy shoulder. Meg flicked him a cool glance, but nodded respectfully. The Barrowby staff seemed unsure of how to treat Elliot now that the engagement had been announced.

It was a bit dismaying to see the wildfire manner in which the news had traveled.

"Common doings." The cook regarded him sourly. "The fair folk don't always know what's upstream."

Elliot grimaced. "Gad, I suppose not. Could be pigs for all you know."

Meg narrowed his eyes. "Aye, pigs . . . or a gent takin' a piss."

Elliot held up both hands. "Not I, I vow." Well, he'd certainly be more careful in the future at any rate.

Elliot looked up to see Marcus studying him. That was fine, for he'd been studying Marcus from the first. It was becoming increasingly evident to Elliot that Marcus was encroaching on his fiancée.

Elliot wouldn't have minded so much if Julia hadn't been so obviously smitten with the big lout. Elliot liked him, too, which made it difficult to loathe him properly.

Would this incessant fondness for people never cease? It was going to make things hard for him in the end, he simply knew it.

The last Igby flopped down beside the pump,

exhausted. The well had been pumped, scrubbed, allowed to fill and then pumped again. Marcus and the other Igbys rolled the unwieldy pump away on its sturdy cart. Meg settled the cover on his filtering system and strode away without a word.

Elliot remained where he was for a long moment, treasuring the quiet and the lack of perspiration it implied. Was the hard labor truly finished? What a heavenly thought. All he wished for now was a hot bath and a cold tankard. He ambled forward to gaze down into the well. Even now, he could hear the trickling waters of the earth filling the depths of it.

The cover of the cistern was still awry. Made of wide, heavy planks strapped together with iron and sawed into a rough circle, it was heavy and awkward to lift.

Elliot looked about—for surely he'd done enough today?—but there was no one in sight to haul it back into place. He should call for some help.

Then again, he wasn't in the mood to see that amused glint in Marcus's eyes. A "coatrack," indeed!

Flexing his hands, Elliot blew out a breath and grimaced. The cover was stained green with damp and still dusted with ash from the stable fire.

None of his new things were going to outlast this hubbub, were they?

He bent to grip the iron rings that served as handles on the thing and gave a mighty tug. The round cistern cover began to slide back into place.

He was concentrating so that he never heard the intruder come up behind him. There was simply an agonizing explosion in his head and then the fading of consciousness as he felt himself fall forward into the open well. As he fell on and on, he heard the grating noise of the cover sliding into place. Then he hit bottom and there was nothing.

Elliot was cold.

No, strike that. Elliot was *freezing*.

He opened his eyes. Then he closed them and tried again.

It seemed that Elliot was also blind. Or . . . he put out his hands to feel slick, icy stones to either side of him. Well, hell.

Elliot, it turned out, was down the well.

He put a hand to the back of his head to find what was sending splitting pain into his skull. There was a sizable lump that still seeped something sticky onto his probing fingers.

"Ow." His voice bounced back to him strangely, at once loud and muffled.

"Lucky I didn't fall on my face," he muttered, for he was sitting in two feet of icy water. If the well was filling the same as before, that meant he'd been down here for at least an hour. Using his hands, he stood shakily to get out of the chill.

He looked upward. There was a faint ring of light far above that told him the cistern cover was tightly in place. "Hello? *Hello!*" His call rebounded madly from all sides of the well, causing him to cringe as it spiked the pounding in his head. Unfortunately, he doubted that his voice made it past the heavy cover.

"Well, this is quite the predicament." He tried to breathe deeply against the panic that was making him gasp.

He shut his eyes against the darkness and tried to think. He was an intelligent bloke. He could figure this one out.

One—if no one had realized where he was by now, then it wasn't likely they would. At least, not in time. Two—the well filled at about two feet per hour, he and Beppo had calculated yesterday. If he wasn't found in the next two hours and some, the water would be over his head. Three—he wasn't a bad swimmer and he could likely keep afloat for a few more hours, but how long could he fight the chill that even now made his bones ache?

Oh, the chill probably counted as the fourth factor. Or did it? He rubbed at his temples, but the pounding didn't abate.

Five—the slick, tightly fitted stones gave little purchase for climbing.

So, by the time the water rose to a level where he could conceivably reach the cover, he would already be dead of exhaustion or freezing.

"Marcus, if you've murdered me to win the fair lady, I'm going to haunt you until you're an old, old man." Blighter would still likely be handsomer then, too.

On the plus side of the ledger, the Barrowby staff would be dipping directly from the well for a while, for the pipe that pierced through halfway up one wall would not be usable for several hours.

Then again, if he was Igby—or Igby, or Igby—he would use up the last few barrels of tepid lake water before bothering to haul heavy water buckets up thirty feet.

The water had risen well past his knees while he was pondering his situation. Elliot stared up at the ring of light, willing someone to develop a sudden uncontrollable thirst for nice cool well water.

Julia rounded the corner into the front hall and nearly ran into Marcus. "Have you seen Elliot?" she asked without preamble.

He grinned at her. "Elliot has disappeared? There must be a bit of perspiration in the offing."

She didn't smile back. "I'm worried. He promised he would help me with the horses when the well was finished."

Marcus frowned slightly. "Why did you not ask me for help?"

Julia looked away. How could she explain that she didn't trust herself to do *anything* with him, for she kept finding herself overcome with the desire to . . . well, *desire* was as specific as she dared be, even to herself.

"That is beside the point. I know he would not have forgotten. Furthermore, his horse is still here."

Marcus folded his arms and leaned one shoulder against the wall. He looked like a lord.

She blinked. Where had that thought come from? She knew the peerage of England as well as she knew her own family tree. There was no Marcus Blythe-Goodman in the House of Lords.

"I know you're fond of Elliot, my lady," he said. "But we both know he's a bit unreliable."

She tilted her head. "We do? How do we know that, pray tell?" She folded her arms as well, aping his stance. "He worked as hard as you to haul water, and he was right with you during the stable fire last night, and he has spent the entire day cleaning the well at your side."

He scowled. "That is true. I wonder why I have such an impression of him, then?"

She raised a brow. "Because he works very hard to cast just that impression. I should think you would have noticed."

He blinked. "I'll have you know that I take Elliot very seriously . . . especially the fact that he was out of sight when the house was searched, as well as when the stable caught fire."

She shook her head. "I have already dismissed those suspicions. Furman at the inn confirmed that he was indeed in his room during the ransacking and when the well was tampered with, and you know very well that his poor horse could never have made it back to the house ahead of ours to set the fire."

"How . . . efficient you are." He grimaced slightly but she could tell she had convinced him. "So what do we do, mount a search? Isn't that a bit extreme? He's a grown man, after all."

Julia chewed her lip. "He was assisting you at the well, was he not? That is where Meg and Igby last saw him."

Marcus nodded. "That is where I last saw him also."

She spread her hands. "Then let us begin at the well."

12

I long for a strong hand to lift me from the darkness of my melancholy.

The yard was deserted and everything seemed perfectly normal . . . but there was one thing out of place.

Marcus bent swiftly to retrieve something from the ground. "This is the mallet Meg used to pound together the sieve box."

Julia leaned over to peer at it. "Don't be silly. My staff never leaves valuable tools lying about." Then she gasped. "Is that—"

Marcus touched the head of the mallet. His hand came away with a smear of blood on one fingertip. "It is. It seems our prankster has just graduated to attempted murderer."

She caught her breath. "Murder?"

"There's no sign of struggle. He must have been knocked unconscious immediately." He straightened and looked all about them. "Look for marks where someone might have dragged a bod—Elliot."

They circled urgently but carefully, desperate for

some sign of where Elliot had been taken. They met on the other side of the cistern.

"There is no sign of anything of the sort," Julia said, her voice tight. "There is a great deal of ash on the cobbles. You would think we'd be able to detect *something*."

Marcus worked his jaw, frustrated. "Elliot is not a small man. I'm not sure I could carry him off that neatly."

"But if he wasn't carried off, then he would still be here—"

As one, their gazes shot to the neatly covered cistern.

"Oh, no."

Horror shuddered through Julia. Marcus didn't bother with a reaction. He simply acted, flinging himself at the cistern cover and dragging at it with all his might.

"Beppo! Meg! Igby!" Julia ran to pull at the other iron ring.

The Barrowby staff piled out through the kitchen door and came at a run. "My lady?"

"Get a strong rope, quickly!" Julia gasped. Meg took over at her ring and the cistern cover was lifted and dragged aside.

Julia flung herself down on the edge. "Elliot? *Elliot?*" She looked up. "We need lanterns. I cannot s—"

"Well, I . . . can't either," a rasping voice echoed from the darkness. "You just . . . bloody blinded me."

Igby came running with a lantern. They lowered it quickly down. Finally they saw him, clinging to the slippery side of the well, only his gray exhausted face above water.

"Oh, thank God!" Julia brushed away the blurring in her eyes. "Elliot, dear, are you injured?"

"My . . . head hurts . . . and I'm cold . . . and I'd sell Marcus's soul for a hot toddy . . . but I'm well enough."

Beppo came running with a length of sturdy rope. Marcus threw one end down the shaft. "Elliot, tie it about your chest!"

Julia watched as Elliot made a grab for the rope—and slipped completely under the water. She held her breath for him, but he did not reappear for a long moment.

Then his head broke water, but he seemed disoriented. He fumbled weakly with the rope for a long moment.

"Do you have it?" Marcus called.

Elliot seemed to be fading before their eyes. "Hands . . . can't seem to . . ." He slipped beneath the surface once more.

Julia looked up at Marcus in a panic. "We're losing him!"

"No we're not." Marcus pulled the rope back up in a few swift motions. He tossed the dry end to Meg and tied the other about his own chest. "Beppo, bring another rope. Meg, lower me in. I don't want to land on him."

"Heaven . . . forbid."

Elliot had resurfaced. Julia laughed damply. "Hang on, dear. Marcus is coming for you."

"I . . . knew it. Always . . . the damned hero."

Marcus was lowered in by Meg and Beppo. The Igbys took the other rope and made a loop for Elliot in the end. They passed it down to Marcus, who quickly had Elliot ready to raise.

"He's losing consciousness," Marcus called. "He cannot climb."

"You stay put then, sir," Meg called back and let Marcus's rope go to help the others with Elliot. Julia stayed where she was, pressed to the opening of the well.

"Are you all right, Marcus?"

"It's b-bloody cold down h-here," Marcus said calmly.

Julia raised her head. "Pickles, have hot baths ready for the gentlemen!"

"Already got the water heatin', milady."

Elliot's soaked head crested the lip of the well. Julia reached to wipe wet hair from his eyes. "Oh, God. He's as cold as death."

Meg hefted him out. "I'll plunk 'im in that tub then."

Igby, Igby, and Igby began to pull Marcus up. Julia heard muffled cursing and one sharp "Ow!" but after a moment, Marcus had climbed the well using his feet and was hefting himself over the wall.

He was dripping icy water and one hand was bleeding, but he was grinning. "You're going to have to pump that again, lads," he told the Igbys. "I don't know about you, but I don't fancy drinking Elliot pot liquor."

Julia slapped him on the bicep. "Don't laugh! I'm worried about him."

Marcus laughed. "I wouldn't be too worried. Before he passed out, he told me that he could see directly into your gown when you were leaning over."

Julia gasped and clapped her hands over her bodice, but then she ruined her "offended lady" bit by snickering. "I was simply trying to give him something to live for," she said loftily.

Marcus shook his head. "That would revive a dead

man," he said with a short bow. He turned to stride after Pickles to his bath, leaving Julia to ponder the flash of dark intensity that had crossed his face.

She had the feeling he wasn't jesting anymore.

Her fiancé was warm and dry and had been inspected by both the Middlebarrow physician and Quentin.

"He's had a bad chill and needs a great deal of hot tea, but he'll fare well enough," the doctor said.

"If 'n 'e was an 'orse, I'd feed 'im 'ot gruel and cover 'im with good wool blankets," Quentin had stated.

To be on the safe side, Julia took both judgments to heart until Elliot pleaded with her to stop. Perhaps it was guilt over the way she'd come to prefer another man while she was promised to him, or guilt over the way he'd come to danger through his association with her, or guilt over the way she'd planned to use him for her own convenience, but Julia could not overcome the compulsion to fix Elliot.

Now he sat in the parlor with her, wearing a suit of Aldus's antiquated clothing and grudgingly downing yet another cup of hot tea.

"Elliot, you must leave Barrowby," she said abruptly. "I cannot have you risking your life for nothing."

Elliot blinked, then put the tea down before he scalded himself. "It is not for nothing."

"Yes," she insisted, her voice filled with gentle regret. "It is."

He frowned. "No, it is for you. You and I—" He stopped, awareness dawning in his eyes. "Ah. I see now. This is the bit where you ask if we might remain friends, isn't it?"

She bit her lip. "I'm caught out. I'm so sorry, Elliot. I'm doing this badly."

"As if anyone could do it otherwise." He swore beneath his breath. "You've taken a fancy to Blythe-Goodman, haven't you?"

Julia closed her eyes. "I—"

He snorted. "I knew it the day I brought him to call on you. Big, good-looking bloke like that—what chance did the rest of us have?"

She opened her eyes to give him a tenderly repressing glare. "I'm not a game of chance, Elliot."

He crossed his arms. "My lady, winning you is the very definition of the term 'lucky bastard.'"

She laughed shortly, shaking her head. "Ah, Elliot, you truly know how to sweep a girl's feet from beneath her."

He looked down for a moment, then raised his gaze, all superficial hardness gone from his expression. "My lady, exactly how well do you know Marcus?"

She drew her brows together. "Odd. That is precisely how he asked me about you."

Elliot did not relieve the intensity of his gaze. "There is more to him than meets the eye."

She blinked. "I vow I've had this very conversation before." Then she sat and folded her hands on her lap. "Elliot, do you *know* of any reason why I should not continue my association with Marcus?"

Elliot's gaze slipped from hers. "I don't know anything . . . precisely. I have some suspicions that he is not simply the man he seems."

"As do I." She smiled at his evident surprise. "Elliot, do you think I would risk myself and Barrowby in the hands of someone I know nothing about?"

He frowned slightly. "And what do you know?"

"I know that he is brave enough to break open a lion's den to save its life." She began to list on her fingers. "I know that he is honorable enough to help save *you* even though he took exception to our engagement. I know that he is not afraid of hard work, or of wading knee deep in privy muck, or of admitting that he is in the wrong, or—"

Elliot held up a hand. "Pray stop, before I fling myself back into the well. Sir Flawless might have to leap in and save me. Again."

She took that hand in her own. His gaze fell to where they touched. "Elliot, you are my friend. I don't know everything about you, but I trust you. Do you have that same trust in me?"

He raised his gaze. "I do. I shouldn't, but I do."

She smiled. "Then trust that I *know* Marcus. I see the man inside the cheap superfine, behind the handsome face. I don't know everything about him, but I know he is a good man, in the same way that I know you are a good man."

He shook his head. "I'm sure I haven't done a thing to give you that impression."

She released his hand and stood. "Elliot, don't be a dolt. Now go find some wealthy lady who will appreciate you properly!"

He stood as well and grinned at her. "I did, and she threw me over for an oversized lout with a penchant for hairy beasts and privy muck." He bowed over her hand. "My best, forever, my lady."

Watching Elliot ride away in her carriage was a relief,

but only a temporary one. His suspicions of Marcus had
sunk beneath the spell of attraction Julia had been under
for days and triggered a few questions of her own.

The man concealed on the hillside watched as one of
the gentlemen was carried away from the house, followed dejectedly by his pathetic old mount tied behind.
So, she'd rid herself of the dandy. The fellow had been
a mistake, one that she would thank him for correcting
when she found who awaited her instead.

As he watched, the other one, the larger man with
the irritating swagger, brought his finer horse out onto
the drive and mounted easily. Ah, leaving with his
friend after all.

It seemed as if his work here were nearly done. She
would not wish to stay much longer, he'd wager, alone
on her troublesome estate.

He would give her a day and a night to stew in her
solitude, then he would arrive with proper fanfare, introduce himself, and offer her the world.

As soon as she emptied her accounts into his keeping, of course.

Very neatly done. Pity it was over so soon. He'd enjoyed seeing the pain on her pretty face.

Then again, he had one more bit of bad news to look
forward to. He wished he could see her face when she
discovered that her precious pet had been captured and
killed by angry farmers in the next dell.

In the village taproom, Marcus joined Elliot where he
sat morosely drinking his ale.

Elliot didn't look up. "She jilted me."

Marcus sat opposite him. "I know."

Elliot shrugged. "That isn't the worst of it—she told me to leave Middlebarrow entirely. She said it wasn't a good situation for me at the moment." Elliot dropped his head and laughed bitterly. "*She's* protecting *me!*"

Marcus raised his head to gaze across the table at the dandy, his eyes narrowed. "Now, why would you say that with such irony?"

Elliot blinked, then quickly brought his ale up for a deep draught. "Don't know what you mean," he mumbled.

Marcus leaned back in the splintery settle. "I say, Elliot," he said with false nonchalance. "Might you be acquainted with a bloke by the name of Montmorency?"

Elliot choked on his ale.

Marcus shook his head. "I ought to have known. Only one of you lot would have such boneheaded staying power in the face of mortal danger."

Elliot wiped his chin with the back of his wrist, eyeing Marcus warily. "I haven't a clue what you're speaking of."

Marcus twitched his lips sourly. "Of course you don't." He leaned forward. "When you get back to your club, do be sure to describe me *very* well. Better yet, do one of those sketches you lot take such pride in."

Elliot leaned back in his seat as well. "I have been known to sketch from time to time. Most gentlemen do. I never keep them, however."

"Meaning you've already sent one in." Marcus nodded. "You'll get a new set of instructions any moment, I expect."

Elliot tilted his head and slitted his eyes. "I do believe

I've had enough to drink. Every single thing you're saying sounds like nonsense to my ears."

Marcus waved him away genially. "Go on, then. Tell that bloke I mentioned earlier that I would appreciate hearing from him soon."

Elliot stuck a pinkie in one ear and wiggled it. "Utter gibberish. It's like you're speaking a different language altogether."

Marcus stood and dropped a coin on the table. "That ale is on me. Do take care not to dawdle back to London." He turned away but Elliot called him back.

"I wonder if you might let me borrow your fine horse," he said blandly. "Since you're in such a hurry for me to leave and all. I can leave it with that bloke you mentioned."

Marcus rolled his eyes. "Liars." He tossed several more coins to the table. "Talk to the hosteler. He'll make sure you don't get a nag. I don't let anyone ride my horse. Ever."

"That's too bad," Elliot said with a grin. He idly slid one finger across the tabletop in a quick motion. "Her ladyship expressed an interest in tacking your stallion."

Marcus gave a short laugh. "I don't think so. My mount would be far too much horse for her."

Elliot's grin became more pointed. "Not for me to say. But watching her ladyship on horseback is like watching a bird soar. As if it were what she was born for." He tossed back the last of the ale. "That's a curious thing, don't you think?"

"Most ladies ride."

Elliot stood. "Not as if they'd marry the beast if they could." He swept the coins from the table and deposited them in his weskit pocket. "Thank you for the contribution to the happiness of my buttocks." He tipped his hat. "Good hunting, *my lord.*"

Marcus let the dig pass and only nodded. "Safe journey, Elliot. Mind the well in the yard."

Elliot shuddered delicately. "Spare me the well. I'll never swim again." He bowed again and sauntered away, whistling.

Marcus leaned down to pick up his hat. There was a design drawn in the small puddle that had dripped from the ale mug. He leaned closer. In the liquid, Elliot had drawn a single symbol—a perfect numeral 4.

Marcus swiped it away with the side of his palm. "Not yet, old man," he breathed. "Not quite yet."

13

I lie in bed. The night is fair, so the windows are wide to the sky. I cannot rest, for the aroma of climbing roses sweeps my thoughts and makes my body restless. I rise from the linens and go to the balcony to soak the scent of the night into my skin.

I lean on the stone balustrade and look down onto the garden where I last saw my lover. The garden is empty and dark, yet I can still smell his sandalwood through the roses.

"Can you not find your rest, my lady?"

I close my eyes at the deep voice behind me. He always knows when I need him.

"Exhaust me," I whisper toward the night. "Tire me to collapse."

Large warm hands cover my shoulders and pull me back onto his broad chest. "I would not want to be forceful with you, my lady."

I shake my head urgently. "Be forceful with me. I will not break."

His hands tighten on me in response. I revel in his strength. "As you wish, my lady."

In one motion, he turns me toward him and presses my lower body to the balustrade with his. His hot mouth comes down on my neck and I feel his teeth scrape my skin. It is not pain I feel, but need.

I need to feel him, to be taken, to be owned. He pulls my nightdress from my shoulders, trapping my arms to my sides. I cannot resist now, I do not want to resist and my imprisonment frees me to be his prey. I close my eyes and surrender to his hot mouth and hard hands. He pulls my braid free and wraps it about his fist, controlling me with the reins of my own hair.

"Take me," I demand. "Possess me."

With a single hard tug, my nightdress falls to the garden below, ruined beyond repair. I am bare to the night now, naked before him. He remains fully dressed tonight, my master, my possessor . . . my lover who always recognizes what I need.

Marcus rode back from the village slowly. He'd done it.

Julia could say that she ended her engagement for Elliot's safety, but Marcus knew why she had done it. He'd won.

Having accomplished the goal he'd set out to accomplish from the beginning, now he had to decide upon his next step.

Of course, if he were to complete his mission, he must learn everything about her. He must dig deep into her thoughts and bring out all her secrets. Only then could he, and the Three, be sure of her motives and her capabilities.

In the beginning, he'd assumed some sordid bits were lurking just below the surface of her beauty, sure to trip her up and expose her for the manipulator she must be.

Unfortunately, he had come to see precisely why old Barrowby had chosen her. God, if he ever became the Fox, he would be looking for an apprentice with precisely the combination of qualities that Julia possessed in abundance. Intelligence, deep loyalty, honor—she wouldn't do more than allow a brief stolen kiss while unofficially engaged to another man!—and twist-minded as all the Four must be.

She worked as hard as anyone in her staff and never let a complaint pass her lips. Her humor never failed her, yet she never lost control of the people she directed. She was clever and thoughtful, gathering all her facts before making an informed decision.

And she was the most beautiful, sensuous woman he had ever seen.

Truly, a woman to tempt the gods.

And yes, he was tempted. Tempted to woo her for himself, to have her as his lady, to keep her forever as his own.

And tempted to let her be the Fox, curious to see where she would take the Four and the nation, intrigued to watch her mow Liverpool's objections down with the swift blade of her quick mind.

But what of the danger? What of the cost to her as a woman? Why should she be put through that deprivation and toil when she deserved to be cosseted and protected and sheltered from it all?

He was faced with a choice. Complete the seduction, or walk away. He knew he could worm his way beneath her defenses—he'd read every word of those diaries. He knew the one absolute way to fulfill her every dream.

The problem was, could he do that to her? He didn't have to. He could turn about this moment and ride away.

Yet that would mean leaving her forever.

Julia could not help but watch the hands of the clock, waiting for Marcus to return. After she had seen Elliot off, she had told Marcus what she had done.

He'd nodded thoughtfully and then informed her that he wished to give Elliot a proper farewell.

Julia raised a brow. "You mean, you wish to make sure he actually leaves."

She received a brief, white-hot glance in return. "Indeed," he said huskily. "For I would not be so obedient."

With that nerve-wracking response—dear Lord, she was in deep trouble now!—he'd ridden off to drive his rival most politely from the vicinity.

Men and their territory.

The thing that Julia had learned a long time ago about men—bless 'em, every one—was that they were never the sort to think about why they were thinking about what they were thinking about. A woman might wonder why her mind was preoccupied with a certain thought, but a man was a simpler creature. He merely had the thought and then moved on with things.

That noted, it had become easier for Julia to "think like a man" as Aldus had so often instructed her. Male minds did not indulge in tangents of thought, so neither did hers—or at least not while she was working.

It was only after a long day of sifting through intelligence reports and records of meetings of the House of Lords—a place she would never see the inside of, that was sure, although she held all their lives in her female hands—and newssheets, even the tawdry ones, for one never knew where the next bit of information would come from, that Julia even had time to think of herself as a woman, much less to luxuriate in dreamy ponderings of love and life and lovemaking . . .

She hadn't written in her diaries since . . . since when? Since the night Aldus had his first attack?

Three years. Her secret fancies had lain in the dust for three—

Or had they? Alarm shot through her. *The intruder.* Or worse yet . . . *Marcus.*

He couldn't have, yet he always seemed to *know*, in the garden, in the lake—oh, God! Hadn't she once written a passage about the lake?

She leaped to her feet and ran down the hall so fast that the wind in the wake of her fluttering wrapper made the candles flicker in their sconces. She ignored the leaping shadows and took the stairs two at a time, not bothering to touch the handrail on the way down. Her bare feet skidded on the marble but nothing slowed her.

The morning room was dark and cold, but Julia didn't need the light. She dropped to her knees beside her sewing basket and scrabbled beneath the embroidery goods for the false bottom, her fingertips missing the catch the first time. She took a breath and forced her hands to calm. "You won't know until you open the bloody thing," she told herself.

The catch moved beneath her searching fingers and the bottom lifted. She ran her hands over the small space beneath—

The key was there, cold and solid to her touch.

Julia let out a great, slow sigh and dropped her head. She ought not to have left such damning material so accessible—in her front parlor yet! What if the Royal Four's henchman had found those scorching entries— what would they make of her then?

Oh, the things she'd written about, the wicked, seductive things she'd written of herself doing!

She must burn them all, immediately.

She removed the key and let the false bottom fall shut, carelessly pushing the now tangled mass of skeins and needles back into place. Never mind. She hated embroidery, anyway.

Her short journey to the front parlor was slow enough for her to become aware of the chill on her bare feet. She turned back to gather a lit candle from the last sputtering sconce.

She used the candle to start the kindling in the parlor. There was no point in bothering with coals, for she wouldn't need the fire long. She opened the inlaid box and removed the nursery key, then went quickly up the cold stairs to retrieve the trunk.

Setting it down by the hearth back in the parlor, she pulled out the first of her diaries. In fact, it was not the very first. There had been one other, the one she had begun when Aldus had taken her and her mother in. She'd burned that diary when she'd wed Aldus and left Jilly behind forever.

She closed her eyes, remembering the pages filled with the large looping handwriting and unrepentant misspellings of Jilly Boots. The many hours sitting by her mother's bedside had caused the words to pour from her young heart.

Pain at her mother's deterioration, fear of being alone in the world, first impressions of the luxurious Barrowby, descriptions of the mysterious but magnanimous Aldus. One page in particular needed no paper, for it was inscribed in her heart forever.

"Mum died tonight. Like a whisper, she went. It's good she won't hurt anymore." Then, scrawled in deep impressions that had nearly torn the paper, *"What am I goin' to do now?"*

Julia sat back and opened her eyes. She'd done what Aldus had instructed her to do, of course. She'd married him in the Barrowby chapel the day she'd turned eighteen, her hands cold and shaking, his not much better. They'd shared a silent dinner and then they'd shared a bed.

Jilly had been curious and willing, although nervous. Aldus had been reluctant and in the end, incapable. They'd made a better success of it later, when they'd come to know each other more, but there had never been any satisfying resolution for her. Aldus had been quick and shamefaced about the whole business, never at ease with the difference in their ages.

Eventually, when his best efforts failed to bring about an heir, he'd let the endeavor go entirely with ill-concealed relief.

Leaving Julia—as she then had begun to think of herself—to expend her considerable sexual drive in her "scribblings."

Her hands caressed the embossed leather cover of

the diary she held in her hands. The most lurid fancies began with this, the second diary. Julia turned resolutely to the now crackling fire. "Sorry, but there's no getting around it. They must go."

Her voice was firm enough but her hand didn't seem so sure. She ought to burn them. It was the only way to make sure someone sent by the Royal Four didn't get their hands on them.

Then again, she'd been well taught never to ignore any source of information. Along with her lonely fancies, these diaries contained insights into herself, something she felt sorely in need of now, with no one to advise her.

Very well, then. She would read them all first.

Then she would burn them.

She turned to the first page of the second diary and began to read. In moments, she was completely absorbed. Heavens, she'd forgotten all about *that* intriguing scenario!

Marcus returned late and let himself into the kitchen after setting his stallion up in temporary quarters—a stall made of stacked water casks and hay fresh from drying in the field. A bag of grain and a pat on the rump was all that was needed.

Once inside, Marcus ran a hand through his hair. He'd argued with himself on the entire ride to Barrowby, yet he still hadn't come to a decision. He was unused to such dithering. He was more the sort to make snap decisions and pay the price later, but then, rarely had his options so fought with that place inside him he was beginning to think of as his heart.

At the moment, it was his stomach that was speaking. Meg usually left some provisions available in the larder. Marcus grabbed a hunk of dry bread from the bread bin and poured a mug of milk from the pitcher in the larder. A cheese caught his eye and he grabbed that, too. His hands full, he backed from the larder with the makings for a plain meal.

The unmistakable click of a pistol being readied cut crisply through the silence.

Marcus froze.

"Drop what you've stolen," commanded an imperious voice.

Marcus let out a slow breath. "If I do that, Meg'll have my hide when he sees the mess tomorrow." He twisted his head over his shoulder to grin at Julia. "Can't a bloke have a meal after a hard day of saving lives?"

Julia tipped her pistol up but didn't relieve the hammer. Her gaze was shockingly cool. He'd thought—

"This is not the first time you've wandered my house in the dark, is it, Mr. Blythe-Goodman?"

Oh, hell. Bloody, bloody *hell*. She'd deduced he'd read her journals. God, he'd shoot him, too! He opened his mouth to save his arse, but his mind failed him. "Er . . . I . . ."

Her lips twisted to one side. "Meg told me someone has been raiding his kitchen for days. Now I know who."

"Ah . . ." Oh, criminy, was that all? Relief swept him, turning his alarm into a rush of something else altogether as he realized what she was wearing.

Not a great deal. Her shoulders were nearly bared by the tiny cap sleeves of her nightdress. She looked like a goddess, standing there in that flimsy gown that draped enticingly from every curve.

His mouth went entirely dry. He didn't know what it was made of but he blessed the weaver for allowing the dim light from the hall to frame her body in misty silhouette.

From within the haze of his sudden lust, he felt the round of Camembert slip from where he'd stuck it under his elbow. It rolled across the floor and spiraled to a stop at her bare feet. Marcus swallowed and grimaced weakly. "May I . . . offer you some cheese?"

She gazed at him somberly. "Is there any gooseberry jam left?"

To his relief, she pushed back the hammer of the pistol and set it upon the heavy worktable. Although the image of her capably holding a pistol while gowned in a translucent nightdress was going to haunt his dreams for a bit, he could tell.

Definitely his sort of girl.

They sat facing each other, tailor-fashion, on the table—"Don't tell Meg"—and devoured a picnic of bread, cheese, and jam, washed down with a shared mug of milk.

Julia ate with good country appetite, something else Marcus admired in a woman. He couldn't abide seeing ladies picking at their food as if nothing were good enough for their refined tastes.

"I left Elliot in good health," he told her. "He'll be on his way by now."

She sent him a knowing glance and swallowed. "Are you sure you didn't speed him along?"

Marcus smiled slowly, letting her see his attraction.

"I might have . . . a bit. I cannot deny that I was glad to see him safely gone."

Her gaze locked with his, her tongue licking a crumb from her lip. "Marcus . . ." Her voice was suddenly husky.

It sent a welcome tingle up his spine. "I like the way you say my name," he said softly. "The way you speak slowly, as if you want to be sure every word is perfect."

She blinked, breaking the spell. She pulled back and cleared her throat. "What a thing to say."

Marcus allowed her room to breathe. He'd had enough of manipulation and seduction. His attraction was real enough, but he wasn't going to use it to win.

From this point on, he would use no weapon against her heart but his own.

He smiled at her, suddenly sure of himself and of her. Whatever might happen, this amazing, valiant, brilliant woman was more than able to hold her own against any man, including him.

"Hold still," he told her. He reached out with his thumb to caress a smear of jam from the corner of her mouth. He let his thumb linger, then slowly slid it across her lower lip, enjoying the texture of her full mouth.

Her eyes were very wide and she looked as if she might bolt, so Marcus pulled his hand back. He couldn't resist licking the jam from his thumb, however—an action that made her swallow hard.

Julia couldn't bring breath into her lungs. His touch—his smile—oh, heavens, those eyes . . .

Her heart was racing and her body ached with

longing. She let her tongue slip out to clean the sticky place on her lip and watched him watch her.

Then she whispered, "Good night, Marcus," and slipped off the table to flee to the safety of her room.

14

The day that I look into his eyes, I will know him for mine.

Once in her bedchamber, Julia pressed her hands to her heated cheeks. That abrupt departure—very well, *escape*—from the kitchen hadn't been prudence, or caution, or anything but naked, panting terror.

Oh, she truly shouldn't have read every single page of those diaries! She was stimulated almost past bearing, as if her body hummed like a hive of bees!

Yet, for all her fancies and longings, for all her dreams and wicked, sensuous thoughts, Julia had abruptly realized that she was scarcely more practiced than a virgin. Here was this man, this virile, worldly male, who would have expectations of her. She was a full-grown woman, a widow.

What if she fumbled it? What if he laughed? What if she couldn't please him? What if he expected her to get *completely* naked? Oh, she wished now she'd resisted her daily enthusiasm for Meg's iced lemon seed cakes.

What if she couldn't catch her breath and died of unquenched lust right here and now?

She ran to the balcony doors, hitting the latch with one hand and springing them wide. The cold night air swept into the room, cooling her cheeks but not the heat in her body. She stepped out into the night and leaned both hands on the balustrade, gulping the icy air into her lungs.

She was a fool. Marcus wanted her. He'd made it entirely clear. She wanted him—oh, sweet heaven, she *wanted* him!—and there truly shouldn't be such a fuss over the matter. She could take a lover if she wished . . . and she wished with all her heart.

What if the Three find out?

Bugger the Three, that's what. The Lion and the Co-bra had their brides, the Falcon must have *something*—a sword collection, or Restoration codpieces, or some such cold-blooded passion—and even Liverpool had his sweet, shy lady whom he was deeply devoted to.

Well, then, she would have Marcus . . . if she dared.

The cold was finally dimming the glow of her lust and allowing her to think. She wrapped her arms about herself and tipped her head back to stare at the endless night sky. She was sorry she'd left Marcus in the kitchen—he must think her an idiot! Still, when he returned to his room, if she could keep from making a fool of herself again, then perhaps, just perhaps—

She smelled sandalwood.

"Can you not sleep, Julia?" His voice was deep and soft in her ear. He was so close she could feel the warmth of his body behind her.

Without thought, she turned and wrapped her arms about his neck, pulling his mouth down to hers.

If Marcus had thought stealing a kiss from Julia in the garden had been exciting, then being wantonly, abandonedly kissed by her was a revelation! Her supple, delicious figure was pressed fully to his body, her hands were buried in his hair, and her lips and tongue were passionately trying to dismantle his.

Unfortunately, he had something to tell her before he could allow himself to partake. It was time to tell her who he was and why he was here . . . that is, if he had the courage.

He took her by the shoulders and detached her, inch by inch, though it cost him dearly. "Julia, I—"

"Marcus Blythe-Goodman, make love to me at once," she panted. "Or I swear I'll fetch that pistol again!"

He laughed, a lust-hardened bark. "Much as I love your sweet talk, darling, I cannot—"

She reached for him again and he weakened. She was so hungry and he'd wanted her for so long—only days, but it felt like a lifetime. Then he shook off the spell and pressed her back again.

"Julia, I need to—"

She shoved away from him and turned around. With her hands pressed over her face, he couldn't hear what she said, but it sounded something like, "Idiotidiotidiot . . ."

He moved behind her and wrapped his arms about her waist, tugging her into the warmth of his body. "Darling, you're freezing. Come inside and we'll . . . talk."

He felt her shake her head violently.

"Julia, stop being an ass. Come inside."

Her head came up sharply and she twisted to stare into his face, fury shining through her damp embarrassment. "Did you just call me an *ass*? How dare you!"

Relieved to see a spark of the Julia he knew, he grinned down at her. "If you don't like the name, then don't act the part."

Her mouth opened and shut, then she pushed past him and stalked back into her bedchamber. He ran a hand through his hair, trying to think quickly. He didn't know what the hell he was doing, he didn't know what the hell he meant to tell her.

All he knew was that if he made love to her now, it would be wrong. He'd spent the last week being the man of her dreams, using her diaries against her. She was too good and too fine to be made a fool of like that.

Of course, if he told her that he'd broken into her manor and read her diaries, that he'd come to discredit her and win the seat of the Fox, she'd likely fetch that pistol back in truth! Not to mention that she'd never look at him the way she had over the bread and cheese—as if she wished she could spread *him* on a slice of bread.

And as if he were her hero.

God, what a thing to live up to! He wasn't feeling any too heroic at the moment. He was feeling like a fool and a sneak. The worst of it was, in order to keep her, he might have to tell her the very thing that would lose her!

He couldn't do it . . . yet, perhaps there were some things he *could* tell her. Things that might make it easier for her to understand and forgive . . . someday.

Coward.

Oh, yes. That I know.

When he reentered the bedchamber and closed the balcony doors behind him, she was clad in her wrapper and seated in the big chair before the fire. He joined her to lean one elbow on the mantel. They both stared into the fire for a long moment. Finally she stirred. "Was there something you wished to say to me?"

You're lovely. You're astounding. I lo—

He blinked and shook off that thought. Then he took a deep breath.

"You're not preparing to leap off a cliff, are you, Marcus?"

He turned to see her gazing at him with wary curiosity. He blew out that breath and smiled slightly. "Perhaps I am." He went to one knee before her and took his hand in hers. Her eyes widened and she drew back in surprise.

"You're not planning on proposing, I hope. I do think it's a bit much to announce *another* early engagement."

He realized he was indeed in the classic pose of the entreating suitor. He laughed and stood, then pulled her to her feet. He took her place in the chair and swept her into his lap. "There. That's better."

She went rigid and leaned away from him. "Marcus, you needn't—"

"Julia, you're an amazing woman and I admire you enormously. But for once, let me be in charge, I beg of you."

"This is my house." She scowled at him. "I think I—"

He kissed her protest silent. At first, she pushed at him irritably. Then after a long moment, she went warm and soft in his arms.

And then she uttered that throaty sound, the one she'd made in the garden, the one that sent his mind vague and buzzing with lack of blood flow as his groin swelled . . .

He pulled away. She clung to him, gasping, still supple and compliant in his grasp. He settled back in the chair and cradled her. It felt very natural to do so.

"Before you and I embark on this . . . affair, I want to tell you something."

She let out a long unenthusiastic breath that tingled his neck and then settled her head on his shoulder to listen. "Go on."

He stroked her hair with one hand. "I am a second son, as you know. I am also a bastard-in-wedlock. My father is not my father and my brother is only my half-brother . . . and all my life, the two of them never let me forget it."

He waited for the bitterness to rise, but the scent of her hair distracted him. "Ah . . . yes." He went on. "The family secret was never common knowledge, never even openly discussed, but there are a thousand ways to make someone feel like an outsider. Being blamed for someone else's mischief, for instance. Learning through the years that no matter how hard you try, no matter how you scrap and study and fence and ride and run faster than any other boy, you will never be anything but second best."

He felt her take one of his hands in hers. She nestled it between her breasts and held it like the child he'd been. Oddly, it seemed to help for he didn't feel the sharp ache that always came with those memories . . .

"The worst of it was that I didn't understand why. If

I'd known about my parentage I think I might have given up years earlier. It wasn't until I found my mother with her lover—a tall man with green eyes and my chin—"

Julia pressed herself to him as if she could protect him from that moment when he'd walked into the greenhouse to see his mother in the arms of a stranger.

"They were only kissing, but then he turned and looked at me as if he knew me, as if he knew all about me and was proud of me! He looked at me the way I'd always longed to be seen by the man I thought of as my father."

He shook his head. "I realized at that moment that it would never happen. I would never be my father's son . . . ever. I cared nothing for the stranger's regard. It was my mother's husband I revered. All those years of struggling to merit his approval had always been in vain, had I but known it."

"So you blame him," Julia said quietly.

"No." Marcus laughed shortly. "I blame *her.*" He paused a moment. "Or at least, I did."

He let out a breath. "That was the day I went into the army—thinking I was walking away," he added slowly, realizing it for the first time. "Yet still trying forever to prove myself."

Julia pulled her head back to gaze at him. "Marcus, why are you telling me all this?"

He tucked her head back down with one hand, leaving it there to stroke her hair. "I wanted you to know, so that you would understand when . . ." He couldn't say it, but he felt to make some sort of apology for how he'd used her own secrets against her.

"When I first met you, and even before I met you, I

made assumptions. The beautiful young widow of the elderly lord—well, it's a bit of cliché, isn't it?"

She gave a sigh of resignation. "Only for those inclined to think in clichés."

Then she shook her head, wrinkling her nose. "I am all right, but I am no beauty. My mother was beautiful. I'm well enough, I suppose, but my nose is too long and my hair is utterly maddening." She spread her fingers. "And just look at my hands!" She sighed. "I cannot seem to keep the calluses away. I believe you may need spectacles, Mr. Blythe-Goodman."

The alias rang harshly against Marcus's conscience. He cleared his throat. "At any rate, I've been told I had a blind spot when it came to women. I'm considered to be a bit . . . judgmental." He shrugged, causing her to resettle herself. "I simply wanted you to know that I no longer care. I am not without fault. I no longer expect the woman I . . . I no longer expect saintliness."

"Well, that's very big of you," she said, gazing at him doubtfully. "Precisely which of my debaucheries have you decided to ignore?"

He laughed. "Julia, my point is that I simply don't care either way. Madonna or whore, it matters not. I want *you*, wholly and completely. All of you."

15

All of you.

This time it was no fantasy, but truth. *All of you.*

All of her? The bossiness and the bad singing and the way her littlest toes stuck out from all those years running barefoot?

Her past? For that matter, her present?

Her heart stuttered a beat. Her future?

She kissed him, this time pinning his hands down so he could not press her back again. He struggled a bit at first, but she persisted, taming his mouth until he didn't want to talk for one more blessed instant.

Keeping her hands over his, keeping his lips busy with hers, she shifted in his lap until she sat astride him and could devote her attention more fully.

When she let him come up for air at last and sat back, he remained limp with his head fallen back on the chair. "If I'm dreaming, don't wake me," he whispered. He swallowed hard, which reminded her that she wanted to remove his cravat.

"Stay," she ordered, as she began to undo the complicated knot.

His deep breathless chuckle bounced her intimately against him. "Yes, my lady. As you wish, my lady. I live to serve."

"Then shut it and let me concentrate," she said as she frowned at the knotted neckcloth. It had always just melted away in her fancies. "Bother this thing," she muttered.

Marcus opened his eyes to see her glaring at his cravat with the concentration of a surgeon, one end of the cloth in her teeth and her fingers busy out of sight beneath his chin. "I can—"

"Sit," she ordered tersely around the cravat in her mouth. "I'm going to get this . . ."

Suddenly the cravat loosened and she drew it free triumphantly to wave it like a banner over her head. "Done!"

Marcus reached up and took it from her easily. "My lady, we have only begun."

He took her wrists in his big hands and began to wrap the cravat around them. She drew in a breath and gave him a startled look. "Marcus, I—"

" 'Shut it,' and I quote." He grinned at her as he tied the knot. "For the next twelve minutes, until that clock chimes the hour, you are at my mercy."

Her tongue flicked out to wet her lips. He couldn't tell if she was aroused or nervous. "Yes, my lord," she whispered compliantly.

Ah. Aroused, then. Then, just as he began to enjoy his supremacy, she added a codicil.

"Then it's my turn."

He laughed, shaking his head. "Then I suppose I ought to use my time well." He put her admittedly loosely bound hands behind her head. "Stay," he ordered. She drew a deep trembling breath that swelled her bosom enticingly, which reminded him that she still wore her wrapper. He took one end of the tie and yanked the knot free in one motion. "Hmm. I suppose I ought to have removed this before binding you . . . oh, well." He took the silk in his hands and ripped forcefully.

She gasped as he tore the wrapper from her, exposing her translucent nightdress once more. "That's better."

"I liked that wrapper!" she protested. "Just you wait, Marcus Blythe—"

He put his fingers over his lips. Not that name, not right now. "I'll weave you a new one with my own little hands if you'll just shut it." He leered at her. "Don't make me gag you."

Her eyes widened and her tongue flicked out again. "With what?" Her hungry whisper caused a cascade of wicked, unseemly thoughts to enter his head. Hers as well, apparently, for her hips massaged a slow circle in his lap.

"Never mind that now. I want to see you again." His fingers shook slightly as he began to undo the tiny buttons of her nightdress. He didn't want to tear this. He wanted her to wear it always.

"Again? When did you—" She gasped. "The lake! You peeked!"

"Hell, yes."

She frowned thoughtfully. "Then I could have peeked as well?"

"Never pass up an opportunity," he said absently as the last delicate button came free. "There."

He spread her gown wide and sat back to admire. She sat astride him, her gown rucked up to the top of her long splendid thighs, her exposed full breasts jutting high and taunting, her rosy nipples crinkling even as he watched. "I think I might just be the happiest man on earth right now," he mused. Except for the massive erection strangling in the confines of his trousers. And the way his heart beat irregularly when her aroused, broken breathing caused her breasts to sway . . . and the way her bottom lip was so chewed that it plumped and reddened until he couldn't live one more moment without kissing her.

He wrapped one hand over the back of her neck and drew her mouth to his. She bent forward enthusiastically.

"Shh," he whispered. "Let me kiss you."

So she went still in his grasp and he was free to take his time. Her mouth was bruised and hot and tasted of Camembert and lust. He drove his tongue slowly within, tasting her more fully. He had all night to taste her, and he would take every moment—

She whimpered into his mouth and his control cracked. Then the clock chimed the hour. "Take me this minute," she moaned into his kiss. *"Now."*

Her husky command, uttered in that dulcet voice that made even the simplest of topics sound sexual, was more than he could resist.

With one hand he found her damp center and tested her readiness. She uttered a sharp cry of joy as he slid a long finger deep.

She was ready for him. He continued to touch her deeply within, distracted by the range of lovely animal sounds she made as he slid his finger in, then withdrew. He found her pleasure center and manipulated it tenderly with the tip of his thumb as he thrust deep with two fingers.

She exploded in his hands. He had to hold her with his other arm wrapped about her waist to keep her from slipping from his lap. She shivered with bone-deep paroxysms that only served to enlarge his own lust as her quivering body rubbed his.

Through the fog of his aching need, Marcus was a bit stunned. As she fell forward onto him, only the occasional shiver racking her now, he stroked her back soothingly.

"Julia . . . has it been that long?"

She gasped helplessly into his neck. "Since I have lain with my husband . . . years." She drew a deep breath. "But that . . . that, never!"

Marcus felt at once proud and dismayed. He took natural pride in satisfying his woman, but . . .

Giving her her first true pleasure meant that all those things he'd read . . . could it be that they were nothing but fiction? Merely the detailed fancies of a lonely wife? A sensuous woman left unfulfilled by cruel fate?

If so, then through his manipulation of her, he'd done Julia a more severe injustice than he'd realized.

And more, he feared, than she would ever be able to forgive.

He closed his mind against the inevitable price he would pay for his crime. It would be far worse to leave her now. He had this one night to show her all of herself,

to fulfill all the promises he'd made, both spoken and
unspoken.

Tomorrow would be soon enough for confession and
accounting.

Quickly, he rose with her in his arms and strode to the
bed. Then he laid her down and sat next to her to unwind
the cravat from her hands, although truly he'd done it so
loosely she could have pulled her hands free herself. Yet,
the satisfied look in her wide eyes told him that she'd
needed him to take control, at least for a little while.

Then he lay down beside her on the bed. Going up
on one elbow, he gazed down into her eyes. "My lady, I
believe it is your turn."

She grinned at him with that gamine's smile and sat
up to push him flat again. "I," she told him briskly,
"have been positively perishing to see you naked."

She efficiently divested him of every stitch of clothing he wore, until he lay there more naked than she. Julia found that she liked that position of power. She also
liked the way his bare flesh felt to her touch, silky yet
different than her own skin. He quivered as she touched
his body with long exploring strokes, running her
hands from his ankles to his cheek, with a few side
journeys along the way.

"You're killing me," he said tightly.

She kissed him quiet. "Shh, it's my turn." Then she
pressed the cravat into his hands. "Wrap it around your
wrists," she advised him. "It helps." .

He compromised by gripping it tightly in two fists
and raising his hands to rest on the pillow above his
head. This had the interesting effect of exposing
his manly underarms. She explored immediately.

On the underside of the impressive muscles of his upper arms lay the softest skin he had. She impulsively bent to kiss that male vulnerability. She felt him tremble beneath her lips.

Interesting. She moved her mouth to the tender area under his ear. More response, with the addition of a sharp intake of breath. Plus, he smelled wonderful just there.

She continued her exploration using her lips alone. The hollow of his throat, the center of his breastbone, the copper rings of his flat male nipples—

"Oh, *damn!*"

The rippled surface of his belly, which tightened further as she kissed her way down each furrow of muscle until she reached his shallow navel. She dipped her tongue into it.

He jerked and gasped and his erection rose higher, as if begging for her attention.

She'd avoided it until now—after all, it was of a size that took a bit of getting used to!—but now she felt ready to explore further. She took him in both hands, wrapping her fingers firmly about him.

He twitched violently. "I'm going to die," he informed her breathlessly.

Without thinking much about it, Julia bent to plant a soft, wet kiss on the tip of his erection. This time there were no words from her glib lover. This time, he merely ripped his cravat in half.

And the clock chimed the hour once again.

Marcus sat up, his eyes glittering and his jaw hard. "My turn."

Julia yelped in mock alarm—well, mostly—and dove

for the other side of the bed. He was too fast for her. He wrapped one arm about her waist and deposited her flat in the center of the bed. He pressed his naked body over hers to quiet her nervous struggles and kissed her hard.

With one swift motion, he sat up and pulled her gown over her head, tossing it aside. Then he flung his long hard body between her thighs and gazed down at her with half-lidded eyes.

He watched her carefully as he pressed the head of his erection into her wet slit. She made no further protest, but only let her head fall back as she slid her hands up his arms to cling to his neck.

He was so thick that her flesh stung as he stretched her, but she was so hungry for him—so alone for so long!—that she only spread her thighs wider and strained toward him.

He pressed onward, not stopping until he filled her completely. Julia wrapped her arms about him, pulling him down upon her. She raised her legs to wrap her thighs about him and held him close. Pressing her face into his neck, she took deep breaths as she waited for her body to adjust.

It did not hurt so much as ache, yet she felt as though her virginity had been returned to her at some point in the last few years, given back so that she could gift it to this man.

Which was nonsense, however charming the thought. He wouldn't be in the circle of her body now if she were a virgin.

"You're very narrow," he whispered. "Are you all right?"

She held him harder, not wishing him to see the tears that ran down the sides of her face. She was not generally a weeper. The tears surprised and dismayed her, and she was afraid what he would think if he saw them.

The problem was—and it was a problem in truth—that the moment he'd come to rest inside her, she'd known.

She was in love with Marcus Blythe-Goodman. Not simple, uncomplicated lust, not "isn't he handsome I want him as my lover" desire, not simple admiration for his finer qualities, but *love*.

It ached. It burned. It made her want to throw everything she'd ever wanted away with one careless wave, just to sink into his skin and disappear forever.

It slid away logic and good sense as wave after wave of impossible fantasies ensued of life with Marcus. Fat, green-eyed babies playing on the lawns of Barrowby. Sharing a single wide bed until they grew old and gray together. Living a long and happy life as ordinary Mrs. Blythe-Goodman—

The Fox was far away. She felt it slipping from her grip, for her hands were full of Marcus.

The most alarming thing about all this was that she was not alarmed at all. That frightened her deeply, but not enough to let go of the man she clung to so tightly.

Then he began to move inside her and she forgot to think at all.

With every stroke, the pleasure increased, rippling from her center to run glittering through her veins. "Oh!" She had never—in all her wildest imaginings— it was—

Beyond speech, beyond thought, she could only hold on as each deep thrust sent her higher and deeper within herself. She was dimly aware of her own sharp cries, but cared nothing for the danger of discovery. She was nothing but a ball of quivering response, held in the hands of a man who knew precisely how to touch her.

Her passion stunned him. She gave herself over to him so trustingly. If Marcus had been a better man, he would have walked away. If he had been a saint, perhaps, for what man could leave such a woman? She was all giving response and wordless passion. He'd never experienced making love to someone so free and unquestioning. Her cries of innocent discovery shattered his heart even as they drove his own passion higher. She was his tonight, no matter what. Tonight, she held nothing back from the traitor in her bed.

He wrapped his hands over her shoulders and drove deeper still, just to make her eyes roll back and her cries come anew. Her trust made him want to cherish her, to keep her safe—yet it also made him want to press her farther, demand more, extort more wicked acts for both their satisfaction.

"I want you to take me in your mouth," he told her huskily as he drove her to madness.

"Y-yes," she gasped.

"I want to take you like a stallion takes a mare."

"Yes! Oh, please—yes!"

"I want to take you in the lake."

She fell apart beneath him, shaking and clinging and crying out wildly. Her tremors grabbed his own passion by the neck and threw him over the cliff. He cried out sharply as he lost himself in her in the most profoundly intense orgasm of his life.

Somewhere, in the back of his mind, alarm bells rang.

Then thought slid away as he spent himself into her quivering, throbbing body and threw himself to her side.

She turned wearily into him, throwing her thigh over his hip to keep his fading erection within her. Marcus tugged her closer, wrapped her safely in his arms, and slept.

16

How can I bear to find him, only to let him go?

When Julia awoke, it was to find herself still in Marcus's strong embrace, her head on his chest. She'd never actually slept with a man in her life. It was surprisingly comfortable, as if she and he had been made to fit together.

"Pieces of a puzzle," she whispered to herself.

She felt him move, then felt him kiss the top of her head. She lifted her face to gaze at him with a smile. "Good morning!"

He grinned sleepily. "Good middle-of-the-night, more like."

She smiled and snuggled deeper into him. "Mmm. Wonderful."

"Oh, are you Lady Lie-abed, then?" he teased. "And here I'd thought you the industrious type."

She poked him. "I'll have you know I've had an exceptionally wearing week."

He let out a breath. "True enough."

"I've scrubbed privy stuff. I've hauled water. I've fought fire and rescued someone from a well."

"To be precise, that was me."

"Yes, well, I helped."

"Indeed. That gaping bodice was an inspiration to us all."

She smacked him in the ribs with a gentle fist. "I lost a fiancé."

"Yes, you did," he said with great satisfaction.

"And I took a lover."

He rolled her over swiftly, until he had one muscled thigh pressed between hers and his lips were inches from her mouth. "I think," he said slowly, "that the lover took you."

She chuckled. "Oh, very well. The lover took me. Still rather tiring, no matter how you phrase it."

He kissed the tip of her nose. "But you are well? I did not hurt you?"

"I am entirely well," she said, and stretched languorously beneath him. The motion made his green eyes go forest dark, just as she'd hoped.

"You are entirely beautiful," he replied. "And you are entirely *mine*."

Julia felt something give way, deep inside her heart. Could it be that she had found the one man whom she could be—almost—entirely truthful with?

Or—and she scarcely dared think it—had she found someone she could share *everything* with?

The Four were forbidden from sharing their roles with their families . . . but the Fox would need a protégé. A rising thrill ran through her.

Marcus was just the sort the Four needed. Honorable

and brave and intelligent and . . . well, she would worry about the required investigation later. He wasn't strictly highborn, but he was high enough.

It was so simple and yet perfectly brilliant. For her first act as the Fox, she would marry Marcus *and* tap him for her apprentice!

Unfortunately, she couldn't tell him yet. She dared not break any more of the conventions of the Four than necessary. After all, they were going to have enough to do to warm up to her presence among them.

Yet she wanted to return his confidence with something of her own . . . something that would show him that she understood his need to prove himself.

"Marcus, do you remember when I told you about the Hiram Pickles Variety Show?"

"If you start to carry on about your maid dancing in the altogether, you'll find that nothing can douse my flame tonight." He wiggled his eyebrows in comic lust.

She put a hand to his cheek and gazed into his eyes. "Marcus, listen. This is important. I am trusting you with something that could do me a great deal of damage."

He sobered instantly. "Julia, perhaps you shouldn't—"

She smiled. "I'm not worried."

Something was hurting Marcus, deep down inside.

Julia went on, oblivious to the chill that had entered his gut.

"I did not grow up with all this." She waved a hand about the luxurious room. "I grew up in a wagon, eating my dinner about a campfire, with only my mother and the fair folk as my family."

Yes, there was definitely something wrong inside of him.

She smiled absently, lost in recollection. "So now you know. Once upon a time, Lady Barrowby was Jilly Boots, a trick rider for the Hiram Pickles Variety Show."

Ah. The confession explained everything. Her way with horses, her unusual staff, her bizarre pet. Even her careful speech.

It also destroyed her.

He had her now. He could take that simple admission straight to the Three and be confirmed as the Fox by noon tomorrow. It would be so simple.

He heard himself as if from a distance. "Tell me more."

Yes. Tell me how it is that the most beautiful and accomplished lady I have ever known could be a common-as-dirt fair performer. Tell me so I can tell them how it is that you are unfit for the office you hold.

She told him, leaving out nothing about her life with the ragged band of travelers who were her family. They worked the roads in summer, with their show of animals and acrobats.

"Then, when I was seventeen Mama got sick with a rattling that wouldn't leave her chest. I left the band to get the gold to take her to Bath. I took the plate from a grand country house that had almost no servants and no family about. Easy mark, until I got inside. There wasn't a thing in the safe box, and there wasn't a thing in the secret drawers. I was desperate, searching every room that didn't have a sleeper in it. Finally, I found a— well, I ought not to say. I found a treasure trove, holding jewels and banknotes and papers, too. I took it all, not willing to stay a moment longer to sort through it. I left just in time, for the servants were moving about."

She smiled in recollection. "I thought I'd made it clean away. It wasn't until I tried to pass on the rubies that I was caught. Aldus simply walked into our squat as if he owned it and sat down at the table. Mama was sick on the cot and I was in my nightdress, yet he simply bowed and introduced himself.

" 'You've taken something of mine and I'll be needing it back now.' he told me.

"I didn't argue. I fetched everything that I hadn't sold and poured it into his hands. He shoved the jewels aside and checked the files first. Then he nodded and sat back in his chair. 'I ought to call the law on you, my little miss, but I'll consider letting the matter go, provided you turn your cohorts over to me now.' "

" 'Naught helped me, sor,' I told him. I couldn't let anyone else take the blame for what I'd done. Of course, he didn't believe me."

" 'Tell me quick, girl, or tell the magistrate!' "

"I swore I'd done it alone and he finally seemed to believe me. He leaned forward. I remember the eagerness in his eyes. 'Then tell me how you did it, for I must guard against it happening again—and I shall take my goods and leave you be.' "

"That made sense to me, so I took the deal. I told him every bit of how I gained entry, how I searched the rooms and then found the—well, that doesn't matter. I could tell I was impressing him."

"Then I made a mistake. I let slip something I could have only known if I had read those papers he wanted back so desperately."

" 'You can read?' he asked me."

"I should have realized why that mattered so, but I was proud of my ability and I admitted it comfortably.

"Then the look in his eyes made me stop and I remember how the fear froze me inside. I knew who he was, because I'd read every word of those files. The knowledge frightened me, but I loved knowing—no, I craved knowing. I felt the power of that information."

Marcus nodded, his gaze distant. "Knowledge is a heady brew."

"Aldus must have seen it in my eyes, for he shook his head. 'Pretty cat, but too curious for your own good, aren't you?' He stood then and said, 'You must come with me.'

"He took Mama as well. I thought he was taking me to the magistrate and I fought him, but he wasn't weak then. He held me by the arm, never hurting me but never easing his grip.

"His man carried Mama, sick and damp and smelling of vomit, right into the grandest carriage I've ever seen. He gave Mama a beautiful room and called the physician, but there was nothing to be done. She held on for a few weeks, for she was desperately worried about me, but I think Aldus finally convinced her that I was in safe hands, for she died peacefully then.

"Aldus allowed her to be buried here, in his family's resting place. Then he wed me within a fortnight." She snuggled back into his arms and yawned. "And that is how I became Lady Barrowby."

It was every bit as bad as anything he could have imagined. The first rule of the Royal Four was high birth. There must be no climbing, no ambitions, no

such leverage on such powerful leaders. There was
nothing he could do but report the truth to them and
cost her the Fox's seat.

*And this has nothing to do with the fact that you will
be the Fox?*

Marcus realized what it was now. The thing that was
hurting his soul? It was the pain inflicted from being
sold.

Julia woke at the first scarce glow of morning. He was
already gone.

There was a note lying on her escritoire. "I have
business in London. My deepest regards, M."

She pulled on her wrapper and padded barefoot
across the chill room to look from the window. In the
faint gray dawn light there were only skeletal trees
standing among misty hills.

Well, that was . . . unexpected. She sat on her bed,
blinking at the note in her hand. Should she be angry?
Injured? Grateful that he had saved her from herself?

Or ought she simply to go about her day and look
forward to his soon return?

She smiled slightly. Of course he was coming back.
She could not be wrong about his level of attachment
to her, not after last night. And wouldn't Marcus tease
her when he returned in a day or two to find she had
imagined her own bit of melodrama with him in the
starring role?

She laughed and shook away her uncertainty. What
a ninny she was. This was *Marcus*.

So she matter-of-factly tucked the note away in
her desk and dressed herself. She would set herself to

putting Barrowby back in perfect order. The new privies had been dug and the sturdy sheds could withstand even the Igbys. The well had freshened and the extra fair folk would arrive today to help keep watch for further sabotage. The horses were fine in the north pasture until the weather turned, and Sebastian . . .

She bit her lip. Sebastian had not returned, nor had any local farmers complained of chickens gummed to death. It was possible the lion was lurking in the Barrowby woods, nursing a petulant grudge against all things people—Sebastian could be a mighty infant sometimes—but he must be so hungry by now . . .

There was nothing to be done for it except wait for him to return. At least her darling had not burned to death, thanks to Marcus.

She smiled and set about her day with good heart. When Marcus returned she would ask him to hunt for Sebastian. She could just picture his expression!

17

*Honor and loyalty are magnificent concepts, but what
good do they do if one is alone?*

Julia was called from her duties by the arrival of surprise guests.

"Their lordships are back," Beppo told her.

Julia started, then smiled. She'd been thinking of little but Marcus for the past day and a half and had
nearly forgotten about the verdict of the Three.

She was not worried. She had passed their tests with
honors, and as soon as she was confirmed, she intended
to give them all an earful about putting innocent servants in danger. She removed her apron and smoothed
her hair—pity she hadn't more time, for the scrubbing
of the paneling made it frizz so—and donned her Lady
Barrowby serenity.

She entered the parlor with a smile. "My lords, how
lovely to see you all again so soon."

They turned to her as one and her belly went to ice.
Their expressions were not congenial at all. The Cobra,

the Lion, and the Fox stared at her coldly. Lord Liverpool's expression was more haughty satisfaction.

The Falcon stepped forward. "Lady Barrowby, we will not waste time. It has come to our attention that you are not, in fact, of noble birth. We have recently discovered that your real name is Jilly Boots and that you are, in fact, a member of a traveling troupe of actors."

She swallowed. "Fair performers, actually." Oh, dear. This was not good, not at all.

How could they have found out? All these years, and no one had found out—

Marcus, of course.

No. It simply wasn't true. Marcus would never do that to her, she would wager her life on it. It had been someone in Middlebarrow, some gossip spreading tales of tightrope-walking butlers and bouncing footmen. That knowledge reinforced her, calming her panic.

She raised her chin. "I very much doubt that you can produce an unimpeachable source for such an outlandish claim."

"And yet, we can." The Falcon raised one hand. "May we introduce you to our new Fox?"

That hit Julia like a blow to the gut. She'd been replaced? She turned to the door. Who—

A dark man clad in somber, expensive clothing entered the room and turned familiar emerald eyes her way. He bowed. "Lady Barrowby."

Marcus. Julia felt her heart break, right in her chest, just the way people had always described. Yet somehow the stories had not adequately portrayed the pain that sliced so deeply she could not breathe. She staggered very slightly, reaching for the back of a chair to steady herself. Even in her breathless agony, she could not bear to let them see it.

Marcus knew it the moment he saw her again. It hit him deep in his chest, in his gut, like a spike through his heart.

Regret.

For she'd trusted him completely. He'd seen her perfect belief in her face when he'd walked in the room. Until that moment, she'd had no doubt that he had held her confidence, that he was coming back to be with her, that he was the one person in the world who she could give her full and complete trust.

He'd taken that trust and dashed the perfect, fragile thing on the cobbles—and why?

Naked ambition, of course. He had very nearly convinced himself that he was doing the honorable thing— saving the Four from a mistake, saving Julia from danger and strenuous demands, saving England from the possible manipulation of one of its leaders . . .

His capacity to lie to himself was astonishing. He'd wanted nothing but the Fox's seat all along. That aim had driven every action, every word, every single moment of the last week.

His own ruthlessness sickened him.

You did what needed to be done. That's who the Fox is.

I broke her heart.

She'll recover.

Possibly. Will I?

He didn't think so, for her wide shocked eyes would surely haunt him to his grave. She stood there, absolutely frozen, betraying nothing but surprise to those around her.

He could see it, however. He could see the crumbling of her spirit, like the wall of a beautiful, besieged castle giving way at last. All the trials that had been thrown at her, all the losses, all the attacks, had not been enough to strip away her strength. The anguish in her eyes squeezed the air from Marcus's lungs. He'd done this to her, fully aware of the price he would pay.

Yet he hurt so much more than he'd thought possible. Every endless second that she gazed at him, the surprise in her eyes shifting to horror, then to grief—now, as he watched, to self-loathing as well.

He'd not realized how angry she would be with herself. He ought to have expected it, for it would be his own reaction as well.

He could hear her now. *Idiotidiotidiot* . . .

To all present, her still beauty betrayed nothing but thoughtful assessment of the situation. Only Marcus could see the spiraling despair behind her lovely eyes.

He had done it with two words.

"Low-born," she said finally. She straightened and turned away from him to gaze at the others, letting her eyes slip from him as if he was beneath her notice.

"Yes, my lady. Marriage to a peer is not enough to raise you that high, I'm afraid." Lord Liverpool did not sound regretful at all.

Julia blinked at the Prime Minister for a long moment. "I see."

The hell of it was—the blasted, outrageous irony of it—was that she was being wrongly cast out. And on the very premise that she didn't dare tell them wasn't true.

Then, in the depths of her loss, things got much, much worse.

"You know too much," Lord Liverpool was saying. "You cannot be allowed to continue thus, especially now that you've been dismissed." He glared at her. "How do we know you won't take your vengeance by exposing us?"

"Perhaps because I'm not the vengeful sort." But her voice was too faint to carry over the Prime Minister's rant.

"You are to spend the rest of your days in a convent of our choosing. You will not have access to the outside world, or to your staff, who are even now about to be investigated by the Liar's Club as to the level of their knowledge—"

"They are loyal British citizens! They could no more betray this country than they could betray me!"

"Nonetheless, they pose a serious security risk. The Liar's Club is close behind us. They will round up your staff for questioning and determine how much they know."

The fair folk knew far too much. Her stomach knotted, thinking of her free and easy trust. She'd drawn them all in too deep—

It was so much worse than she'd thought. Broken heart aside, shattered dreams aside, now the Four were going to shut her up behind stone walls and destroy her family! Aldus had warned her, he had taught her and he had told her everything—and still she had remained the stupid girl she had once been. She had set her heart free—and Marcus had put an arrow through it.

The Royal Four would quietly dispose of her family and they would be quite right to do so—for without her at the helm, the group would soon disperse, and someday, someone would relax his tongue for just a moment . . .

And it was all her fault.

She couldn't do it. She couldn't abandon them like this, even to save herself. All for one, one for all.

"I . . . see." She drew herself up as tall as she could, seeing as she'd been gutted. "Very well. For the good of England, I will comply with your wishes. My only request is that I—" Why was there no air in her lungs? Oh, yes—she was contemplating treason, that was why. "I should like to be allowed to make my farewell to my people here. You'll find them more cooperative if they believe me to be in good hands."

Liverpool's eyes narrowed. "No."

She saw Marcus's jaw tighten. "Yes."

The Lion was looking at Marcus with sympathy. Why? "Yes," the giant said.

The Falcon was gazing only at Julia. She gazed back as openly as she dared. He was too bloomin' perceptive. "No," was the Falcon's verdict.

The Cobra stood with arms folded. He'd not said a word through all of it. Now his single word was, "No."

She was surprised. He'd seemed to be the most likely one to vote in her favor. Well, then, there was nothing for it. She bowed her head in acquiescence. At least now she knew something she'd not known before: Marcus had feelings of guilt for what he'd done—or at least regret—and the Dane was letting Marcus make the call on this issue.

That was two things—two things that changed the odds so very slightly. Perhaps, in some outlandish dream world, it was enough.

"May I pack?"

Liverpool stepped forward. "The sisters will provide you everything you need. The Order of St. Clara operates under a vow of poverty, so you will need very little."

From pauper to princess to pauper again.

Something woke in Julia—something bold and desperate and long lost. With giddy relief, Julia recognized and welcomed the intruder.

Jilly.

Jilly scoffed at the threat of rags and gruel. No crumbling convent walls could hold Jilly. And no loyalty to a group that had betrayed her would keep her from saving her family.

Her heart beat fast with a welcome, reckless rhythm and she beamed a wild-child smile on the gentlemen before her. "Damn you all to hell," she said cheerfully. Then she threw back her head and gave voice to the wild girl within.

"Hey, Rube!"

There was nothing but shocked silence for a long moment. Only Marcus looked properly alarmed. "Ah, my lords—"

The door to the parlor burst open and the Barrowby staff piled into the room, brandishing pokers and rolling pins and whatever had been handy.

They didn't bother waiting to find out the situation. Meg took a swing at the Falcon, who ducked the rolling pin and drove a fist into the cook's impressive gut. Meg grinned.

Beppo had tackled the Prime Minister himself with a broom and was driving Liverpool back with a complicated swinging routine that Julia recognized from his tight-rope days.

"Run, my lady!" Pickles brandished a poker at Marcus, who gazed at the elderly maid in consternation.

Julia backed from the room. "Players, time to knock down! The magistrate is on his way!" she called as she left. They would know that she meant it was time to knock down the wagons and get out of town as fast as possible.

It was the best she could do for them. They were seasoned mischief makers all, and could take very good care of themselves, once they were dispersed on the wind.

The Liar's Club would never find them now.

18

"My lady, would you care to walk in the wood with me?"

He reaches for my hand and I allow him to take it, though we wear no gloves. His skin is rougher than mine, the hands of a horseman, not a dandy. He does not let go as we turn toward the trees, but only wraps my fingers in his as though he owns them. We walk silently into the dimness, the shadows the only watchers.

I close my eyes and breathe in the smell of cool, damp loam and green growing things. When I open them, he is watching me. I know he watched my bodice swell and I breathe deeply again, simply to make him notice once more. His eyes flicker to where my nipples now press through the thin muslin of my gown and I let him gaze on me, shoulders back and chin high. I want him to look, to want.

His gaze grows hot as he steps closer. I see his organ swell his trousers and I revel in the knowledge of my power. He wants me—and not in some polite, "leave your gown on I'll manage" sort of wanting. He wants to rip my bodice to free my breasts. He wants to devour my rigid, aching nipples with teeth and tongue, he

*wants to lay me on the ground and take me right where
we stand.*

The dark wood might have seemed threatening to a
stranger, but this was Barrowby. Julia ducked and wove
through the tangled branches stretching through the
mist as if she didn't need eyes at all.

Here, jump the tiny streamlet. There, scramble over
the fallen oak, avoid the open pit where the roots once
delved. Her own breaths sounded loud in her own ears,
but she knew that her feet made almost no sound on the
loam floor of the wood.

There was a thicket ahead, thorny and wonderful for
hiding if one knew the way the deer had pushed
through to get the best berries in summer—

A weight fell upon her from behind, carrying her
hard to the ground. The breath left her lungs, but she
didn't hesitate to turn on her attacker, hands curved
into claws. She took a strip from one cheek before she
found herself flat on her back with her hands pinned
above her head.

Marcus.

The sight of him—oh, God, the *feel* of him—covering
her sent her into renewed struggles. She writhed beneath
him, desperate to rid herself of his weight.

She didn't realize she was weeping until he kissed
away the tears streaming down one cheek. His lips
were warm on her frozen skin, but fatal on the ice she'd
surrounded her heart with.

"Julia, Julia—" His voice was a moaning rasp.
"What am I going to do with you?"

"Let me go."

She'd meant her voice to be hard. The raw need she heard from her own throat shocked her silent. But then, she had no pride left, did she? She had nothing left to lose by begging.

"Please . . . Please, my lord, let me go," she gasped. His lips pressed to her eyes, then her temples, his own panting breath hot on her ears. She twisted her head away, forcing herself to deny him. "I would never betray England. You know that—you know *me*!"

He paused in his consumption of her and dropped his forehead to hers. "I know that you would never *want* to betray England . . . but you cannot simply walk away, Julia. You know the danger is far too great. You were the Fox long enough to know that we are only doing what we have to do."

Duty. She writhed anew beneath him. "Is it your duty to rape me on the ground?"

He let his cheek slip down hers and kissed her ear. "No."

She twisted away as best she could. "Then let me up!"

"If I let you up, will I ever lie with you again?"

"No!"

"Then I'm in no hurry to let you up." He kissed her neck. "A man has to take what he can get."

"Marcus, if you turn me in now, you know I'll be hung—or have some curiously convenient accident!"

"If I let you go, they'll set the Liars on you all. Have you ever seen what an assassin can accomplish with nothing but a throwing knife and a straight shot?"

He was right. If she went back willingly, she might still have the option of the nunnery, although she didn't think so.

Marcus had his hand on her breast. When had he released her wrist? And why was she lying there, acquiescing to his bald encroachment?

Because it felt too bloody good, that was why. After everything he'd done, she was still melted wax at his touch, still easy takings.

His mouth still teased her neck, sending shivers of need through her. She forced herself to breathe against the weight of him, when all she wanted was to sink with him through the earth forever. "Get off," she demanded weakly.

He released her other hand and slid his down her arm to caress her cheek. "I cannot let you go," he whispered.

"Then stop." Her demand lacked force and she found herself teasing his curly hair through her fingertips.

"I cannot do that, either," he said, and kissed the hollow between her breasts. Her bodice had come awry, she noticed absently as she twined her fingers through his hair to press his mouth lower. His knee had shifted and was now pressing his hard thigh between hers. She writhed against that pressure, pleasuring herself against the muscled length.

"I want—" She stopped, for what did she want? Oh, yes, she wanted his hot mouth on her nipples. She slapped his hand away and tugged at her neckline until her breasts were freed to the chill in the air. Marcus, being an intelligent fellow, took advantage of the situation. She let her head fall back as the shudders of pleasure gripped her. Hot hard hands, clever fingers, hot wet mouth, big muscled body covering and dominating hers . . .

"I want you."

He moaned against her breast. "I'm here." She felt him reach down to hike her hem above her knees. She slid her own hands down between them to free him from his trousers. The buttons slipped from her shaking hands and she nearly cried. Her need for him went so deep she felt as if she'd never be whole again if he didn't take her right this minute.

He brushed her fumbling hands away and freed himself. She took him greedily in both hands, his hot flesh jerking at her cool touch. He hissed when she wrapped her fingers about him and squeezed. He throbbed larger in response, filling her hands with hot, pulsating male flesh.

Her female flesh responded, turning to molten liquid as she pressed the large head of his erection into herself. He thrust deep, wrapping his hands over her shoulders to keep her still.

Her own hands were trapped between them. It was all she could do to clutch at his coat and gasp as he spread her wide from within. He thrust again, deeper and harder, his own need taking the fore. "I cannot let you go," he gasped. "I cannot!"

She held on tight as he took her with all the broken love in his soul. She knew he had done what he had to do, and that he would continue to put his duty first. He would make love to her on the chill ground, and then he would take her back to the Four and turn her in.

The worst of it was that she didn't care. Marcus was in her arms, and in her body, for the last time. She wasn't going to waste a moment on pride or regret now. She wrapped her arms about him and held on for the tumultuous ride as he slipped and thrust into her wetness.

"I love you." He didn't hear her, for her whisper had been soundless. She pressed her face to his shoulder and whispered it again. "I will always love you."

Her heart ached, but her body trembled with the pleasure of him. She released the pain, released the heartbreak, and only let the pleasure shine through as Marcus's heated thrusts increased. She rode the cresting ecstasy higher, lost in pleasure, her keening cries shameless and animal in the forest air.

Marcus couldn't bear it. He had to devour her, own her, make her his! If he lost this woman, he could not see anything but gray disillusionment and agony for the rest of his life. Unbearable. Unacceptable. She was his.

When she welcomed him into her heated softness, he took her with everything he had in him. Every ache, every lonely hollow ache, every desperate adherence to empty duty, every loss—he gave it all to her, holding nothing back.

When she whispered her love, after everything he'd done to her, after his betrayal and now his crude seduction in the dirt, after he'd ruined her entire world—his heart broke beyond repair. He didn't deserve this amazing, astounding creature.

He took her anyway.

When they were spent and panting on their bed of leaves, Julia turned her face away and wiped at her tears. She did not want him to see her like this, weeping and weak.

Although he'd always seemed to see too much. He'd

known within days what her nearest beloveds had not discerned in years. He'd known precisely what she'd wanted and needed—

The intruder on the grounds. The canny seduction. The lake, the horse race, the balcony—even the woods!

She pushed him from her and rolled away, her body racked by deep bitter laughter.

"The diaries! Oh, my God, you read the diaries!"

He hesitated. "Yes."

Her laughter raked her throat. "And I fell for it. What a perfect mark I was. What a perfect, gullible, romantic fool." She viciously rubbed the tears from her face and stood. "You said you had misperceptions about me. You thought it was all real, didn't you?"

He cleared his throat. "They were remarkably detailed, but I eventually realized they were only fantasies."

"Well, *of course* they were fantasies! No man is so understanding, nor so strong and tender as that." She wrapped her arms about herself. "As you have so thoroughly proven today."

"I confess, I wanted to believe they were real," he continued doggedly. "I wanted to think the worst of you, for it's much easier to destroy a wicked woman than a good one."

"And that goes well for you, does it?"

He flinched from her sarcasm. Good.

He stood, adjusting his clothing. "This plan of theirs—ours—I knew nothing of this. It must have been decided before I was confirmed this morning."

She looked up. "Then you can convince them to change it."

He shook his head. "No. It is binding. There is no

way through it . . . but there might be a way around it."

She pushed back her hair. "I'm listening," she said
warily.

"Marry me! Wed me at once!" He stepped closer.
"If you are my lady, they will have to reconsider your
sentence. It will solve everything!"

She closed her eyes, that small hope slipping away.
She put a hand to his face and gazed into his eyes.
"Now who is being gullible?"

He pressed his hand over hers. "It might work."

"And it might get you hung alongside me." She went
up on tiptoe and kissed him softly. Then she spun
quickly and kicked high, knocking him flat with a blow
to the jaw.

Marcus rolled with the blow, his brain spinning in
his skull. He rose to his feet and staggered, then froze
as he spotted her.

She stood upright on the rump of his stallion, long
reins held neatly in one hand. "Good-bye, Marcus,"
she called, and gave him an insouciant wave.

She rode away on his startled mount, still standing,
a golden-haired goddess in black. He watched her until
she was out of sight, but never took a step to stop her.

"Damn," he said faintly. "That was my favorite
horse."

19

With Mum dead and gone, I decided to stay on with Himself and learn what he wants to teach me. How bad could it be? Besides, I can always go back to the fair . . .

"You're a very fine horse," Julia told her weary mount. "Most horses would have given out long ago."

The stallion flicked an ear backward at her voice and continued his plodding gait down a muddy country lane Julia wasn't sure she was recalling properly.

"I'm sorry about the steeple chasing," she added. "It was important to get far and fast. The Liar's Club was right behind us."

The stallion huffed a disbelieving snort.

"Oh, very well. Not right behind *you*." She straightened wearily in the saddle. Horseback had once been as comfortable as any chair for her, but she'd not ridden so hard and desperately for many years. She would most definitely be feeling the consequences when she woke tomorrow.

The stallion drew in a giant breath, expanding his ribs against the inside of her legs. Julia winced. Her skirts were of necessity rucked up to her knees and her stockings were shredded from their wild cross-country escape. The fact that her skin stung and throbbed beneath the tears didn't bear thinking about just yet.

"We ought to be close now," she told the stallion. "There are always traveling fair folk at the Dunston harvest fair about this time."

The stallion ignored her, since she'd been saying that same thing for the last hour. "No, truly," she assured him. "Oats and hay for you, bangers and mash for me." She sighed. "And perhaps a bit of liniment for my arse."

"Well, now, I think I can 'elp you with that, pretty lady." A figure stepped from the bushes into the last of the evening light to leer at her. "Rubbin' in the liniment, anyways."

Julia halted the stallion quickly and peered at the thickset, bearded man before her. Then her lips tilted. "And won't Petunia have something to say about that, John Wald? She still has that rolling pin of hers, doesn't she?"

The man started, then blinked at her. "Jilly Boots? Is that our skinny little Jilly-girl?" He laughed out loud and threw open his arms.

Julia let him haul her off the stallion, for she doubted she could get down with her stiffened limbs. "Hello, John," she said around his bear hug.

He set her back and took another look at her. "We heard you'd married up, fine lady now and all. Folk still havin' a 'Say' about how you caught yourself a lord. Always meant to go take a look at that man of yours, see if he was treatin' you right."

Then he seemed to see her black gown for what it

was. Widow's garb. "Well, now, don't tell me you lost 'im already?"

Julia nodded, not trusting her voice. She'd lost Aldus and Marcus both in less than a fortnight. If there was such a thing as a blacker black, she'd wear it.

"I've lost a great deal, I'm afraid," she said finally. "All I have now is what I'm wearing." She tilted her head at the stallion now cropping grass by the side of the road. "And someone else's horse."

John gazed at the stallion speculatively. "Those are the best kind," he mused. Then he looked back at her. "Then what of the Pickles folk? I heard you gave 'em all monkey suits and salaries. Did you lose them, too?"

She sighed. "Had to knock down and get out of town."

That was all she needed to say. He threw an arm over her shoulders. "They'll be about, then," he said comfortingly. "Come and use our second wagon. Petunia'll be over the moon to see ye." He glanced back at the stallion. "He any good? It's too late to start a new show now, but a trick act would sure bring 'em in next season."

Julia looked at Marcus's stallion blankly. She'd not thought so far ahead. Could she simply turn herself back into Jilly the trick rider? Was such a thing even possible? She wrapped the reins about her hand and clucked the stallion into following her to the campsite ahead, where the colorful wagons of the fair folk were gathered.

It might not be much, but it was more future than she'd had five minutes ago.

Petunia was indeed "over the moon" and eagerly bestowed the second wagon, her best nightgown and she and John's second best set of tin. "I'd give you the good'ns, milady," she said apologetically, "but they're still on the fire."

Julia smiled at the homey sights and smells of campfire cooking and took the battered set of pots and pans. "This is lovely. And please call me Jilly, just as you used to."

Petunia bobbed. "Yes, milady—I mean—" Flustered, Petunia turned her ire on John. "Don't just stand there, you dolt. Lady Barrowby's wantin' a plateful, or I miss my guess!"

Julia shook her head, laughing. "I think I'm too weary to eat. If you'll do me the favor of spending a bit of that pampering on my horse, I'll take my rest now."

Petunia and John watched every moment of her climb into the second wagon. Julia waved and smiled, then closed the narrow door on their overeager hospitality before she could lose her poise. Once alone, she leaned her forehead against the flimsy door and took a deep breath.

"Imagine that!" she heard Petunia exclaim. "We've got a real lady in our wagon!"

"She's still Jilly, though, ain't she?" John sounded doubtful. "She's so fine now . . ."

This was home, and yet not home. Her family, yet she was so different now. Julia sighed. Perhaps a simple future as Jilly the trick rider was more complicated than she'd thought.

She removed her battered widow's gown and donned the nightdress, which was too short and too wide. The wagon had been hurriedly emptied of John and Petunia's extra belongings and the bench bed had been made up with a faded but clean quilt. Julia stroked it, remembering sleeping beneath a nearly identical one all her childhood.

"I'm back where we started, Mama," she whispered. She dropped her head into her hands. She felt like a pendulum, moving from one extreme to another, her life a pattern of gains and losses.

Had she ever been as low as now?

No, she decided. This was indeed the worst day of her life, for this time she had nothing to carry her on. No husband, no family, no estate, no lover, no work. Her hands and arms and heart had never been so empty.

"Well, tomorrow will surely be a step up, then."

She dropped back onto the quilt, pressing her hands over her eyes. Now that she had stopped moving, it seemed that all the emotions she'd held at bay during this endless day were coming up to ambush her.

Marcus.

She would not cry. She would *not*. She'd taken her leave of him, she'd had her last taste of his love and she'd kept his horse. There was nothing to be gained from tears.

Yet there was no denying that he'd caught her when she'd thought herself clean away. The last thing a man like Marcus wanted do was fail. He could find her again, for he'd wormed his way deep inside her. He *knew* her, in just the way she'd always dreamed of having a lover know her.

Unfortunately, her lover was now her enemy.

Oh, what the hell. Sometimes tears were the only way for a woman to know she could still feel.

◆ ◆ ◆

A roar split the morning quiet.

"Sebastian?"

Julia threw back the covers on her cot and sprang from her borrowed wagon without sparing a moment to don her wrapper. Carelessly running through mud and muck with bare feet, she crossed the camp in mere seconds to where the menagerie was housed.

Behind the cart where the monkeys sat dolefully scratching at one another, Sebastian sat morosely in a battered, wired-together beast wagon. His mane was matted and his eyes were running and he had never looked thinner.

"Oh, sweet baby," Julia breathed as she knelt in the mud next to the bars. "Don't you worry, Mummy is here now."

"Oy! Get away from that beast!" A burly fellow in muck-spattered canvas trousers ran up to pull at her arm.

Julia slapped him away and turned back to Sebastian. "Don't worry, my darling. I won't let the bad man hurt you."

"Hurt 'im? Miss, I paid a year's profit for 'im! Bought 'im off a farmer what was set t' kill 'im. But 'e won't eat and he won't let no one near 'im!"

Julia was working at the twisted wire holding the wagon door shut. "You must chop his meat fine and take out all the bones. He needs brushing and he has a cold. Lions are from Africa, you idiot! You cannot leave them out in the chill night air!"

A big dirty hand appeared before her intent gaze, blocking her. "Miss, yer ought to go back to the girly wagon and leave the beasts to them what knows their business."

Julia turned on him. "Girly wagon? *Girly wagon?*" The man took a step back before her fury. "My family owned their own show, you muck raker! I'm Jilly, the trick rider, and this is *my* bloomin' lion!" She took another step and poked the man in his grubby waistcoat with one finger, hard. "Now go chop the meat!"

"Y-yes, ma'am." The man ran for his life, followed by a rousing roar from Sebastian.

Julia reached through the bars and ran her hand through Sebastian's mane. "That's right, sweet darling. You tell him."

Sebastian took her wrist in his great, toothless jaws and tugged gently. *More.*

Julia laughed damply and pulled her hand from the cage. "On my way, love." She wiped the spittle carelessly on her borrowed nightdress and bent to the tangle of wire once more. "If the idiot ever meant to tend you," she muttered, "he would never have tied this up so."

"Someone who doesn't love the Beast?" The deep voice came from behind her. "I don't believe it."

Julia's heart stuttered in its beat. She whirled to see Marcus standing there. "How did you find me? The fair folk would never—"

Marcus shook his head. "They didn't. I tracked Sebastian. People don't soon forget seeing their first lion." He tilted his head and gazed at her for a long moment. "You love that mangy beast. I knew wherever he was, you would not be far away."

"Marcus, you must leave."

He stepped closer. "You know I cannot," he said softly.

I cannot let you go.

Marcus above her, inside her, on the damp ground. The ache in his voice, the need in his eyes—

There was no point to those thoughts now. Her mind was firmly convinced, her heart was too shattered to voice an opinion, but her body still felt the pull of his nearness. She lifted her chin. "I want you to leave. I can make you go, you know I can. The fair folk will come running at a word."

The corner of his lips lifted a fraction. "Two words, actually. Now I have two words for you. Marry me."

The mere mention of such an impossibility cut deep into her heart. "I will not bring you down so."

"Would you say yes if I left the Four?"

She crossed her arms to hide her chill. "No one leaves the Four."

"Etheridge did."

"Within himself, Etheridge will be the Cobra until he dies. He's simply fulfilling his duty as our—your spymaster instead. You must serve as the Fox. There is no other."

No one leaves the Four. The truth was, the Four never left them. She *was* the Fox now, and she always would be. Could she ever simply be Jilly again, knowing what she knew, having tasted the power and profoundly exalting commitment of the Four?

"Isn't it wonderful?" The wistful words escaped her before she could stop them. Before her stood the one person in the world who understood what she'd lost.

He raised his hand slightly as if he wished to touch

her, then abruptly aborted the gesture. "Sometimes it is. Sometimes . . . it is not."

"I think I finally understand why I cannot be the Fox," she said softly.

"Because you think with your heart?"

She looked up to see the utter understanding in his gaze. It ruined her inside. She reached out impulsively.

He moved back slightly, avoiding contact. "It is no bad thing to feel so deeply," he said. "But such passion does not belong in the Four."

She put her hands behind her back. "No, of course not. The point is moot, however, for I can never be part of the Four."

"Perhaps, but you have changed us, like it or not. It turns out that we would have considered allowing a highborn woman to take the seat. That is a vast relief to those of us who find scant possibilities for successors in the current crop of young men."

She blinked. "Would you choose a woman to succeed you?"

"It is a possibility." He didn't smile, but his eyes grew brighter. "I have the highest esteem for intelligent women."

She smiled at nothing in particular. "You'll never guess who I had decided to appoint."

"So that is all." He took a breath. "We'll not meet again, you and I."

She swallowed. "So final. Yet, how else can it be?" She held out her hand. "I shall always . . ." She stopped. "Well, perhaps that's best left unsaid. I shall always remember you," she finished.

He took her hand so briefly, it was almost as if they hadn't touched. "And I, you."

She bit her lip. "Is that all we should say?"

"Is there anything else?"

She shook her head. "No . . . yet, how can it be that we can simply decide this? I'd become rather used to having no control over my heart."

Marcus said nothing. He still had no control over his heart. It was only the rest of him that would be riding away.

She raised her chin and gave him a watery smile. "I am not sorry, not for a single thing."

I am. Oh, God, I'm so sorry for everything I took from you.

"I'm glad," was all he said.

I'm sorry that I shall live the rest of my life with a rip in my soul, just penance though it be. I'm sorry that you will never become who you were meant to be. I'm sorry I wasn't who you thought me. I'm sorry I am not actually Marcus Blythe-Goodman, destitute gold-digger and free man.

I'm sorry I caused you to love me.

She took a breath. "I will keep an eye on the gossip sheets for you. I'm sure there will be notices of . . . marriage and such."

"I will have no such resource."

She looked around the encampment. "You could always ask the fair folk. They won't tell you where I am, but if I allow it, they'll let you know if I live or die."

Marcus had a moment of his future flash before him, where someday he would rise from before the hearth fire in Ravencliff to find a graying Igby at his door with terrible news. In his imagination, the house was cold and empty.

There would be no marriage—not even for the required camouflage of the Four could he bear to do that. In his heart, he felt as wed as if he and Julia had stood before the Bishop of Canterbury himself. He gazed down at his beautiful, maddening, brilliant Julia.

"Be well," he said. *Live forever,* his heart echoed. *Be happy.* He reached a hand toward her, but did not touch the flyaway strand of hair that had escaped her workaday braid.

She gazed up at him, her helpless pain in her eyes.

"How did we come to this?" she whispered.

He swallowed. "Fate, I suppose. We were simply not meant to be."

She shook her head. "No. Fate brought us together. And I will always believe that for at least one night, we *were* meant to be."

There was nothing more to say. Marcus took one last look into her pain-glazed eyes and then turned away. His lungs felt tight, as if there wasn't enough air to breathe. Somehow, it didn't seem like punishment enough.

20

Perhaps it is better to be alone, for I cannot bear to be left again.

As Marcus walked back to his horse, the grounds of the encampment seemed oddly sharp in his vision, the colors jarring. Pulled to the edges of the circle were the plainest wagons, yet even they were brightly painted once upon a time.

The fading colors told a story of long years on the road, as did the shabby curtains hanging in the tiny windows. Julia's had been a hard life, it was obvious, yet the people who worked and laughed and gazed openly and curiously at him as he passed seemed quite the happiest crew he'd seen outside of Barrowby itself.

No conservative village restraint here. The laughter was loud, the voices were boisterous and full of rough humor. The children ran happily about in their varying degrees of dirtiness. One naked infant sat, fat bare bottom in the dust, sucking a finger as it watched Marcus with unblinking absorption.

Marcus spotted his stallion. The beast was tied to a

shabby wagon, absorbed in his nose-bag of oats, being buffed to a gleaming shine by several admiring children standing on overturned pails. He'd never looked happier.

Marcus hesitated. He'd paid a king's ransom for that horse, who was meant to be the stud of the Ravencliff stables someday, not some nomadic angel's show pony.

Then again, Marcus was leaving behind his heart, cut from his chest and left in the hands of the above mentioned fallen angel. He turned and went on his way. His best horse seemed a small loss after that.

She'd be gone in minutes, he knew. Even now, she was likely pouring last minute instructions into the beast master's ear. In less than an hour, she'd be headed down whatever fast road would take her as far from him as possible.

Forever.

He didn't realize he'd turned around until the menagerie wagons came into sight again. Julia stood with the beast master, just as he'd pictured her, burdening the fellow with all the facts of the tender care of spoiled, toothless lions.

Marcus came up behind her. "Julia."

Julia spun about, her lips still parted around her last words. Her first thought was that he'd come back to kiss her goodbye forever. Her second was that he'd come back to clap her in irons and carry her off.

Frankly, she didn't know which was worse.

"Yes?" She hated the breathless, hopeful tone of her voice.

"I don't know what to do," he said simply. "I cannot turn you in. I cannot let you go."

She licked her lips. "Are you asking for my advice?" She truly hoped not, for she strongly suspected she might do the stupid thing and help his career by turning herself in.

"We only had one night together. If I must live the rest of my life without you, then I want one day to match it." He reached out again, and this time he stroked his finger down her cheek. "I'm asking for time. I want one day. With you."

Her heedless heart leaped. "With me?"

He smiled and turned his palm to cup her cheek. The heat of his skin on hers threatened to melt the vault in which she kept her tears.

"With you," he whispered.

Julia clung to her sanity and will. She raised her chin. "Not if you're going to browbeat me into marriage or the nunnery."

He grinned. Her heart spun in her chest.

"No browbeating. No national crisis. No nunnery, no Fox, no Royal Four." He removed his palm with a last, lingering touch of his fingertips, then held out his hand to her. "Only you and I, together. Will you grant me that?"

Julia looked down at his open hand, then up at his face. He looked so weary, just the way she'd felt last night until the warm hearts of the fair folk had lifted her hopes.

She put her hand in his. "Stay with me."

"The toff's stayin', is 'e?" A big voice boomed from beside them.

Julia turned. "John." She introduced her burly, bearded childhood friend to the immaculately dressed

Lord Dryden with a smile. "Marcus, may I present John Wald?"

Marcus stuck out his hand, only to find himself drawn into a bear-like embrace.

"Marcus, you won't find a better lady than our Jilly-girl! Now, it's time you come help me shovel horse—" John glanced at Julia. "Shovel horse-apples," he finished.

Marcus looked down at the muddy shovel that had appeared in his hand, then up at the brawny man standing next to Julia.

"Ah . . ." Julia seemed taken aback. "John, I don't think—"

The big man crossed his arms. "It's our way, re-member? Now, come on, then," the man said to Marcus with satisfaction. "There's work to be done."

Marcus blinked. "But—"

Julia was backing away, one hand raised, fingers waving, a small helpless smile on her face. "I shall see you at my wagon for dinner."

Marcus took a step to follow her, then looked down. His boot was inches deep in a steaming manure heap that could not have come from a mortal horse.

"Told ye there was work to be done." John chortled deeply. "Pile's not getting' smaller with you standin' there."

Marcus watched Julia disappear in a flutter of ill-fitting linen and sighed. Horse-apples it was, then. Not quite what he'd had in mind when he'd asked for one day. Still, the brightness in her eyes told him he wouldn't be alone for long.

Julia watched John put Marcus to work from a dis-tance. She hadn't been able to bring herself to tell him that this was the custom when two of the fair folk were about to marry. The others kept the two apart, busy with other things all day. In a small encampment, where two lovers might well have grown up side by side, it was a way to increase anticipation and renew the joy of being together.

She could not tell him and she couldn't bear to explain to her friends, so she let him be drawn away and put to work. The separation did not matter, for there was nowhere in the camp that she could not find him in a moment. As it was, she could feel his nearness like the warmth of a campfire on her skin as she went about the tasks she was set to as well.

Petunia watched her with mingled humor and worry, for she at least realized that a man like Lord Dryden would never stay. Julia smiled at her old friend and shook her head. "Let them play. He could use a day at the fair."

Julia strolled the Fair, looking for Marcus. She'd caught glimpses of him all morning as he'd been put to one dirty chore after another.

Without her telling them a thing, the fair folk had taken Marcus in with laughter and good-natured teasing. They addressed him very formally, all the while ordering him to the worst tasks.

"If you please, milord, there's a pisspot that needs emptyin', if you would be so kind."

"Thank you, milord. Here's the new privy hole needs diggin', milord."

All the while, Julia kept an eye on his progress from afar. She'd seen him go from appalled dismay to easy calm to cheerful laughter as his work worsened.

Then the tide had turned on her. Now it was she who was kept too busy to think. Enough was enough, Julia decided. She longed to be with Marcus anyway.

If she could only find him.

She found him in Sebastian's pen.

He was sitting with his back against the wagon wheel and his cap pulled down low over his eyes, relaxed and very nearly napping if his slumped posture was any clue. Julia held her breath, wondering if he realized that Sebastian had his great heavy head resting on Marcus's lap and was sprawled at his side like a giant golden hound.

Then she saw Marcus lazily lift a hand and bury it in Sebastian's mane, scratching in just the right place behind the cat's ear.

My lads.

Marcus yawned. Sebastian followed suit immediately, in all his toothless grandeur. Julia shook her head fondly. "Lazy sods, the both o' ye," she whispered.

She returned to their—her—wagon and began to peel potatoes for a filling camp meal. She paused somewhere around her twelfth potato and gazed down at her hands, struck by the contrast to herself a week ago. Lady Barrowby had slipped from her like an unwanted wrapper, leaving behind someone else entirely.

She was Jilly, yet she was far more than simple Jilly with her common speech and her fearful secrets. She was more than obedient Julia as well, for all that she had loved and worshiped Aldus.

It was as though Julia and Jilly had been blended and strained through, leaving only this new, purer creature behind. She had never felt stronger or more at ease with herself as she did sitting tailor-fashion on the wagon's apron, peeling potatoes for Lord Dryden's supper.

It was too bad she was no longer to be the Fox, for she felt as though she could perform those duties better now than ever before.

She smiled and returned to her task. Then again, she might find it hard to resist the common urge to spit in Liverpool's eye now and again. "Oy," she murmured to herself. "What a stick." The occasional lapse into vulgarity was proving to be good for her soul.

"Who's a stick?"

She looked up to see Marcus lounging against the wagon's side, smiling at her.

She raised her brows and pursed her lips. "Did you lads enjoy your nap?"

He snorted and rubbed his neck sheepishly. "Sebastian's not so bad under all that hair."

"Is that so?" She threw a piece of toweling at him. "Wash the lion off yourself. I love Sebastian, but I don't want to smell him in our wagon tonight."

He caught the cloth absently, watching her oddly. "There's something . . . you seem different, somehow."

She smiled up at him. "I've simply realized who I am."

He blinked. "Oh. All that since this morning?"

She picked up the pot of peeled potatoes and hopped down off the wagon. "You know me. I ponder and mull and cogitate—"

He grinned. "And then you assume control of the world."

She leaned close and tilted her face up for a kiss. "I prefer to think of it as sort of a boiling point."

His eyes darkened. "Boiling. Fire. Heat. Let's pass on dinner, shall we?"

She gave him a sultry look. "Trust me, you'll need food to keep up your strength."

He closed his eyes in a pained expression. "Ah. You're going to do me in, you temptress."

She laughed and pulled away. "Stop. You'll make me spill these."

He peered into the pot. "What are those white things?"

She blinked at him. "You don't know?"

He wrinkled his brow. "Um . . . eggs?"

She rolled her eyes. "My lord, you may be a splendid raker of muck, but you have obviously never set foot in your own kitchens."

"Should I have?"

She hesitated. "No . . . no, of course not." She'd almost forgotten who he truly was. He was one of the most powerful men in England. He was the Fox.

And he wasn't hers.

She smiled to cover her sudden sadness. "Now get thee to the basin, O Lord of Lion's Breath."

He snapped the towel at her bottom as she walked away. "You're a cheeky little sausage, my lady of the peeled potatoes."

She turned. "So you did know—"

He was gone, leaving only the faint echo of his laughter behind.

Julia bit her lip. Dear God, how she loved that man. She would love him forever.

Even if she would only have him for now.

* * *

After their simple dinner, Julia gazed about the camp, challenging the eyes that she knew were watching. "I've had a trying morning," she said loudly. "I think I'll have a bit of a nap."

Marcus blinked. "Ah, certainly. I'll just—" He hesitated. "Should I—"

Julia rolled her eyes. "Good heavens, Marcus," she hissed. "Are you a spy or aren't you?" She stood and shook out her borrowed skirts, then turned to climb the steps into the wagon without another word.

She was naked beneath the quilt by the time the trapdoor in the floor lifted. She rolled onto her stomach and propped her chin on her hands to gaze at Marcus in exasperation. "You must be the slowest lover to sneak into a wagon in all of recorded history."

He grinned as he clambered into the narrow confines of the wagon. "I think I did it rather nicely. They all think I'm back at the beast master's."

Julia raised a brow. "They all know you're in here with me. The point is to be discreet so they can pretend they don't."

His eyes darkened as he took in her nudity beneath the faded cotton coverlet. "Stop talking. Now."

She smiled coyly at him and threw back the quilt. "Shutting up, milord."

Unfortunately, Marcus had never tried to undress in a space more like a coffin than a room, much less do so in a great hurry. He still had one arm tangled in his shirt and one foot stuck in his boot when he looked over at her in desperation. "Help."

She sighed, wiping the tears of laughter from her eyes. "The show is over then." She reached for his hand. "Sit."

He sank to the low bench, flushed with his exertions. "This is most embarrassing."

"You've had a humbling day, haven't you, my darling?" Julia tempered her sympathy with a hot, wet kiss to his neck as she removed his shirt. "Poor, disadvantaged Lord Dryden."

She was all lithe, naked woman and quick fingers. Marcus couldn't get a proper grip on her until she'd made him as naked as she was. Then she landed on his lap, facing him, with her long thighs wrapped about his back and her slender arms twined about his neck.

"All better?"

He pulled her tightly to him, hands spread on her back. "All best."

And it was. They proceeded slowly, cherishing the sensations of skin on skin and kissing deeply. Once Marcus tried to speak, his pain dark in his eyes, but Julia put her finger over his lips. "One day," she whispered. "Let us not waste it."

So they stayed silent but for sighs and cries and wordless passion. There was no ending and no beginning again. There was only touch and scent and helpless, heartrending pleasure. He moved above her. She moved above him. Their skin dampened and heated and melded together until there was no separation.

Time hung suspended elsewhere, for this one moment had to last forever. Every minute was strung tightly, humming like a wire, thrumming in time with her heart beating against his.

She took him in her mouth and he closed his eyes in surrender. He savored her with his lips and tongue and she cried out his name. He delved into her with aching solemnity and she gazed into his eyes as he took her flying somewhere beyond awareness of their fate.

It was time to forget.

It was time to remember.

At long last, somewhere between loving and mourning, they slept.

A tapping on the wagon door brought both Marcus and Julia awake in an instant. Marcus reached for his pistol but Julia waved him back. Her belly felt like ice. There was something amiss.

"Milady?" John Wald's whisper came through the thin wood. "Milady, I know it's late, but I wish you'd come talk to Petunia. She's in an awful fit."

Petunia didn't take fits.

Julia spoke through the door. "I'll be right there, John." She turned back to smile at Marcus. "You needn't get up. John and Petunia have a tumultuous marriage, but they're mad for each other really. I'm sure she just needs a bit of soothing about something or another."

He grinned and lay back down. "When you're done, I could use a bit of soothing as well."

She returned his lazy smile with an ache in her heart. There were only two reasons that would spur John to wake Lady Barrowby at this hour. One was fire. The other was worse.

The other meant that she would be forced to choose again.

She threw on the mismatched clothing the fair folk

had given her—sturdy boots that nearly fit beneath a faded muslin gown that hung at the waist and dangled inches above her ankles—and pulled a threadbare cloak about her. "I'll be back soon," she whispered to Marcus, who was watching her dress with sleepy appreciation.

"Sooner," he said. "I can't bear to miss a moment."

She put one palm to his cheek in a last caress. "Today was the most glorious day of my life."

He blinked, drawing his brows together. "You're very serious all of a sudden."

She forced a wicked smile. "Dead serious, love. Now rest up. I'm a woman of high standards."

He nodded, relief flashing in his eyes. "I live to serve."

She kissed him hard, with all the promise she could never keep. Then she left him in her bed to wait for her return. On the way out, she furtively slipped his pistol into her pocket.

John and Petunia awaited her by their fire with a stranger.

"Oy," the wiry tinker man said, nodding vigorously. "That sounds like 'im alright. Small bloke, young face, deceivin'-like. Coughed like 'e were sick in the lungs. Soon as I 'eard the 'Say' tonight, I know'd him for the bloke in the story."

Julia was not surprised by the confirmation. She'd always known somehow, hadn't she?

The Chimera was alive.

"Me cousin was fixin' tin for a village in the north. That fellow were stayin' at the inn there and he come to 'Enry for a knife. He didn't 'ave no blunt for it, but damn if 'e didn't talk 'Enry out of it anyway. Same w' the innkeeper's wife. Talked her out o' payin' for 'is room and all—or maybe scared her out o' askin' for it."

The man shook his head. " 'E were a cold one, by all accounts. 'Enry said it strikes ye when he's walkin' away, like. Feels as if ye found a snake in yer boots."

Julia nodded. "Indeed." Her heart felt like a stone in her chest. The moment had come. No longer could she convince herself that it didn't matter. Now, there was no denying that she must have confirmation of her own.

If what she suspected was true, then she must act without regard to her own future. Every shred of information was needed if England had any hope of defeating the Chimera.

Her only hope was that she could rescue Marcus from the consequences. She must save him.

The Four—and England herself—needed him more than Julia had the right to.

She took the wiry man's hand in hers. "I cannot reward you for the information, as much as I wish to, but know that you have done a great service to us all."

The tinker stared down in awe at her elegant fingers wrapped about his blackened ones. "Th—that's all right, milady. You ain't but asked a question."

Julia smiled. "And you answered it." She bent forward to kiss the man's weathered cheek. "Thank you." She stood. "John, would you saddle my stallion for me, please?"

The little man put a shaking hand to his cheek. "*Cor*," he whispered. Petunia gave him a sympathetic pat on the shoulder.

"I know it," Petunia told him. "She's an angel, I tell you."

Julia turned away. An angel wouldn't walk away from the people who had helped her. An angel wouldn't do what she was planning to do with the stolen pistol in her pocket and the stolen horse John was leading toward her even now.

She felt something pressed into her hand. She looked down to see a small, worn purse, then looked up to see Petunia's watery smile.

"We had a bit saved up."

A very little bit, by the weight of the few coins in the purse. Julia closed her hand over the cracked leather. She was loath to take their savings, but she could not give in to sentiment now. Those paltry coins might make the difference in her success or failure.

She took the stallion's reins, ignoring the beast's irritated lipping at her hair. There was no time to indulge in oats now.

John tilted his head at her wagon. "What you want me to tell Himself?"

Julia bit her lip. She couldn't bear to face Marcus. He cared for her, she knew. Unfortunately, there was no possibility that his attachment could ever withstand the knowledge of who she truly was.

"Tell him to go to Barrowby. It holds everything he needs. Tell him to look beneath the lake." She turned away, then turned back. "Tell him . . . tell him to be happy."

Then she rode into the night, alone.

21

Why does contentment seem so possible in the moonlight, then so unattainable in the light of day?

A thunderous bellow broke the spell of sleep. Marcus stretched, wondering precisely when he'd become accustomed to waking to a lion's roar instead of a simple cock's crow or the rattle of a milk wagon on the cobbles.

Julia wasn't in the wagon. Marcus smiled. Off to tend to her giant tufted infant, no doubt. Then his grin faded as a few tiny anomalies came to his attention.

One, Julia had not woken him when she came back from seeing to Petunia.

Two, there was a strange silence about the wagon, as if he sat alone in a wood, not in a busy encampment.

Three, his pistol was not where he'd left it.

In seconds he was dressed and at the door. He thrust it open and bent his head to pass through. When he straightened outside, it was to see the two wagons and only the two wagons where the night before there had been dozens.

John Wald sat on the steps of the other wagon,

whittling listlessly at a piece of wood. He looked up at Marcus. "Morning, milord."

Marcus's jaw hardened. "She's gone, isn't she?"

John nodded. "Left in the night."

Marcus flicked his gaze about the littered clearing with its blackened fire rings. "With the others?"

John shook his head. "No, she left first. Happens like that sometimes. Fair folk can't help it, like a flock o' swallows. One flies off, the others fly, too, though they don't know why."

"But I heard Sebastian."

John scratched at his head with the tip of the knife. "The beasts left last. 'Bastian was just sayin' goodbye, like."

"Why did you stay?"

John shrugged. "Well, yer in me wagon. And Milady said t'give you a message."

Marcus waited. John blinked. "Well, now, first ye best listen to what I got to say to you. Ye won't like it, and Petunia says I'm oversteppin', but it needs sayin' just the same."

Marcus didn't think there was any way he was going to get Julia's message without listening, much as he wanted to wring if from John with his bare hands. He sank to sit on his own step and clasped his hands over one knee. "Go on then."

"You'd best watch yerself with her. Milady ain't like the rest of us. Never was. She used to act like it, and talk like it, but ye only had to look at her to know there was more. Sharp like a razor, that Jilly-girl. Rough as she might've been, she was fine underneath the dust— finer even than you."

"I'm aware that Julia has come a long way—"

John threw his abused stick to the ground. "Ye don't know nothin'! *Julia*." He spit. "That ain't even her name."

Marcus reached for patience. "I'm aware of that. Jilly—"

John snorted in disgust. "'Jill' just means 'girl' among the fair folk. You think you got her all pinned down? You think you're the mighty lord lying with the travelin' girl after she cleaned up a bit?"

Although that was a crude but accurate summation, at least in terms of social status, Marcus narrowed his eyes. "You mentioned overstepping'?"

John stood and shoved his knife back into his belt, obviously exasperated. "Petunia were right. Thick as a plank. You got to figure this one out by yerself."

John folded his arms over his wide chest. "Milady said for you to go t' Barrowby, that everything you need is there. She said to look under the lake. She said for you to be happy." John spit again. "Now get out of me wagon and be on yer way . . . milord."

Barrowby. *Everything you need is there.*

She'd left him. He could not blame her for tearing herself away, for it struck so deep to be the one left.

Be happy. How could he be happy when "everything" did not include Julia?

Or ever would.

Once Julia reached London, she left her exhausted mount in the last affordable hostelry before entering the boundaries of Mayfair. Then she pulled the hood of her cloak up and ventured out. Her hood covered her

face, and the foul weather made her concealment un-
surprising.

She had known this moment might come since she'd
received the drawing of the Chimera provided by the
Liar's Club. She'd hoped she was mistaken, for he
looked no older than she did now. So she'd convinced
herself it was a chance resemblance, and prayed the reports of his death were true . . . and searched for him
anyway, just in case.

Now she dared not let the matter rest any longer. If
he wasn't dead, how could he have survived? How
could he be so mystically forever young, forever powerful?

She had to know for certain so she was taking her
evidence to the artist herself, the one who originated
the sketch, someone who had seen and come into close
contact with the valet named Denny.

There was no one to send in her stead, for she could
not chance her friends being captured, and she must keep
Marcus as far from this matter as possible . . . for now.
She dreaded to see the inevitable revulsion in his eyes.

Her walk into Mayfair proved uneventful.

She bought a tatty covered basket from a scullery
maid on an errand—one more than happy to take Julia's price.

That, along with a slump and a creaking voice, was
the only disguise she needed.

She knocked at the front door of Etheridge House.
A grizzled man with a military bearing opened the
door. The Sergeant, of course. His eyes narrowed immediately. "State your business, madam."

Julia offered the basket. "Is this the lady's moggie,

sir?" She made sure her quavering voice carried. "I found it in the street outside, hurt bad."

"Oh, what a pity," the Sergeant said without conviction. "But these things do happen." He moved to shut the door on Julia.

"Marmalade?" A woman's voice came from behind the butler and then a pretty face popped around him, brow wrinkled in concern. "Or is it one of the kittens? Oh, it doesn't matter—come in, come in!"

The small, dark stout Lady Etheridge pushed the butler aside with ease. "You won't get rid of my darlings that easily, Sergeant!" She dragged Julia into the closest parlor where a fire cheerily fought the chill outside. Taking the basket, the lady knelt at the hearth to open it.

Finding it full of nothing but a rag-wrapped rock, Lady Etheridge, once Clara Simpson, anonymous political cartoonist and now the bride of one of the most dangerous men in England, turned to find herself at the point of a pistol.

Clara's gaze immediately shot to the door. Julia shook her head quickly. "I locked it. The Sergeant didn't seem inclined to stay."

"He doesn't care for cats," Lady Etheridge said faintly. She rose slowly, her hands pressed protectively over her belly, her features gone ashen.

Julia felt sick. She ought to have remembered that Lady Etheridge was increasing. She felt doubly guilty for frightening the woman with her empty pistol. She lowered the firearm slightly. "I do not wish to harm you, my lady. I need information, that is all."

"I have no doubt you do." Clara raised her chin. "I will not aid the French, no matter what the cost."

Julia sighed. "Neither will I, my lady." She raised the hood and dropped it down her back. "Now please stop being stupidly valiant and listen to me. I need to know more about the Chimera."

Clara's eyes widened and her fingers twitched. "You are quite lovely. Have you ever had your portrait done?"

Julia snorted. "Only an artist would think a thing like that at a time like this."

Clara waved a hand. "In my experience, if you haven't shot me yet, you probably aren't going to." She pressed the other hand to the small of her back. "Do you mind if I sit?"

"If you are so accustomed to being at gunpoint, then go right ahead." Julia pocketed her useless pistol with amusement.

"Lady Barrowby—"

Julia flinched. Clara smiled slightly. "I saw a sketch of you, by one of my best students. You aren't going to kill anyone, Lady Barrowby, unless perhaps it's that idiot Liverpool." Clara's eyes brightened. "That isn't your plan, by any chance?"

Julia laughed shortly. It became a bit damp at the last. "I don't want anyone dead but the Chimera."

Clara nodded, subsiding. "Yes, of course, as do we all."

Julia shook her head. "My lady, you have no idea." She sat opposite Clara and leaned forward urgently. "The Chimera lived in your household for months, serving his lordship's nephew Collis Tremayne. I need to know everything, every insignificant thing you remember about his habits and his mannerisms."

Clara frowned slightly. "He was in his Denny

persona," she said. "I'm sure he's dropped that disguise by now." She laced her hands over one knee. "Let's see . . ." Her gaze went vacant. "He disliked women of all classes, that was something he was not able to hide. Little Robbie Cunnington told me once that he heard Denny cursing in French, but I assumed Denny was only being pretentious."

That was not reassuring. Julia felt her carefully constructed doubt begin to crumble. "And what of his appearance? You are an artist. You notice things others do not."

"I always thought his hair was a bit thin for a fellow his supposed age, but that does happen to an unfortunate few. And life on the streets can age one's face. I thought little of the lines around his eyes and mouth."

Julia felt her stomach clench. "If you were to guess at his true age, according to your observations?"

"He could be as old as forty-five, as young as twenty, I suppose." Clara shrugged, frustrated with herself. "I saw so little of him, for he served Collis exclusively—" She frowned. "Then again, he always seemed to be about, didn't he? We all feel terribly stupid, you know."

Swept by new certainty, Julia shook her head. "He is entirely brilliant and deeply diabolical. You would not be the first person to be hoodwinked by him."

"You sound as if you know him personally."

Julia glanced away. "I—I know I have no right to ask it of you, my lady, but I must beg you for your help." She reached into her neckline and withdrew the locket. She opened it and regarded her mother's face for the last time. She doubted she would be allowed to keep the locket in prison. Her father's she did not let her eyes linger on. She handed it to Clara. "Is this the man you knew as Denny?"

Clara took it and held it to the light of the lamp on the side table. After a long moment, she looked up, her eyes sharp. "This is your mother. The resemblance is extraordinary, but she was softer in her features."

Julia smiled sadly. "She was but sixteen in that portrait, sold in a political marriage to my father, who was but twenty years of age himself."

Clara looked back down at the locket, shaking her head in amazement. "He is so unchanged, even now in his forties. It is positively unnatural—it almost makes one believe in magic. Yet it is most assuredly him."

Julia closed her eyes. "You have no idea how much I hoped your analysis would be the opposite."

A deep voice came from behind Julia. "I was rather hoping for that myself."

Julia whirled, fumbling for the unloaded pistol in her pocket. Lord Etheridge stepped from the shadows, pointing his own—and undoubtedly loaded!—pistol at her heart. Julia went very still.

From beside her, Clara smiled fondly at her husband. "My knight has arrived. Hello, darling. You were right, those secret doorways came in very handily."

Keeping the pistol aimed, Lord Etheridge rounded the settee and pulled his wife close with one arm. "Are you well?" He breathed the question into her hair.

Julia felt a twist in her heart at the desperate worry in his husky voice. "I would never have—"

He shot Julia a fatal glare without lifting his face

from his lady's. "Lady Barrowby, I am a split second from ending your life. Do shut up."

Clara poked her husband in the chest with one finger. "Dalton, your manners. Her ladyship is here on important business."

"Then she ought to have come to the club. Coming here, tricking you, locking you in like this, locking the Sergeant out—I can only construe it as an attack." He looked a bit shamefaced. "I stole someone's horse to get back here faster. I pulled the poor bloke right off it."

Clara sighed. "Men." She looked at Julia. "He's right, you know. You should have gone to the club. Now he's going to be very unreasonable about all this."

"I had to be certain I would be heard. And I cherished the faint hope I might be able to bluff my way to escaping once more." Julia gazed at them both helplessly. "I needed *you*, Lady Etheridge, not Cunnington or Tremayne or—" She had a thought. "Or Elliot. He's the student you spoke of, isn't he? He's a Liar." She threw out her hands. "Dear God, is there a man in this world who *ever* tells the truth?"

Lord Etheridge pulled back the hammer of the pistol at her sudden motion. Lady Etheridge grabbed his cravat firmly in her fist to get his attention. "Don't you dare, Dalton Montmorency, or I vow I'll name the baby after Lord Reardon!"

Lord Etheridge winced. "Please, not that." He sighed and lowered the pistol slightly, carefully uncocking it. Julia could see that his lordship's first protective rage had faded. She doubted he would now be able to kill her in cold blood.

She hoped.

She held her open hands wide. "My lord, I did hold a pistol on your lady, but I swear to you that it is unloaded."

Clara's eyes narrowed. "Unloaded, is it? I should have hit you with the poker after all."

Julia sighed. "Don't worry, my lady. I'm sure I'll come to a very bad end anyway." She dragged a shaking hand over her frizzing hair. Her body ached from the brutal ride and at the moment her knees were like water. "I—"

"You need a cup of tea and one of the Sergeant's special teacakes," Clara said firmly. "Sit." She bustled to the door and unlocked it. "Sergeant, emergency rations, immediately," she barked into the hallway.

Julia sank back down on the settee, exhaustion and panic making her a bit giddy. "You make an excellent general, my lady."

Clara snorted and caressed her belly. "Too right. General Mummy. I intend to breed my own platoon."

"*Clara,*" Lord Etheridge said with stern embarrassment.

Clara propped both hands on her hips. "*Dalton,*" she imitated, glaring at him fondly.

They were so in love it shone from them like sunlight. Julia laughed, hiccupped, and abruptly began to cry. She held her breath and swiped angrily at her tears, but when Clara's concerned arms came about her, she couldn't hold it back any longer.

After far too long, she pushed back from Clara's embrace and drew a long, broken breath. She wiped her eyes with the handkerchief that had magically appeared in her hand and looked up to see a visibly uncomfortable

Dalton and Sergeant gazing uneasily about the room, everywhere but at her.

A short gasping laugh broke from her. "I shan't dissolve or anything, you know." She took a breath and straightened.

"There is work to be done. I have a great deal to tell you about my father."

Barrowby was just as Marcus had left it—and entirely changed.

The great house was dark and silent. Marcus's boot heels rang loudly on the marble floor of the entrance hall. The sound seemed to report forever through the chill and vacant halls.

For all its elegance, the place had the eerie feeling of a graveyard. It was dead without the opulent use of candles, without the buoyant energy of the oddment staff, without—

Without her.

He had been lost since the moment he'd seen her miniature and the vulnerability in those wide, gray eyes.

He'd done everything wrong. He'd lost all perspective, lost sight of his goal, lost himself in the beauty and warmth of her—

And yet here he was, the Fox. He'd won.

He caught a glimpse of himself in the sizable looking-glass which dominated the front hall. Even in the dimness, he looked every inch the lord and leader.

He turned away. *Liar.*

Yes, he'd lied. He'd lied to the Three when he hadn't told them immediately how to find Julia. He'd lied to

Julia when he'd pretended that all was well for that one perfect day. He'd lied to himself when he'd pretended he would be able to walk away afterward.

She'd known, obviously. She'd poured all her love into one day with him, then made his decision for him. Rescuing him from himself.

Again.

Wouldn't she make a marvelous Fox?

He threw his hat to the side table and ran a hand through his damp hair. "Shut it," he muttered.

What was done was done. She'd made her choice, and who could blame her for preferring a life on the road to putting herself in his hands.

When had he ever given her reason to trust him?

Yet she'd trusted him to be the Fox.

Under the lake.

The lake had been covered in mist when Marcus had ridden in. He didn't relish the idea of diving into it in search of the Fox's records.

Under the lake? Perhaps John Wald had mangled the message. It simply didn't make sense. Although submerging something in a lake would be an excellent way to hide it, how would one be able to preserve it properly? What about the constant use and referral to the files?

John must have mistaken Julia's words. Which left Marcus with nothing.

Too much to think on—too late at night—too heartsick to care . . .

He drew himself straight and blinked. He had duties to attend to. He must find the Fox's files and then he would make his way to Ravencliff. He had a difficult task before him. Never had a man taken over a seat without years of involvement with his mentor.

Marcus's estate on the moors was isolated. He would tend to his neglected estate matters and use the silence to absorb all that he had not learned at the Fox's side.

Julia's side.

Julia had truly been the Fox. With all her abilities and intelligence, Julia had been far, far more than an old man's mistake.

Or a younger man's regret . . .

For the rest of his life.

22

When I leave my lover behind, I never allow myself to look back. Perhaps I fear he won't be there after all.

Julia pulled her new borrowed—and much too short—wool coat about her.

"Are you sure you wouldn't like for me to find you something more . . ." Clara's brow wrinkled. "More fitting?"

Julia's lips twitched as she looked down at the dress and boots Clara had obtained from one of her taller housemaids. "I think this is perfectly appropriate for me." She flashed a brief grin at Clara. "I much prefer it to a nun's habit!"

Clara snorted. "Who wouldn't? That's just like Liverpool. A woman stirs from her designated place in the world and all he can think to do is to lock her away!"

Julia shook her head. "He isn't against women, Clara. He is against change—and that makes him much more dangerous."

Clara narrowed her eyes. "I think Mr. Underkind will have something to say about locking up women."

Julia straightened. "Clara, your fingers are twitching again."

Clara smiled and it was not a nice smile. "I can be rather dangerous myself, you know."

Julia pointed a finger at her. "No. No political cartoons about me or my fate. You must not ever let the Four think you know as much as you do. It isn't safe."

Clara tilted her head. "You might have been one of them. What would you do to me if you were?"

Julia drew a breath, then shrugged and answered honestly. "I would watch you like a hawk. If you did not show good sense and keep to your societal issues, I would probably recommend that the Four take steps to neutralize you."

Clara blinked. "Well . . . perhaps you made a good Fox, after all."

I helped take a throne from a king. Julia gazed at Clara evenly. "I made an *excellent* Fox."

Clara moved back a fraction. "Julia, you give me the most uncanny chill at times." Then she smiled. "I'm rather used to it, you know. Dalton is much the same."

"Your husband is very fortunate. He is the only member of the Four ever to step down—unless one counts Lord Liverpool stepping sideways to become Prime Minister."

Clara nodded. "Dalton misses it sometimes, I think. He was not the Cobra for long, but sometimes I think . . ."

"You think that he is the Cobra still." Julia sent her a sympathetic smile.

Clara smiled. "I suspect that Dalton always will be, a bit."

"Always will be what?"

Clara turned to smile at her lord where he loomed in the doorway. "Always will be a bit tardy, darling. We've been waiting for you."

"I took a moment to load your pistol for you, Lady Barrowby." Etheridge frowned at Julia. "I will give it to you as soon as my wife is no longer in the room."

Clara sighed. "You're never going to leave that be, are you, darling?"

"No," he said, his voice grim.

Julia raised a hand to divert the lover's quarrel that was brewing. "Clara, I more than deserve his suspicions. The pistol was uncalled for. I did not know you, or I would simply have asked for your help." She turned to Etheridge. "What will you say when you report this evening's events to the Four?"

Clara stepped forward. "Oh, Dalton won't—"

Julia glanced at her. "Of course he will. I would." She turned back to Etheridge, who didn't bother to mask the respect dawning in his eyes. "Will you give me time to get out of London?"

Etheridge nodded. "I cannot keep it a secret forever, but perhaps I can delay my report until you've had a chance to disappear again."

Julia nodded. "Do not wait long. The Four must have this information." She drew a breath and smiled at them both. "Thank you. I did not think I would have this chance."

This chance to run . . . forever. She would never be able to rest, never be able to live a true life—never be able to see Marcus, ever again.

Are you sure the nunnery isn't preferable?

But in the convent, she would be of no use. At least this way, possibly, she might still work for England, even if it was only in the collection of useful information by way of the traveling folk. Perhaps, in some small way, she might still be a shadow of the woman Aldus had taught her to be, who Marcus had loved, who—for a little while—had held the reins of a nation in her hands.

Clara embraced her quickly. "Go. Let us know how you fare."

Julia smiled, but she knew she wouldn't dare risk them that way. She had already put them in enough danger.

Etheridge was watching her closely. "Do not worry for us. We told you nothing. You gave Clara information, then disappeared before I could detain you. I hear you're quite crafty."

She nodded. "I hear the same about you. After all, you sent Elliot to me."

"I knew who Barrowby was from my days in the Four. When he died, I sent Elliot to find out the lay of the land. There is a practice of keeping the spymaster on an information string."

He gave a sour smile. "I have learned not to take everything the Four says on faith alone. There have been too many losses—and near losses—" He gazed at Clara with fierce love in his eyes. Then he turned back to Julia. "Like you, I keep my own avenues of intelligence open."

Leaving the warm circle of Lord and Lady Etheridge made Julia all the more aware of the cold outside. She regained her rested horse and picked her way down the back alleys of London, eager to be free of the city yet uncertain about where she might go next.

The only thing she was sure of was that the road to Barrowby was closed to her.

She rode the day away, traveling north up the Great Road, keeping alert for signs of the fair folk, though she saw none. She was not sure she could go back, in any case.

There must be somewhere in the world for her. She only wished she knew where it was.

She found herself on a northern road anyway and chastised herself for a fool. What did she think Derbyshire had to offer her? Other than the opportunity to be apprehended by the Royal Four.

Her cheerless thoughts were interrupted by the realization that the stallion had stopped his listless plodding and was now pulling at clumps of dry grass along the road. She pulled his head back. "You'll get your oats this evening," she said soothingly. If she let him have his head, she'd never be able to control him.

He was too much horse for a poverty-stricken traveler like her at any rate. She'd be better off selling him to the next hosteler she saw and bargaining for a less memorable mount.

But Marcus loves him so.

"Which has nothing to do with the price of apples," she told herself. If she needed to sell the horse, she would do as she must. She simply didn't see the need to sell him quite yet.

She heard the clip-clop of hooves behind and looked back to see another soul on the road. Although this was a post road and was well used in most seasons, she'd not seen another person for hours on this grim evening.

Whoever it was had better places to be, apparently, for the mount was being pushed at a good steady clip. She decided to halt the stallion to let the rider pass, for the less time someone had to look at her on her very fine horse, the less chance they would remember her later.

The stallion took to the grassy bank with some relief and the other traveler came even with them in a few moments.

The other rider was huge, a giant man on a mount that was nearly the size of a draft horse. Julia felt a moment of natural caution at being alone on the road with such a person, until she noticed the scarred visage beneath the brim of the rough hat.

Then icy horror drenched her gut. Kurt, the Liar's Club assassin, was looking her right in the eye.

Julia looked down quickly, letting her cloak hood cover her eyes. Her hair was covered and her outsized clothing completely disguised her shape. If she was lucky, Kurt the Cook would think her no more than a rather stout old woman.

The larger mount passed with a horsy whicker of greeting and Julia could hear the distance growing between them by the hoofbeats. She held her breath and her fear in a tight grip until she could no longer hear the other mount.

Only then did she risk looking up.

The giant rider had halted his mount in the middle of the road and was staring back at her. Even as she watched, he turned his mount completely and kicked it into a gallop.

No.

Her booted heels hit the stallion's sides with every ounce of power she had in her and the horse spun about and shot forward with a surprised squeal, stretching his high-blooded legs out in an ears-back gallop that stole the breath from Julia's lungs.

She lay low on his back and tangled her fingers into his mane. She was smaller and lighter and her mount was of racing stock—*oh, God, give me wings!*—but Kurt could pin a fly at fifty paces with one of his throwing knives!

A smaller target has a better chance.

The thought had scarcely crossed her mind before she was out of the saddle and hanging on the far side of the stallion's great lunging body with only one leg crooked over his back. He started and nearly slowed at the peculiar shift of her weight.

"Yah!" she screamed, nearly in his delicate ear. He flinched and put on more power, probably hoping to leave his mad rider behind. She clung to his side like a flea and lifted her head to see behind them.

The giant charger was matching their pace, despite Kurt's greater weight. She couldn't believe it. If any horse could outrun the assassin's powerful mount it would be Marcus's stallion. Kurt had likely been riding at a good pace all day to have reached her so soon after Lord Etheridge had reported her location to the Four.

How Marcus must have hated making that choice—and yet he'd made it. He truly was a better Fox, for she was not sure she could have killed someone she cared for, no matter what sort of security risk they posed.

Unfortunately, she wasn't going to live long enough to answer that question. The stallion was maintaining his powerful gallop, but so was the charger. No advantage gained, just an exhausting race of equals until her horse dropped dead and Kurt killed her.

A lunatic giggle bubbled up from Julia's aching lungs. Oh, dear. She had that Jilly feeling again.

Then again, what had she to lose?

She put herself to rights in the saddle and urged the stallion off the road, sending him leaping wildly into the wood.

She didn't look back, although she knew from the crashing hoofbeats behind her that she was being followed. She kept low, praying that she and the stallion could squeak through the forest and lose her much larger pursuers.

Unfortunately, the wood began to thin and she found herself racing through open pastureland. The stallion took stone wall after stone wall, uphill and down, racing through herds of sheep whose bahing protest was lost in the wind. Still the assassin kept pace.

The stallion began to tire, and in an act of desperation, Julia set him to a wall too high for the draft horse to manage.

It was too high for the stallion as well. They went down, taking much of the wall with them. Julia threw herself to one side. The horse landed hard and tumbled. Julia landed badly. Agony shot up from her ankle.

The big horse leaped easily through the gap they'd made in the wall and came to a puffing halt before her. She scrambled back desperately, unable to run, unable to even cry for help that wasn't there. The giant assassin dismounted and turned to walk toward her.

A gunshot came from nowhere at all.

The assassin froze. His eyes widened and he gazed at her with stern surprise. "Weren't goin' to kill y—"

He fell facedown in the grass. His sturdy mount started and reared at the thud.

Julia couldn't believe it. For a long moment, utter silence reigned. Then, as her shock faded, she began to crawl toward him. Whatever he'd been attempting, Kurt was a valuable and loyal soldier of England. He might not be dead. She must get to him—

"A fair bird caught in my net." A pair of very clean but worn boots stepped into her vision.

"Oh, thank God!" Julia looked up. "You must help that man—"

The bottom fell from the world. Day turned to night, good switched to evil, the dead walked the earth.

Or at least, one dead man walked the earth.

"Now why would I render assistance when it was I who shot him?" He knelt before her, a slight smile on his rounded face. "Pretty bird. So like your mother." He reached to gently stroke a lock of fallen hair from her face. It *was* him.

Pure shock froze her too thoroughly to flinch away when his fist slammed into her jaw.

23

The halls of Barrowby can be so dark and chill in winter. How glad I am not to be alone here.

Julia woke to the smell of coffee. Someone pressed a cup to her lips and she groggily took a sip. Strong and sweet and full of milk, the way her Parisian mother had made it for her as a child—

She opened her eyes in surprise, only to see *him*. She jerked back, turning her face away. She spat the offending coffee from her mouth. She wanted nothing from him.

Then again, it didn't seem as though he were in a giving mood, for she realized that she was tied to a bed in a shabby room with the anonymous air of a cheap boardinghouse. She was sitting up against the headboard and her hands were tied to each post. Her ankles were also bound and there was a rope around her middle anchoring her tightly.

She was helpless in the presence of evil.

Panic threatened to consume her, leaching the strength from her spine and the starch from her soul.

"You are more beautiful than she."

Julia's fear burned away like paper as pure rage erupted in her heart. She lifted her gaze to the bastard who stood by the bed. "You know nothing of beauty. All you know is evil."

He smiled. "Harsh words when we have only just met."

Julia didn't take her hot gaze from his. "I've known your wickedness for years. It isn't too difficult to recognize it when I see it formed in flesh."

"Lovely *and* observant. That is useful." He walked to a rickety table across the room and set the coffee upon it. Then he turned to regard her with cool consideration. "Yet much too intractable for my purposes."

Julia tilted her head. "It seems I was born that way."

"You've been given your head much too often, I see. Still, twenty-three years is but a moment." He flicked away her life with his fingers. "It might take some time to retrain you to proper obedience, but I find I am at a loose ends presently." He smiled. It was like ice down her spine. "I believe I am looking forward to it."

"You're going to beat me into *submission*?" Julia felt wild laughter rising within her. "Oh, dear, I hope you have nowhere to be in the immediate future!"

Her defiance clearly angered him. A voice within cautioned her, but Jilly was back at the reins. "You probably ought not to break my jaw," she said conversationally. "I require a great deal of feeding. And of course, if you want to keep the 'lovely' intact, you probably should stay away from my face altogether."

His eyes narrowed slightly. She went on cheerily. "I'm simply trying to help, you understand. Let's see . . ." She gazed at the cobweb-strung ceiling as she mused. "Whipping might leave permanent marks . . . and broken arms and legs never do seem to heal straight . . ."

His fist crashed into her stomach. She bent double, sagging from her bindings as she wheezed.

The next strike caused her to vomit on her gown. The following blows strung together like a nightmare until she thankfully lost consciousness at last.

Standing on the cold, gray shore of Barrowby's lake, Marcus was beginning to feel the impossibility of taking over for the Fox. It seemed that the key to all the Fox's intelligence was locked away in Julia's mind, for there was nothing in the house, nothing on the grounds, nothing contained within the boundaries of Barrowby.

Now it seemed there was nothing under the lake as well. Marcus had hired several sturdy fellows from the village to swim the chill water in search of the records of the Fox, even taking to the water himself until his bones ached and his fingers wrinkled.

Then he'd had the bloody thing dragged. Boats pulled a heavy iron rake along the bottom, finding the bones of livestock, wildlife and a few people, but nothing that could possibly contain written records. Barrowby itself seemed to mock him, winter dead and unbeautiful as it was.

"Sorry, milord. Whatever you're lookin' for, 'tisn't there." The village smith, who'd forged the rake for Marcus, gazed dolefully at the pile of debris dragged from the lake.

Of course, the man's sympathy and sorrow might

have much to do with missing out on the obscenely
high reward Marcus had offered to the man who found
the "object."

Marcus clapped the big smith on the back. "My
thanks anyway." He turned to walk away from the fruit-
less effort.

"Milord?" The smith caught up with him. "Milord,
is our lady coming back to us?"

Marcus stopped. "The search for the heir of Barrowby is still underway," he hedged. "I'm sure you'll
have a master in place soon."

He moved on. The smith stubbornly kept pace.

"But our lady—do you know if all is right w'her? She
wouldn't leave us without a farewell, not if all was well."

Oh, really? Seems to me she makes a habit of it.

The smith went on, but Marcus put his head down
and strode away. He couldn't bear to gaze into one
more inquiring face, to look into one more set of wondering eyes.

Where is our lady?

He could show them, if they cared to look, for she
was everywhere. She sat in the front parlor, she was in
the stables—she haunted Barrowby like a specter. Her
scent lingered in the halls and her gamine smile shim-
mered just out of his vision.

She danced in the temple in the barren garden, kissing him back with sharp and surprising hunger. She
walked the front hall, her brow crinkled, telling him
that Elliot was missing. She stood on her balcony in
the night, her lovely face raised to the stars with the
wind cooling her flush.

Where is our lady?

He didn't know. He didn't want to know. Wherever she was, he wished her free and happy. For himself, even his ascension to the Four was simply another dreary day in what looked to be a long and colorless future, his achievement tainted with guilt and loss and mind-bending regret.

A band tightened about his chest as he remembered her last words to him. *"Today was the most glorious day of my life."*

One bloody day. One in which he'd spent much of his time covered in privy diggings and lion spittle. The hell of it was, there was no denying the fact that it had been the best damned day he'd ever known.

So where did that leave him—other than alone?

"Milord, you have a visitor!"

Or perhaps not as alone as all that.

It was Elliot, but a completely different man from the effete dandy Marcus had previously known. Soberly clad in black, with only the deep blue of his weskit to break the darkness, he was a far cry from the peacock of old.

Elliot performed a crisp bow. "Good afternoon, my lord." Gone were the languid gestures and the heartfelt ennui.

Marcus regarded him with some amusement. "Nice weskit."

Elliot's lips twitched, showing a hint of the old version. "Thank you, my lord. I thought you'd like it."

"So the other rig was courtesy of a certain valet?" The fastidiously stylish Button served former spymaster Simon Raines but also did his duty as costumer for the Liar's Club, a fact the Liars sometimes secretly lamented.

Secretly, for Button was known to take vengeance on anyone who criticized his flair for fashion. Marcus shook his head in sympathy. "What did you do to deserve that?"

Elliot made a face. "I'd rather not say, my lord. He might be listening even now."

Marcus laughed. "So you're here as yourself. To make your report directly to me? That isn't procedure."

"No, my lord. The Gentleman asked me to convey his apologies personally."

The Gentleman was Lord Etheridge's code name among the Liars. "Apologies? For stepping on the toes of my investigation?"

"I was here first," Elliot pointed out.

Marcus grinned. "So this apology goes more like 'Why the hell don't you lot ever tell us anything? How are we supposed to operate if you keep us in the dark?'"

Elliot bowed his head slightly. "Well done. That was nearly word for word."

"So you must be one of the recent additions to the club. I received that file shortly before—" *Before I met Julia.* He halted himself. "I see that I should have read it more carefully."

"I graduated shortly after the Tremaynes," Elliot said. "I am specializing in infiltration."

"You're very good at it," Marcus said with a laugh. "I suspect your 'Elliot-the-dandy' will be making many appearances in the future."

Elliot sighed. "Now I've done it, haven't I? I'll be wearing poison-green weskits for the rest of my career."

"It could be worse. I've heard that valet is very fond of rosy hues."

"Pink." Elliot closed his eyes briefly. "I must be very nice to him, I can see."

Marcus let Elliot into the study and shut the door. "Now, tell me what you really came to say."

"It concerns Lady Barrowby. Have you found her again, my lord?"

Marcus worked his jaw. "At the moment, her ladyship is still at large." He most seriously hoped she stayed that way—invisible.

Elliot rubbed the back of his neck. "My lord, I wish I could ask this more delicately—"

"Speak," Marcus ordered, his tone dangerous. "Do not dance about with me."

Elliot nodded shortly. "Very well, then. I informed the Gentleman that you and Lady Barrowby were engaged in an affair. His response was to wonder—" Elliot hesitated.

Marcus didn't move a muscle, but his expression turned to stone. "The spymaster wished to know if I am in love with Julia. What did you tell him?"

Elliot drew a breath. "I told him that I had never seen a man more so, not even himself. And might I add that Lord Etheridge is most infatuated with his lady."

"I know," Marcus muttered. "They're obnoxiously blissful." He spread his hands. "I cannot deny it."

"Indeed. Upon which the Gentleman sent me to inquire of you . . . what would you do if you learned that Lady Barrowby—and this is purely hypothetical, you understand—if you learned she was indeed highborn?"

"I have never doubted Julia's innate quality, but—"

"Er, perhaps I should have said *very* highborn."

Marcus stopped. "Julia?"

Riding astride, more centaur than horse and rider. Rolling with him in the leaves, as uninhibited as a wood nymph. Laughing with all her being, flopped back on the sofa in the parlor.

Passionate about her people. Devoted to the Four.

Loyal and steadfast to the end.

"I would say I am entirely unsurprised." Marcus lifted a brow. "Hypothetically."

"Would you consider asking her for her hand in marriage—hypothet—"

Marcus interrupted. "I already did, most forcefully."

"Ah. The Gentleman wondered about that. In which case his lady wished me to ask if you remembered to tell her you love her first?"

A jolt went through Marcus. "Of course I did! I'm sure I did." He blinked. "I . . . I don't think I did."

"Her ladyship surmised as much. I am now commanded to call you an idiot." Elliot shrugged, a gleam of his earlier self rising in his eyes. "My apologies, but I was under orders."

Marcus passed a hand before his eyes. "She's right. I am an idiot. That was not the cause of her decision. She knew she'd risk imprisonment or death if she came back with me."

Elliot gazed at him pityingly. "And did it occur to you that she might need a reason that would make coming back worth the risk?"

Marcus felt his jaw drop.

Elliot shook his head. "The fact that you already proposed leads me to the third command. Only on that condition was I ordered to show you this." He strode to the mantel and pressed the upper right three of the carved roses there. With a click, a panel of the wall—which had a painting of the lake—came loose and slowly swung their way. Marcus gaped. "How did you know about this?"

Elliot looked over his shoulder with a grin. "Liar secret. And Lady Barrowby told the Gentleman."

He reached in to extract a leather-bound folder of an unusual green color. "I believe this is the one."

Marcus took it and opened it to remove the contents. He took them to the lamp and began to examine them. "This is a record of a Liar's Club investigation more than six years old—" His eyes widened at what he read. After he'd consumed every word, he gazed up at Elliot in astonishment and growing fear.

"We must find her at once."

24

*If I never again felt the embrace of another's arms, I
should despair indeed.*

Marcus and Elliot had scarcely mounted their horses
and begun to gallop down the drive when they saw a
rider coming from the other direction at a mad, break-
neck speed. When the rider, a scrawny fellow mounted
on a giant charger, reached them he fell to the gravel as
if he couldn't bow to them fast enough.

"Pardon, milords, pardon—" he panted. "I come
from Kettigrew village, up the north road—I've a
message—the man, 'e said 'e'd wring my neck if 'n I
didn't deliver it—'e will, too, milords! 'E's mad,
milords, stark raving mad!"

Elliot glanced at Marcus. "One of your friends, perhaps?"

Marcus sent him an impatient glare. "More like one
of yours." He turned to the messenger. "We have no
time for this—"

"That's Kurt's horse," Elliot said abruptly. "It's the
only one in our stable that will carry him!"

"Again, I have no time for the cares of that lot." Marcus reined his horse around the messenger, who watched him with the despair of a man sure of his own impending doom. "If you want to chase down mad assassins," Marcus told Elliot, "then that is your concern."

"Marcus, don't be a fool. Kurt is rarely employed within England herself. What target do you think he might have been aimed toward—in this locale, at this moment in time?"

An icy shaft went through Marcus. *Julia.* He turned his horse about to face the messenger.

"What is this communiqué?"

The man cowered before the intensity in Marcus's expression, but apparently he feared the giant Kurt more so.

" 'E ain't dead."

Marcus clenched his jaw. "Happy to hear it." He began to turn his horse toward the road—and Julia—once more.

" 'E orta be, after 'e were shot like that."

"Shot? Kurt?" Elliot's shock was apparent.

Marcus sighed and returned to the conversation, such as it was. "This surprises you? I rather think it's the sanest possible reaction to the man."

The messenger nodded fervently. "Too right, milord."

"So he'll recover?" Elliot pressed the man.

Marcus could not have cared less for the merciless Kurt's welfare at the moment. "Did he tell you what he was doing in this vicinity?"

The messenger looked back and forth at the two of them, then apparently decided that Marcus was the more menacing.

" 'E said he come to find a lady—and he found her—"

"What?"

The man shrank and began to edge away. " 'E said 'e found her, then someone shot 'im and took her away."

"Oh, thank God!"

The messenger seemed unsure. "I don't know, milord. 'E—the giant—'e were real worried about the lady. 'E said to tell you—to tell you—"

"To tell me what?" Who could be more danger to her than Kurt himself?

" 'E said to tell you that Denny got 'er."

Denny. The Chimera. Marcus sent one anguished glance at Elliot, who returned it in equal measure.

They turned their mounts as one and raced down the drive, lying low and letting the gravel fly. Marcus had only one thought that echoed beneath the pounding hoofbeats and the racing of his dread-filled heart.

What if I'm too late?

In Kettigrew, they found that Kurt wasn't merely shot, he'd nearly died. If a passing shepherd hadn't paused to investigate a freshly collapsed stone wall, he'd never have spotted the large man lying in the rubble.

Kurt's great mount had lingered nearby, which was fortunate for Kurt, since no other horse could have carried his limp hugeness down the hill to the village of Kettigrew, where the local midwife was able to remove the bullet and stop the wound.

Even so, in her words, "Tha fallow orta died."

From what Marcus could see past the wild hair and the overgrown beard, the mighty Kurt was looking ill indeed.

Elliot immediately went to the large man's side. "Kurt? Kurt, can you hear me?"

Marcus hung back, seized by an abrupt wave of rage as he looked at the massive hands lying limply on the covers. Julia had been in those hands.

She knew what Kurt was. She would have known the minute she saw him what his intentions would be. Marcus couldn't bear it. He pushed past Elliot to grab the giant by the front of his hastily pieced together nightshirt.

"She ran from you, didn't she, you vast bastard!" he shook Kurt in his rage, lifting the man half from the bed. "She knew you'd come to kill her, didn't she? Who sent you?" He leaned into Kurt's hairy face. "Who sent you?"

Elliot pulled at his arm. "Marcus, let him go! Good God, the man's half dead!"

Marcus turned his head to snarl at Elliot. "He'll be full dead if he doesn't speak," he growled.

"Didn't . . ."

Both Marcus and Elliot jerked their gazes back to the man in the bed. Elliot pushed Marcus away to lean over the bed. "Didn't what, Kurt?"

"Didn't come . . . to kill 'er. Come to find 'er . . . bring 'er back . . . Himself said not to kill 'er lessen I must."

Marcus shoved past Elliot's restraining arm. "Who? Who told you to find her? Etheridge?"

A massive hand wrapped itself around Marcus's upper arm. "Shut . . . up . . . milord. Don't matter. Denny . . . took 'er away . . .'e was talkin' to himself . . . she were out . . .'e thought I were out . . . she's 'is ticket 'ome, he says. She's got to give 'im the money.' Passage to France, passage back to his true life' . . . that's what 'e said."

Kurt's hand fell away and his voice began to fade. "'e were real happy 'bout it. Enough to give a bloke the shivers . . ."

"What else? Where did he take her?" Marcus grabbed Kurt again, but Elliot pulled him off.

"He's out, Marcus. Come on. We know enough."

Marcus blinked, trying to marshal his chaotic emotions and teeming thoughts. *Money. Passage.*

There was only one place where the Chimera could expect to gain both the money from Julia's accounts and illegal passage to France.

Marcus straightened. "London."

"What are we going to do?"

Marcus clenched his jaw. "We're going to shout 'Hey, Rube!' "

In the small filthy room above the crowded London Street, Julia feared she was going to lose her will to continue fighting. How could she defeat him? She could not, she realized. There would never be enough power for her to defeat him. She began to doubt everything, her strength, Aldus's confidence in her, her own mind, Marcus's love, everything.

She might doubt Marcus's feelings for her, but her own love for him was a shining light. She understood his difficulty, she didn't blame him for his conflict. He would make a good Fox, a fine and effective Fox, while she was fast beginning to doubt everything that had ever made her think she could do it.

The cracks in the ceiling plaster seemed to waver before Julia's vision. He was starving her now— although if he knew how out of sorts she became when she wasn't properly fed, he might have reconsidered. She struggled to focus her vision on the largest crack, the one she'd named the Thames. It meandered from one side of the grimy room to the other across the stained ceiling.

Once she'd properly brought it into focus, she turned her attention to the lesser tributaries. One by one, she forced her eyes to obey her enough to make them come clear. The Fleet, the Tyburn, the Westbourne, the Black Ditch . . .

Julia sighed. Her body ached and her head throbbed. She would have rolled over onto her stomach, but the chain didn't allow it. She had only the slack she required to lie on the bed and to use the chamber pot.

He hadn't enjoyed cleaning up after the first beating he'd given her and had been forced to change her situation to prevent more offenses to his fastidious nature.

She barked a dry, coughing laugh. Odd for a man who blew up privies.

"Oh, Aldus, I've properly let you down this time," she whispered to the rivers above her. "You were wrong about me. I tried to tell you, but men never listen, do they? You were wrong and Liverpool and Marcus and the others were right. I don't have the strength needed to be one of the Royal Four."

She blinked and drew a harsh breath, looking about her carefully. She'd slipped again. Thank heaven *he* wasn't around to hear her.

Abruptly tears began to leak from the corners of her

eyes. "See?" she whispered. "I'm nothing but a silly girl after all, crying about nothing."

She was weakening by the hour, she could feel it. She was like the child with his thumb in the dike, holding back the flood of information inside of her. Sooner or later, he was going to realize that she was more than a simple widow—probably because she was going to stupidly let something slip—and he was going to get every single thing she knew from her with ease.

When he'd beaten her this morning, she'd ached to cry out the truth, just to make him stop for a moment, just long enough for her to take a breath. If she'd had an ounce of air in her lungs, she would have.

She was a danger to England, just as Liverpool had said. She was nothing but a weakling, best kept locked away in silence because she wouldn't be able to keep her stupid mouth shut much longer!

She slid her feet to the floor and shakily stood. She couldn't allow herself to lie about. It would only make her weaker. She set herself to the task of walking from the reach of the chain, by the bed, to the other reach of the chain, by the window.

She extended her body and reached for the sill yet again, but her arms had not grown in the last hour, nor had the chain stretched. She would have broken the glass and screamed for help long ago if she could have, although from the rough sounds coming from outside and from the other rooms, she didn't know if anyone would even notice another woman screaming.

Certainly no one had heard her yet.

She stood on tiptoe, pulling her full weight against the chain. If she stood just so, she could see people on

the street below. She would have to stop after a few
moments, for the strain on her wrenched shoulder
would become too much to bear, but someone, just
once, might look up into her window. Some curious
soul might see her signaling madly up in her tower and
come to find out about the madwoman in the window.

Unlikely, but not impossible. She was quite prepared to cling to even that slim hope.

Her vision swam and her knees weakened. She
blinked rapidly, pulling herself together with will alone.
She hadn't eaten in . . . three days? It didn't matter anyway. She would eat when she ate. That was not currently under her control, so there was little point in
worrying about it.

Although, when next she ate, she first planned on
having all the bangers and mash one woman could
hold—

Igby walked down the street beneath her window.

Julia blinked, then shook her head. No, it couldn't—

It was, plain as day. He was stopping a washer-
woman with her heavy basket, showing her a paper—a
sketch, probably, for there wasn't a soul within miles
of here who could read—and listening closely to the
woman, who shook her head regretfully.

"Igby!" Julia screamed. Her voice could not penetrate the glass and the street clamor outside. She cast
about for something, anything—

The chamber pot! In less time than it took to think
about it, Julia had grabbed up the filthy thing and flung
it fully through the glass. *"Igby!"*

Her voice was lost in the outcry outside from the people doused with the contents of a well-used chamber

pot. Igby turned to watch what must have been quite the contretemps, then lifted his gaze to see where the object had originated from.

Julia pulled so hard against the chain that it cut into her flesh. "Igby! *Igby!*" She waved wildly as close to the glass as she could manage. She saw him hesitate for a moment, saw his gaze pass incuriously over her broken window, and then saw him turn and amble away, out of her limited sight.

No. Don't go. Gray flecks surrounded Julia's vision and she sank to her knees, her bleeding wrist still stretched out behind her. *No.*

The raucous Cheapside streets seemed sinister, as if every beggar and baker were conspiring against the search for Julia with their jostling and commotion. Marcus fought the despair clawing at his throat. He knew she was near, for they'd tracked the hired cab that had carried a small kindly faced man and his ailing wife thus far.

Knowing that he was in the exact area they had been dropped off should have been a comfort, but as he looked about the crowded twisting ancient streets and the hordes of Londoners who gazed suspiciously at his fine clothes, Marcus wondered how one set about finding the single silver pin in a case of tin ones.

Julia would have won the lifelong loyalty of every Cockney within miles by the time the bells of St. Mary-le-bow chimed the hour and found her quarry in half that.

Marcus had taken Elliot's drawing of her to every shopkeeper and resident and ragman he could find, as

had the old staff of Barrowby, roused by his unabashed
cry for help in the square in Middlebarrow.

Even now, Meg the cook, Beppo and the Igbys were
working other streets in this festering pit of humanity,
all carrying hasty sketches of the round-faced man and
their lost lady.

If she was here, she would be found.

Yet the growing dread in Marcus's soul would not
be appeased by hope or common sense. He'd lost her
too many times—the last because she didn't trust him.

And now she was slipping away in earnest . . . he
could feel the very fibers of their bond deteriorating.
He closed his eyes. *No. I cannot let you go.*

Someone bumped him and moved on without apology. Marcus could hardly breathe for the fetid odors of
these churning back streets. Slop ran down the center
of the lane as if they lived four hundred years ago. The
shouting and clanging and rumbling of coarse humanity swirled about him as he stood immobile as a rock in
a muddy river.

Or perhaps it was sheer panic stealing the air from
his lungs. She was here, in the hands of a brutal, ruthless killer, and he ought to be able to find her, to feel
her, to sense her very heartbeat. If love was enough, he
would fly directly to her side.

He'd seen the work of the Chimera, the wreckage of
the ranks of the Liar's Club, the cold-blooded murder
of the master's own pawns when their usefulness
ended. He knew how ruthless the man could be—and
yet he'd let Julia ride away from him, alone and vulnerable, kept from following her by his own stupid pride.

He could scarcely remember being that man now.

His pride was gone, swept away by regret and agonizing fear for her.

Elliot left a tobacconist's shop and joined Marcus at the foot of the church steps. "The fellow took a quid for information, then told me he hadn't seen either one of them." Elliot shook his head. "It doesn't matter," Marcus said. "It's only gold."

He half-closed his eyes and turned his head slowly, trying to sense her presence. The only thing he sensed was his own growing dread. He worked his jaw, willing himself to regain his cool objectivity, but there was no such thing where Julia was concerned and never had been.

"That's all right then," Elliot said. He patted Marcus awkwardly on the shoulder. "We'll find her yet."

Marcus looked down at the hand on his jacket. From a distance, he recognized the comfort Elliot was offering, but he could not feel it. All he could feel was a great aching void inside him.

Julia.

Julia opened her eyes. *Diamonds.*

She blinked. No, not diamonds. Only broken glass, fallen from the window to the wooden floor on which she lay. She reached for a brightly glinting shard of it—

Red agony from her wrenched shoulder stabbed through her. She gasped and rolled toward the fetters, desperate to ease the strain. It was a long moment before she could do anything but breathe in and out. Then the memory of watching her last hope walk away brought her to tears once again.

After a moment, she drew a deep breath and wiped her face on her sleeve. "Silly infant." She pushed herself into a sitting position and began to work her shoulder carefully. "You've only stiffened up a bit, which is what you deserve for fainting on the floor like a rag doll."

The glittering shards of glass caught her eye once more. The window was entirely shattered, the mullions between the panes snapped and bent as well. There would be no hiding it.

"Well, he's certainly going to kill you now." The thought did not bring her much unhappiness. If she was dead, then he certainly wouldn't be able to get the secrets of the Royal Four from her—

If she was dead. Her breath caught and her vision fixed on the triangle of glass closest to her. She reached for it with a shaking hand. It was unthinkable—yet, here she was, thinking it, so obviously it was at least worth contemplating. If she drew the glass across her wrists—no, better across her throat, for she wouldn't want it to take long—

She ought to have let Kurt do it. He was a professional. It probably wouldn't even have hurt. She was going to make a muck of it, no doubt there, but surely it wasn't all that hard?

She dropped the shard into her numb hand where it lay in her lap, and pressed her other fingers to her throat. Her pulse was best found *there,* under her jaw. She felt it jump beneath her touch.

She took a last look at the gray sky and the grimy rooftops and then closed her eyes. She wrapped her fingers around the shard, disregarding the way it cut into her flesh. She lifted her hand.

Jilly, you must fight. You must always fight, even if it means giving in for a time. Fighting means forever trying to win, even when you know you can't.

Mama had fought, right to the last day, fighting for her breath, fighting for her last moment on the earth. Aldus had fought, years past when the doctor had said he was lost, fighting against the hand of death dragging him into darkness.

How dare she willingly reach for that hand?

The hand holding the shard shook. She gritted her teeth and pressed it harder to her skin. Blood began to drip down her wrist. *There.*

No. Perhaps Igby saw me. Perhaps someone is coming.

You are alone. No one is coming for you. You are forever alone.

Depressing but true enough. Then again, forever might not be much longer.

"*I cannot let you go.*"

Julia's eyes flew open. "Marcus?"

His voice had been so clear, so deep and real. There was no one there, of course. She was mad from lack of food. The beatings had disarranged her brains. She was completely alone.

"*I cannot let you go.*"

Marcus would not like what she was doing. Of course, if he himself ever even thought of such a thing, she would give him a tongue-lashing herself—

No, Marcus would fight to his last breath, just like Mama, just like Aldus.

She let her hand drop to her lap and gazed at it. The tip of the glass was clean and unbloodied. She opened her fingers to see several cuts on her palm and finger pads. The blood running down her arm was only a few drips, not her life's blood pooling on the carpet.

She gave a rusty giggle, her relief overwhelming. She was going to die, she had no doubt, but she was going to die fighting, and *that* she could live with.

She laughed out loud at that outrageous thought, just as the door to her room opened.

25

Is it possible to will yourself to be more intelligent, more capable—to be more?

Julia looked into the eyes of the devil and smiled. "Oh, dear," she said cheerfully. "You're still with us."

He shot a cold glance at the shattered window. "That was not wise. Get up. We must leave, quickly."

No. Leaving was a very bad idea. Her people were near and she still held her secrets close, but if he were to lock her away on a ship and continue his torture over a long passage, she was quite sure her strength would fail.

Julia shook her head. "Will you drag me screaming and fighting into the street? I don't think that even the masses of Cheapside would tolerate that easily." She smiled wider. "Besides, I think you are too late. I'm fairly sure I cannot stand at all."

"That would be a pity. I had plans for you. I have waited here in England for so long. At first I waited out the Terror, hoping the masses would kill a few more of the heirs in the meantime. I never thought the Revolution would take—it was a ridiculous notion, the commoners ruling themselves!"

His lip curled. "Then Napoleon came along, as common as dirt but wily and ambitious. He had great respect for such ambition. Yet he has kept me here, on this moldy, foggy, godforsaken island, promising me my ancestral lands, always keeping them just out of reach."

He sneered. "Until you. You were just what I need. Lovely, blonde, just Napoleon's cup of tea. Now look at you. Who would want a bloody-minded, boney cow like you? You'll never make the passage in this condition. I want nothing more than to be rid of you."

He kicked her, a swift, coldly vicious blow just beneath her ribs. She gasped softly and her vision darkened. When she revived, it was to find him pulling her to her feet. Her stomach rebelled but there was nothing in it. Pity. He deserved to be vomited upon.

He stood her on her feet. She wavered, but remained standing, preferring to tower over him rather than be at his feet like a supplicant.

"You're losing your hair," she observed as she looked down at him. "I daresay you'll be wearing a full wig soon."

He dug his fingers deeply into the flesh of her arm. "Quiet!"

She felt a mad giggle rising in her throat. "Or you shan't like me any longer?"

"Or I shall kill you," he said flatly as he dug the key to the wrist irons from his weskit pocket with one hand.

"Oh, is that all?" She smiled widely. "Then I have

nothing to lose." As he bent over the rusty lock about her one wrist, she drew a deep breath and raised the glass shard high.

A drop of blood fell from her gashed palm to his neck. He looked up. "What—"

She stabbed downward with all her strength. He was quick, but could not avoid a deep cut to his shoulder as he ducked away. "Bitch!" He clapped a hand to his cut. His blood welled, but Julia despaired when she saw it was not a serious wound.

The iron fell from her wrist and Julia stepped back, keeping the shard high. Her knees failed her and she stumbled. How tragic that when she finally had both the will and the weapon, she lacked the strength to use them.

He struck her to the floor with a single blow to her cheek. His was the power of madness, without mercy or caution.

She fought back the dizziness to push herself up on her hands.

It took only one more blow to send her back to the floor. She lay helpless and barely conscious as he dropped to one knee beside her. He smiled slightly as he took her throat in his hands.

"Weak and stupid female after all," he said scornfully. "If I'd seen you born I would have drowned you then."

She pushed at him weakly but he ignored her, intent on systematically squeezing the life from her like a macabre artist creating death from a piece of wood.

I will die now.

The thought came without real fear. The only emotion

that made its way through her fogging mind was rage.
This man had done so much to her, to her mother, to the
Liars, the Four and England herself. That he should win
again—that he should kill her and disappear to work his
evil yet more—that thought filled her with such fury
that she struck out against him.

She didn't even realize that the glass shard was still
in her hand.

The first blow cut through his cheek with ease, the
razor edge needing no strength to wound. He started,
then struck her hand away.

"Bitch!" He wiped the blood away with one hand
and bent to his task with renewed fury, no longer con-
strained by that eerie callous calm.

She was done for. All she wanted was to disempower
him, to remove his invisibility, to burst the bubble of his
enchantment. There would be nowhere for him to hide
with such a hideous mask.

Her vision was beginning to close. No time left. She
struck wildly, slashing at his face again and again—
that face that allowed him to lie so easily and well.

He cursed and fought her off, but dared not release
her throat long enough for her to take a breath. His
blood flowed easily from the gashes. Did he even realize how gravely she'd damaged him with her weak
blows?

She would have laughed, had she air to do so, for his
disguise was ruined . . . slashed away . . . the scars would
run across his face like furrows plowed in soil . . .
ruined . . . now a monster on the outside, too . . .

Her hands fell to her sides, no longer at her command. She felt nothing now, not even the pain of her

throat. He bent over her, shaking her limp form with the force of his choking. His slashed, bloodied face receded from her vision, his enraged eyes—so like hers—giving way to a merciful fog.

Dying . . . so sorry, Aldus . . . Marcus . . . my love . . . missing you . . . already . . .

The sound of thudding footsteps didn't truly register and the breaking of the door meant nothing as she let herself fall fully into the dark.

26

I cannot be philosophical about death. I hate death in every form. Does that make me weak?

Marcus and Igby burst into the boarding house room to see a crimson monster with his hands around Julia's throat.

"Halt!"

The Chimera sprang back from Julia's still form with a laugh. "Too late, Englishman. Or is it?" He leaped for the broken window. Marcus instinctively moved to stop him.

The Chimera laughed again through the ruined mask of his face. "Capture me or save her? You cannot do both!" He knocked away the remaining glass and vaulted over the sill, disappearing from sight.

Marcus let him go without a moment of hesitation. He hoped the bastard dashed his brains out on the cobbles, but it was likely he could climb down well enough. Marcus could not have cared less.

All he wanted was Julia.

To hell with the Chimera, to hell with the Four, to

hell with anyone or anything that ever tried to separate Julia from him again.

She was on the floor, a broken angel on a dirty carpet. "Oh, God," Igby whispered. "Oh, God, the blood—"

Marcus didn't remember crossing the room to drop to his knees next to her. He was just there, reaching a trembling hand to wipe the blood from her face. It was everywhere, running down her cheeks, slashing across her neck, flowing from her brow—

There were no cuts on her face. Marcus ran his hands over her beautiful battered face, but it was whole. A bark of tortured laughter left his throat. "It isn't hers."

He looked up at Igby. "It isn't her blood. She tore the bastard to bits, my girl did."

Igby's face twisted. "That's my lady, all right."

Then Marcus uncovered the purpling bruises around her throat, like a brutal necklace. "Oh, dear God." He pressed his ear to her breast, but his own heart was pounding so from fear. "Julia, oh, please—"

He lifted her half upright, holding her close, pressing his cheek to hers, desperate to feel her breath. He gave her a little shake, his vision blurring in his grief. "Breathe, darling, breathe! Damn it, you stubborn woman, *breathe*!"

He held her close, rocking her limp form slowly as Igby sank to the floor next to him, hands helpless in his lap.

"You have to breathe, J-Julia." He couldn't bear it. She was leaving him. "I don't deserve you, I know, but breathe anyway, my love." He pressed his lips to hers in a desperate, mad attempt to breathe for her, filling her lungs with his own air.

Two, three breaths—then he waited. Nothing.

"Oh, sir—" Igby moaned. "Oh, my lord, sir, I think she's—"

"That's *disgusting*."

The rasping whisper came from the dead woman cradled in Marcus's arms. He pulled back to stare down at her. "Julia?" Her eyes were still closed but she was most definitely not dead. She pushed at him weakly.

"You've been . . . drinking." She coughed, a dry, painful sound. "I don't ever want to taste . . . liquor on you again."

He laughed damply, his heart swelling until he could hear his ribs creak. "As you wish, my lady. Never again."

"I'll hold you . . . to that. I won't tolerate . . . spirits in our house."

He dropped his face into her neck, washing away the Chimera's blood with his tears. "Oh, my Jilly—"

"Stupid pet name," she gasped. "I'm . . . Julia."

Marcus broke down, sobbing his laughter into her skin, rocking her in his arms in the filthy room, vowing silently to never, ever let her go again.

27

A wife is a terrible thing to waste.

In the secret chamber of the Four, Marcus stood unrepentant before his former masters. Two men stood while the other two sat at the grotty old table.

Lord Reardon, the Cobra, appeared concerned. Lord Wyndham, the Falcon, was impassive as usual, and Lord Greenleigh, Marcus's own mentor, stood to one side with his massive arms crossed. Dane had excused himself due to his partiality.

It was the right thing to have done and Marcus didn't blame Dane for it—yet it would have been more helpful to have the Lion in his corner.

As it was, Lord Liverpool had taken it upon himself to provide a quorum. The Prime Minister hovered behind the carved chair that was the traditional seat of the Fox as if he itched to take it for his own.

Marcus restrained a fierce grin. *Not while I'm still standing, Robert.*

The Falcon cleared his throat and stood. "Lord Dryden," he said formally. "What say you to the charges that you withheld information from your peers and aided the escape of a known spy?"

Marcus frowned slightly and scratched at his jaw. "Which one? The Chimera or Lady Barrowby?"

The Falcon did not smile, but then he never did. "At this point we are more interested in the Chimera, although your illicit involvement with Lady Barrowby is most surely fodder for further discussion at another time."

Marcus clasped his hands behind his back and regarded his judges without alarm. "I vote that we discuss it now. I do still have a vote, do I not?" He smiled. "Or have I been officially unconfirmed?"

The Lion narrowed his eyes. "You are still the Fox," he said, speaking for the first time. He reached a giant hand and pulled out his customary chair. "I withdraw my withdrawal," he stated, seating himself. "I don't want to miss this."

Marcus nodded, glad to have his friend back in the game.

The Falcon shrugged. "Very well. We shall table the subject of the Chimera." He sent Marcus a warning glare. "For now."

Marcus bowed. "Thank you. First, I would like to explain my reason for involving myself personally with her ladyship." He shrugged, spreading his hands. "It seemed advisable in the moment."

Reardon smiled slightly. Dane snorted. Liverpool twitched and Wyndham tapped an impatient fingertip on the table.

Marcus doused his grin. "My apologies. My reasoning led me to believe I needed to outmatch her ladyship's other many admirers in order to get close enough to learn the truth."

"Yes, yes," Liverpool said impatiently. "We know that much. It is how you learned about her low beginnings."

Marcus nodded. "Yes. Unfortunately, I did not remain long enough to discover more." He smiled slightly. "As in the fact that I was already in love with her."

Dane blinked. "I thought you were in love with my wife."

Marcus shook his head. "I never loved Olivia. I simply envied you having someone believe in you so completely, without reservation." He looked away. "Then I didn't recognize it when I saw it and nearly killed it all by myself."

Reardon flinched. "Ouch."

Liverpool threw out his hands. "What are we talking about here—romance and the lovelorn, or treason?" He leaned forward to slam one palm on the table. "I want to know why the hell you let that female escape you—thrice!"

Wyndham slid Liverpool a cool glance. "My lord, please remember that you are an observer here.

Liverpool straightened. "I may no longer be the Cobra, but I still take my duty to England seriously." He glared at Marcus. "Unlike some."

Marcus turned the full force of his rage on Liverpool, all easy façade gone. "And you interpret that duty as the right to assassinate a lady?"

Reardon and Dane shot alarmed gazes at Liverpool. Dane stood. "You did what?"

Liverpool folded his hands behind his back. "I sent

the Liars after her." He gazed at them all unrepentantly. "Dryden was too close to the case."

Reardon stood. "And you have overstepped, my lord!"

Liverpool gazed at his own former protégé calmly. "I admit it was regrettable, but we had already seen what a risk she posed, setting her people on us that way."

"She has helped us! Because of her, we know more about the Chimera than ever before. For that you ordered her death?" Remembered fear threatened to choke Marcus. "You sent the Liars' premier assassin, Kurt the Cook, who is above all a consummate professional, who wouldn't hesitate to kill a lovely young woman if so ordered."

"I ordered her apprehended," Liverpool amended. "She would have only been eliminated if she did not cooperate."

Marcus's righteous rage was not assuaged by that, for when had Julia ever been the cooperative sort?

Then he took a deep breath to calm himself. The day was yet to be won. Liverpool's alarming assumption of power would keep. "What is past, is past. Nor am I in a position to criticize, for I am not yet one of you in truth."

"I don't recall our having resolved that question just yet," Dane interjected mildly. "Nor am I convinced we have closed the topic of Lord Liverpool's interference."

"I should say not!" Reardon added.

Marcus held up a hand. "Gentlemen, I cannot possibly be named the next Fox when the current Fox is still living." He gestured to the door. "May I present my wife, Lady Dryden?"

Julia entered the room, her graceful serenity belying

the fact that her body was still a map of garish bruising.

Marcus had never been so proud of anyone in his life. She stood tall and more than defiant—she was fearless, an intrepid tigress in a room of lesser predators.

She was still terribly thin, but the shadows in her cheeks highlighted her aristocratic bone structure and lent dignity to her level gaze. A length of lace hid the still livid bruises about her throat and one hand remained lightly bandaged. She looked like a warrior goddess, fresh from battle.

Yet the final battle had only just begun.

She did not wait for permission to speak. "My lords, I have come to demand my rightful place as the Fox."

Liverpool reacted instantly. "You have no place here!"

She flicked a glance his way. "Shut it, Robert. I helped select you for your current position, so I know quite well *you* have no place here."

Liverpool blustered. "You did no such thing! My appointment was a full year past—" He halted as the truth sank in. "You were acting as the Fox even then?"

"Indeed."

The Falcon gazed at her evenly. "Perhaps he is no longer the Cobra, but the Prime Minister will still be accorded respect by all of us."

She did not back down. "The Prime Minister tried to misuse the Liar's Club to assassinate me, nearly causing the death of one of England's most valuable operatives. I will respect him when he has earned it."

The Cobra pursed his lips and tilted his head. "She has a point there, Liverpool."

Liverpool gazed acidly at them all. "I have explained the misunderstanding that resulted in that attempt. I do not kill women."

"Not this woman, at any rate." Julia gazed at him until he was forced to look away. She turned her attention to the rest of them.

"I do hope you know what you are doing, Lady Dryden." The Falcon watched her. "Liverpool was correct about one thing. If we refuse to recognize you as the Fox we will be forced to dispose of you most permanently." He glanced at Marcus. "Which would pose a difficulty about what should be done about your husband."

She nodded. "We are entirely aware of this." She sent Marcus an expressionless glance, but he could read beneath her composure. His life was in her hands. He grinned easily at her. *Take no prisoners, Jilly.*

She made no response, but only turned back to the Three. "I make my claim on the grounds that I was wrongly dismissed. I am indeed highborn."

Higher than you lot. Marcus stifled his grin and kept his peace, though it cost him. They'd toss him out and he didn't want to miss a thing.

"I was born the Comtesse Joëlle Conti du Boutin. My mother was the wife of the count at that time. They both fled Paris during the Terror to take safe harbor in England. My father was a cruel man who beat my mother so severely that he was forced to abandon her when she could not keep up. Unaware that she was with child, he left her for dead in a ditch, where she was found by the members of the Hiram Pickles Traveling Variety Show. They healed her as best they could and sheltered her from discovery for the next seventeen years. She died five years ago."

"A thrilling tale." Liverpool sneered. "Fit to put on the stage. Where is your proof? Where are your documents of your parents' marriage, the certification of your birth? I fear we're a bit on the outs with France at the moment. You'll never get the records from—"

The thick file hit the table between the Three. Marcus smiled. "Oh, bother. Did I forget to show you those?"

They quickly unwound the tie and spread the contents over the table.

"You are my second." Dane scowled at Marcus. "You ought to have brought these directly to me."

Julia shook her head slowly. "No, my lord. He is *my* second now."

Liverpool leaned forward to peer at the contents. "This means nothing. You could have falsified these."

Julia clasped her hands before her. "Falcon, you are something of a document expert," she said serenely. "Are they false?"

The Falcon was bent closely over the certificate of marriage. "Well, someone very nearly royal wed someone else very nearly royal. That does not seem to be in question."

She nodded. "I am a princess of the blood. Currently I believe I am twenty-fourth in line for the throne . . . if there were still a throne."

"A French countess?" Liverpool went tight-lipped. "All the more reason to refuse your suit."

"I have never set foot on French soil," Julia stated firmly. "Nor do I have any loyalty to my father or his heritage."

"No?" The Cobra spoke up for the first time in a long while. "How can we be so sure of that? What if he were to appear today and appeal to your familial loyalty?"

Julia reached to pull the scarf from her throat. "He has appeared."

The other men inhaled sharply. Even Marcus winced, for the bruises looked worse than ever, dark purple streaked with an evil green.

"The man who did this to me is my father, the Comte Renauld Conti du Boutin, prince of the blood, vicious wife beater, loyal servant of Napoleon—" She pulled the locket from about her neck and tossed it onto the scattered documents. "And the Chimera."

The Cobra pounced on the locket and flicked it open. "Oh, *hell*." He passed it to the Lion, who blinked at it, then passed it to the Falcon. "That is indeed the image of Denny," he said slowly.

"He doesn't look like that anymore," Julia said. "I took a shard of glass to his best weapon." She held out her hands, palms forward. The scars and blood-dotted bandage spoke volumes. "In the future, I don't believe he'll be able to pass himself off as anything but a sideshow player."

The Lion sat back and let out a long breath. "Well, I think we can dismiss the possibility of mixed loyalties."

The Cobra leaned forward. "Did the bastard bleed?"

Julia showed white, even teeth. "Copiously."

The Cobra smiled back fiercely. "Good." He sat back. "Well, I think this removes the objection of her birth. We already know her other qualifications. What say you all?"

"But she's a woman!" Liverpool's protest was very nearly a howl.

"No, I feel fine about that." The Cobra looked at the Lion. "Does that bother you?"

The Lion shrugged. "No. She's a bit scary but I believe I can cope."

They both turned to the Falcon. "What do you think?"

The Falcon looked down at the locket still open in his palm, then up to Julia, who stood calm and silent, gazing back at him. "Since the other obstacles have been disproved and there is nothing in the vows that precludes gender . . . I suppose I concur." A sardonic flash of smile twisted his lips. "Welcome to the Royal Four, our new Fox."

Marcus let out a whoop and dashed across the room to spin Julia in his arms. She gasped a laugh, then pushed at him with her less-injured hand. "Put me down," she hissed. "It isn't seemly."

The Cobra bowed. "My lady, you have the rest of your life as the Fox to be seemly. Proceed to celebrate. If you are feeling well enough from your ordeal, we should like to meet in three days to brief you on the latest reports."

Julia took a breath and gazed back at the Cobra with serene dignity, but her fingers were crushing Marcus's hand. "That is agreeable." She dipped a slight curtsy. "My lords, I bid you good evening."

She made it most of the way down the deserted hallway before she stumbled and sagged in Marcus's grip.

"Darling, are you all right?"

She turned and buried her face in his weskit. "We did it," she gasped. "We truly did it. We're the Fox!"

He tipped her chin up with one finger. "No, my love. *You're* the Fox. I am your eager student."

She blinked up at him, her brow creased. "You don't mind?"

He shook his head, a slow grin crossing his face. "I am ever willing to learn from the master . . . or in this case, the mistress."

Her lids went heavy and she returned his sensuous smile. "Well, there are a few things I never dared write in my diaries . . ."

A startled laugh burst from Marcus and he pulled her close to bury his face in her sweet-smelling hair. She was truly his now—this courageous, astounding, sensual beauty was his forever!

"Forever and ever," she murmured into his weskit. "Now feed me. I'm starved."

He stroked her hair. "I know where they make the best bread and cheese midnight picnics . . ."

Epilogue

After the heat and passion and sweet ferocity, he brings me cool water and strokes my skin to soothe me.

"So what comes next?" Marcus dropped a kiss onto the bare shoulder he was massaging.

Julia let out a luxuriating sigh and rolled her head on the pillow. "No. No more. I'll be walking decidedly oddly tomorrow as it is."

He nibbled on that particular place he'd found on the side of her neck, the place that caused a most delightful reaction. She shivered beneath him, her backside quivering delightfully against parts that were most appreciative of her rounded softness.

"We have nearly half a day left until the Four meets again. Go on," he whispered. "Tell me another one."

"Hmm . . . well, there was one where we douse each other with sweet oil and—"

His eyes nearly crossed. "And?" he begged hoarsely.

"And I happen to know that Pickles put a bottle of sweet oil in that drawer." She pointed without opening her eyes, a small smile lighting her profile.

Marcus was across the room in a flash. The oil wasn't in the first drawer, or the second. He shoved everything about, shifting the accumulated post without regard to the finely embossed quality of the invitations that slid to the floor unnoticed.

Finally he laid hands on the oil and rushed back to the bed. "Shall we lie before the fire?"

It was a seductive question, said in a husky, hungry voice, so there was no reason at all for her to turn her head to laugh riotously into the pillow.

"What is it?"

She lifted her head with a helpless snicker. "If all the post carriers dressed like you, I would pay them a great deal more per letter!"

Marcus looked down to see a slim envelope balanced on his erection. Julia rolled over to pluck it from his dampened skin and began to open it.

"You're going to read it now? Not now. Please, not now. I have oil!"

"It will only take a moment. It must be good news," she said with a grin. "How could it not be, with such a delivery?"

Still smiling, she unfolded the letter and began to read. Her smile faded. After a moment, she looked up at him with brows drawn. "When did this arrive?"

Marcus shrugged. "We haven't left the room in two days. I think Pickles brought it in with the rest of today's post. Why? Who is it from?"

Julia sat up cross-legged on the bed and regarded him with the strangest expression. "It seems that Aldus's solicitor has finally found the heir to Barrowby."

Marcus knelt on the mattress beside her. "You knew

he was bound to turn up someday," he said gently. "And your people will be welcome at Ravencliff, you know that."

She shook her head, chewing on her bottom lip. "That isn't the issue," she said slowly. "He is writing to tell me that he has just fulfilled Aldus's other requirement—the notification of certain individuals—three of them, in fact—of my very excellent lineage."

She looked up at Marcus, eyes wide. "He said that Aldus must have confused the priority of such requests, so he took it upon himself to search for the heir first, and to notify their lordships second."

Marcus gazed down at the letter in her hand. "The stupid sod. Do you realize what you would have been spared? Yet I cannot blame him." He smiled and stroked her curling hair from her dampened brow. "After all, what could be the urgency of proving Lady Barrowby's obviously superior breeding?"

"Oh, stop." She pushed at him. "You have breeding on the brain."

He kissed her neck. She shivered, then she slid him a roguish look. "Hmm. Where's that oil? We have half a day . . ."

Turn the page for a sneak peek
at the final thrilling installment in the
the Royal Four series

Seducing the Spy

Coming from St. Martin's Paperbacks
in August 2006

If ruined and disgraced Lady Alicia Lawrence thought he, Stanton Horne, Marquis of Wyndham and member of the secret protectorate of the Crown known as the Royal Four, would turn such a notorious female loose on an unsuspecting London, she was sadly mistaken.

He would meet her here at the opera and keep her contained within the viewing box she'd selected—and billed to him. She could thus accomplish her goal of putting herself on tawdry display and he could keep an eye on her every move.

Stanton leaned back in his viewing box and regarded the ongoing opera with a level of boredom he hadn't thought himself capable. Oh, the soprano was very talented and the set was extravagant, as was the pageantry of the cream of London society that swirled below him—but Lady Alicia was not here.

Apparently she was making a fashionably late appearance. Since the performance was nearly half over, even the ever unpredictable Lady Alicia must surely arrive shortly.

Sure enough, the orchestra had just begun the next

movement when the curtains parted behind Stanton and an usher bowed someone through.

Stanton turned. "Good evening, Lady—"

It wasn't she. It could not be she. Lady Alicia Lawrence was a blotchy, ill-kempt creature, swollen like a grape and not as appetizing.

Before him stood a faultlessly stylish lady, posed with her head high and her shoulders back, her rich emerald velvet wrap framing a fine-boned face of exquisite porcelain. Her lips curved in a sensual bow and her auburn hair glowed in the light from the stage. She was all that was elegant and polished.

She wouldn't be elegant in his arms. She would be earthy and untamed and shameless—

Stanton blinked. That thought had flown through his mind like an outlaw's arrow, coming from nowhere.

It wasn't she.

Yet, lively cat-green eyes gleamed at him knowingly.

"You seem taken aback, my lord. And rather boring. Do I not seem different? Am I not much improved? In the last week I've spent more money than the Prince Regent's new mistress! Have you nothing to say about my accomplishment?"

She waited. Her eyes narrowed. "Never mind. I've reconsidered helping you with your plan. Piss off." She turned to stalk from the box.

Stanton came out of his trance in an instant. His witness was walking off the case. He caught up with her in a few swift steps. "You cannot reconsider, Lady Alicia."

She turned. "Oh? Can I not? Observe." She moved away from him.

Stanton ignored a lifetime of social training and caught her by the arm. "You belong to me now."

Startled—and angry, he'd do well not to forget angry—green eyes fixed on his. "I beg your pardon?"

"I paid for a mistress—put her in a house, bought her a new wardrobe, a new staff. I demand that certain services be rendered in return."

She gazed at him for a long moment. "Very well. But only once."

Then she went up on her toes and kissed him.

It was a clumsy, untutored kiss—the kiss of a sheltered girl, fervent and hesitant at once. The innocence of her lips on his transported him directly back to his first achingly sweet kiss, to the boy with the shaking hands and the pounding heart, his first taste of female lips on his. Another time and place indeed, another Stanton entirely.

He kissed her back.

It took the booming of the bass drums during a particularly dramatic movement for him to realize where he was—and who he was kissing!

He stepped back abruptly. "Well, that was best out of the way, I suppose." He smiled reassuringly, albeit tightly.

She did not seem reassured. "What are you doing here?"

"Did I not make myself clear? I am to be your escort at all times."

"You were entirely clear. I simply ignored you." She settled herself in the chair beside him warily. "I do that a great deal, you know."

Stanton debated engaging in a bit of timely sarcasm,

but unexpectedly felt no need. In fact, he felt inexplicably light-hearted this evening. He smiled easily at her. "You must be warm. Why don't you let me take your cape?"

She tucked the collar of the cape closer to her throat, though her flushed face was clearly overheated. "I—" She pressed her lips together and gazed at him in irritation. "Oh, I simply do not care what you think!"

She abruptly stood. Stanton automatically rose to his own feet at her side. "Lady Alicia, I fail to see—"

She dropped the cape and raised her chin defiantly.

Stanton felt his mouth go dry. The gown was a titillating scandal in deep green silk. The neckline dipped indecently low, showing off a truly prepossessing figure, if one was inclined to prefer a bit of plump abundance with one's morning cup of tea . . .

She looked like a prostitute—a beautiful, opulent, extravagantly endowed prostitute with sexual fire alight in her eyes.

She was the embodiment—oh, dear God, that body!—of every man's most wicked dream.

Whose dream? Theirs . . . or yours?

The air came back into Stanton's lungs in a rush. "What in the seventh level of hell are you wearing?"

He hadn't meant to bellow and he certainly hadn't realized that the orchestra was just finishing the last movement, and he sure as hell hadn't meant for his question to echo through the opera house like a bass crescendo. The faces below turned their way.

"Oh, well done," Alicia murmured to him.

He turned to glare down at her. She patted his arm with a pleased smile tugging at the corner of her mouth then she stepped away from him in a dramatic flounce of skirts. "You beast!"

Again, her voice carried over the hall as if she stood on the stage itself. Every neck craned to see. A soggy sob followed, and then she turned back to him, dramatically wiping her eyes. "You horrible, cruel . . . man! First you seduce me, and then you denigrate me for it!"

For a horrified moment, Stanton thought she intended to throw herself to her knees at her feet, but then she seemed to realize she would no longer be visible to the people below.

To catch herself, she staggered melodramatically, then teetered as she raised the back of one hand to her brow. "I cannot go on this way," she wailed. "I love you so, no matter how cruel you are to me—"

Stanton wasn't entirely sure how it happened. Perhaps she became too caught up in her own performance, or perhaps it was the trailing skirts of the elaborate gown, but suddenly Alicia lurched sideways, hit the balustrade with her hip and then began to tip over the railing of the box.

Still shocked motionless with dismay at her public theatrics, Stanton almost didn't react quickly enough. It was only when she raised a surprised and horrified gaze to his that he realized she was truly about to fall.

The crowd below gasped in delicious horror and several ladies screamed even as Stanton leaped for her. He caught one flailing hand and wrapped his other arm about her waist even as her feet completely left the floor and she began to flip backward.

Stanton almost lost her when the railing began to crack beneath their combined weight. It ought to have held. *Tampered with.* From the corner of his eye, he saw something fall to the crowd below. Wrapping both arms about Alicia, he swung her high and around, pulling them both back from danger as the railing failed.

They rolled together across the carpeted box, ending with her beneath him. The sound of the crowd rose about them as the people who had gathered to help catch the falling lady fled the falling bits of balcony railing.

Stanton heard only his own racing heart and the gasping breathing of Alicia against his face. He wrapped her tightly in his arms and tucked his face into her silken neck.

She hadn't fallen. She wasn't broken and bleeding on the floor below. She was safe and warm in his arms, clinging fiercely to him and shaking from reaction.

Or perhaps it was he who shook. That moment when his grip had slipped—he'd never felt fear like that before, not even during his stint in the army.

That fact alone was enough to bring him to his senses. He released her smoothly and stood, holding out one hand for her to take.

Alicia gazed up at Lord Wyndham in confusion. He gazed calmly down at her, as if he was merely a stranger helping a lady up a step. She blinked. Less than a second ago he had been holding her so fiercely—

Obviously, her imagination had failed her again, for she now saw no hint of that desperate emotion on his face. Bemused, she took his hand and allowed him to raise her to her feet.

The crowd beneath erupted into cheers, the opera performance forgotten in the drama being enacted above them. Alicia blinked at the sea of faces now revealed by the lack of railing. They were smiling . . . cheering . . . her!

"So turns the fickle tide of society," said a deep warm voice in her ear. "It seems our passionate affair has quite caught their fancy."

Alicia snorted. "And why not, when we deliver such entertaining fare?"

It didn't bode well for her mission, however. How in the world was she to enact her vengeance on Society if they loved her instead of loathed her?

"I'm simply relieved your bodice remained in place, such as it is," he said drily.

Alicia looked over her shoulder and raised a brow at him. "That should teach you not to disrespect the feminine arts. It takes work to look this scandalous. None of it is accidental. I've seen ancient battle armor less formidably constructed than this bodice."

He bowed mockingly. "I concede to the mighty bodice—although I insist that gown must meet its end in the fireplace."

Alicia shrugged. "Its work is done. I could hardly wear it again, lest I diminish its impact."

"Heaven forefend," Stanton replied wearily. "Now, I shall have one of my men escort you home. I have another matter to attend to."

She nodded. "Indeed. I would very much like to know who rigged this box with a trip wire." She bent to hike one side of her skirt to reveal her ankle. "I felt it cut me."

Sure enough, there was a fine bloody slice through one stocking.

Stanton clenched his jaw. He'd not suspected a trip mechanism, although now it seemed obvious. Why else tamper with the railing unless one could guarantee someone would fall against it?

What he wasn't prepared for was the fierce jolt of primeval protectiveness which shot through him at the sight of her bloodied skin. The wound was nothing—a mere scratch—so why did his vision begin to redden at the thought of getting his hands on the perpetrator?

She didn't matter that much to him. She never could. He wouldn't allow it.

Ever.

**Take a sneak peek at any of
the Royal Four you may have missed!**

To Wed a Scandalous Spy

Surrender to a Wicked Spy

Willa hummed cheerfully, if somewhat out of tune, as she foraged in the meadow for a few greens to round out their noontide meal. Traveling with her husband suited her absolutely. Even with Nathaniel's strange aversion to staying at inns and his tendency to monosyllabic conversation, she was determined to enjoy his company.

Besides, she was seeing places she'd never seen before. Even though the new stone-walled sheep fields greatly resembled the previous stone-walled sheep fields of her experience, they were *new*. After a lifetime spent in the same tiny village and its monotonous environs, anything new was delightful.

Furthermore, marriage was *new*. Spending her days with such an attractive man was entirely new, and there was no point in denying the purely female pleasure she took in watching Nathaniel ride, walk—oh, heavens, that leonesque stride!—and basically breathe in and out.

Of course, she'd imagined that by now she and her husband would have managed to put that silly consummation requirement behind them . . .

Willa picked up her sack of found treasure and decided to cross the beck further down to look for watercress. Watching her feet on the damp slope, Willa didn't look up until she reached the water's edge.

When she did, her heart stopped beating, the breath left her lungs, and her mouth went dry.

He was beautiful.

Nathaniel knelt in the beck only a few yards away. With his back to her and her arrival masked by the chuckling water, he was entirely oblivious to her gaze.

He was also entirely wet.

And entirely naked.

The water was shallow, and there weren't enough bubbles in the world to cover the sheer expanse of naked man that rose from the beck.

Willa couldn't breathe. Her knees went wonk at the sight of the sudsy water streaming down his broad back into the crease of his powerful buttocks. She had never seen anything so unbearably delicious in her life.

His back rippled with muscle as he soaped his hair, the cloudy afternoon light doing nothing to dim the sleek shine of soap and water on his male perfection.

Nathaniel bent to duck his head in the water, and Willa could not control the moan that escaped her at the view.

Instantly Nathaniel whirled, one fist pulled back in instinctive defense while his other hand frantically wiped soap from his eyes. Damn, he should have known he was too vulnerable here. He hadn't been thinking with the mind of a spy but had let thoughts of Willa's sumptuous thighs distract him.

His vision cleared and he saw her. The impulse to

fight eased, only to be replaced by another equally ancient instinct.

It was her eyes. They were wide and hungry, with a shining ache in them that he knew from his own soul. She wanted him. He could see it in the way her chest swelled with heavy breaths and by the sheen of perspiration gilding her face and neck.

His own need rose in response to her hungry gaze, and he saw her gaze drop and her eyes widen in surprise. Then slowly, her gaze traveled back up him. Nathaniel straightened and stood motionless for her perusal.

He was the most magnificent creature she had ever seen. She knew that the thrumming within her was because of his male attraction, but the ache in her heart was from his sheer lonely perfection.

I could have her.

◈

Being one of the most eligible bachelors in London Society, Dane Calwell, Viscount Greenleigh, was actually rather accustomed to saving damsels. In fact, they seemed to drop from the sky to land at his feet in various states of distress.

The Season was nearly over, and Society's mamas were becoming desperate indeed. Unbeknownst to them, Dane had every intention of marrying this year. After all, he was in his late thirties and his wild days were long done. A man with his responsibilities needed an appropriately demure, composed, well-bred hostess and mother for his heir. Therefore, he looked on all of this attempted entrapment with amused tolerance. Still, Dane had hope that he'd find a young woman with a bit more substance before the season ended.

So when a young lady fell into the Thames right before his eyes, Dane hadn't hesitated before leaping from his horse to dive into the water next to the struggling miss.

Except that this particular miss hadn't needed rescuing, at least not until she'd nearly frozen while rescuing *him*.

She lay in his arms now as he carried her up the grassy bank of the Thames. He didn't think it was precisely proper for him to be holding her so close, but the unconscious girl's mother—who only now had thought to run back down the bridge to the bank—was currently indulging in a rather overblown fit of panic and there didn't seem to be any servants or footmen with them.

Dane wrapped his sodden coat more closely about the pale chilled form of his rescuer. Her frozen state concerned him greatly. He was feeling deadly cold himself, and he was far larger than the young woman he held.

He glanced up at the gathering crowd—where had all these people been while the two of them had been floundering in the Thames?—and picked out a mild-looking young man at random.

"You there," he called. "Fetch a hackney coach here at once." The fellow nodded quickly and ran for the street. Dane glanced at the woman he was beginning to think of as "the mother from hell" and tried to smile at her reassuringly. This only sent her into a fresh bout of sobbing and carrying on as she clung to his side. She seemed to feel that she was to blame for some reason.

There was no sense coming from that quarter, so Dane tuned the woman out.

A shabby hack pulled up on the grass. It was a pretty poor specimen and small to boot, but Dane was in no mood to care. He ordered the mild young man to load the mother into the vehicle and carried the girl on himself. Seating himself in the cramped interior, he settled her into his lap, keeping a protective hold on her.

Perhaps he ought to be ashamed of noticing that she was a healthy armful and that she fit rather nicely against him. Still, it was refreshing to be this close to such a sturdy female. She felt rather . . . unbreakable. He always felt somewhat uneasy when he came too close to some of the more petite women in Society. His common sense told him that he was not going to crush them during a waltz, but his imagination supplied many an awful vision anyway.

So when his coat briefly fell away from the young woman's bodice during the jostling carriage ride, Dane fell prey to his manly instincts rather than his gentlemanly ones and didn't precisely avert his eyes from what the thin, sodden muslin wasn't covering very well.

Well, well. Very nice. Very nice indeed. He could safely change his description from "sturdy" to "buxom."

Dane saw her open eyes and smiled at her, glad to see that she was alert once more. She likely hadn't seen him peeking, and if she had, he certainly wasn't going to affirm her suspicions by appearing guilty. Besides, the brief glance at her full bosom capped with rosy points that pressed tightly to the translucent muslin had been the highlight of his rather trying day.

Her gaze left his, however, and slid to where her mother sat opposite them, now sobbing somewhat less vociferously.

"Mother," the girl said firmly through blue, chilled lips. "T–tell this nice gentleman that you're s–sorry."

The weeping woman uttered something unintelligible which seemed to satisfy the girl in Dane's lap, for she then turned to look back up at him with an air of expectation. Dane hesitated, having the feeling that he was the only one who didn't know what they were talking about. "Ah . . . apology accepted?" he said finally.

The girl seemed to relax. "You're t–taking all of this very well, I must say," she told him as her shivers continued. "That bodes well f–for your character. You must be a man of g–great parts."

Perhaps it was the fact that he'd recently been peeking at her own rather "great parts", or perhaps it was the fact that his own "parts" were becoming more and more stimulated by the motion of a curvaceous bottom being jostled against them, but the commonplace saying struck Dane in quite a different way than it was intended to. He laughed involuntarily, then covered it with a cough. Smiling with bemusement at the very unusual creature nestled on his lap, he nodded. "Thank you. I might say the same about you."

The girl eyed him speculatively for a moment, then turned to her mother again. "Mama, you should allow this gentleman to introduce himself to you."

"Mama" nodded vigorously, then visibly repressed her sobs and dabbed at her eyes with a tiny scrap of lace that truly didn't look up to the task of drying all those tears.

"That's not necessary, my dear," the woman said, with a final sniffle. "The Earl of Greenleigh and I have already been introduced."

Dane sat there for a long moment with a smile frozen on his face while he racked his memory to place the rumpled, red-eyed woman across from him. Finally, light dawned. Cheltenham. She was the wife of a destitute earl, but the family was of excellent lineage and spotless reputation. "Of course we have, Lady Cheltenham," he said smoothly, as if he'd recognized her all along.

Then he looked down at the self-possessed and voluptuous young woman in his arms. So this was Cheltenham's daughter . . .